When I returned, he was looking out the window toward the birthday cake or, as they say here, L'Hôtel de Ville. "You have a magnificent view, Miss Alyssa. A treasure, surely."

"Thank you. It is beautiful. Did you know my Aunt Isabella well?"

His forehead buckled, and he seemed confused for a moment, tapping his hand to his withered lips. "Is that what you called her?"

"Well, yes. Isabella Manchester. That was the name she was born with in America."

"Ah, yes. Isabella," he whispered, then shook his head. "Non, I only knew her as Sophie, Madame Sophie. She lived in this apartment longer than most people remembered. I moved here a few years ago, and she had been here many years already."

I set down a tray with sugar and milk, tea cups, and spoons on the large square trunk in the middle of the room. "So very strange," I said under my breath.

Monsieur cocked his head to the side.

"You see, our family lost track of Isabella before the war. Never heard from her again after France fell. In fact, most of the family thought she had been killed in the war."

"*Quelle dommage.* In all these years, you have never spoken to her?" His eyes brightened with the question.

"No. Her lawyer contacted us after her death." I poured tea from a Wedgwood teapot with a darling rabbit on the lid. I'd found it under a slew of ratty baskets on top of the kitchen cabinet.

Deadly Commandment

by

Joy Brighton

This is a work of fiction. Names, characters, places, and incidents are either the product of the author's imagination or are used fictitiously, and any resemblance to actual persons living or dead, business establishments, events, or locales, is entirely coincidental.

Deadly Commandment

Cover Art by *Kristian Norris*

The Wild Rose Press, Inc.
PO Box 708
Adams Basin, NY 14410-0708
Visit us at www.thewildrosepress.com

Publishing History
First Crimson Rose Edition, 2020
Trade Paperback ISBN 978-1-5092-2630-6
Digital ISBN 978-1-5092-2631-3

Published in the United States of America

Dedication

For my friends the Armadillos;
again much thanks for your wise suggestions,
ruthless and necessary editing,
and your loving support
while I worked on *Deadly Commandment*.

~

A special thanks to Teri for her rabbit poem
that sent me off in a fun direction.
Also, to my Wild Rose editor, Anne,
for her patient and creative help.

~

To my sweet husband,
who understood why I needed time in Paris to write.
And to all the wonderful people of Paris
for sharing your beautiful and inspiring city.
To Shakespeare and Company bookstore in Paris
for loaning me a desk to work at
and to Notre Dame for calling me to matins
when I needed a break.

~

And, finally to my dear mother-in-law, Vida,
who shared with me her idea
of the Deadly Commandment
and wanted me to write this book.

Prologue

"You have the death certificate?"

"Here, sir."

"Has the family been contacted?"

My sergeant gave a quick nod.

"*Très bien*. Who will make the journey to Paris?"

"The youngest daughter." He slid an eight-by-ten photo across my desk.

I pursed my lips and squinted at the blurred printout. "You would think the FBI might have improved their surveillance photography after all this time."

A snicker. "She should arrive within the week."

I stared at the apartment building across the square from our temporary office in the Marais district. "Continue twenty-four-hour surveillance on the building."

"Yes, sir."

"And request the FBI watch her until she arrives in Paris."

"Of course, Captain."

Chapter One

"Alyssa. Stop complaining and put on the damn dress."

My best friend Georgie narrowed her eyes and glared at me, but her exasperated tone was a put on.

I shrugged and stepped into the black sheath she held before me. It looked perfectly modest from the front with a high, boat neckline. But the back? No way could I carry off the plunging back that barely covered my essentials.

Georgie hitched up the zipper on the side and turned me around to face the hotel room mirror.

"There. Told you." She tossed her head and brushed back her long dark hair. "Perfect. You and my sister are exactly the same size."

"We may be the same size," I said, staring at the strange woman in the mirror. "But we are definitely not the same style." I shook my head and gave her a skeptical frown. "In the first place, I never wear a dress. My legs are too skinny to pull off most of the short ones, and I'm way too tall to wear a maxi."

Georgie tucked in the tag on my shoulder and ignored my complaint. "You should wear them more often. You look fabulous."

"Wearing a dress to work makes me stand out more than I already do. With this mop of curls and these glasses, I belong in Dockers and Polos, not Yves St.

Laurent."

Georgie didn't reply to my rant and pushed me toward the little stool in front of the doublewide mirror. "Sit. I'll do your hair."

I sighed, folded myself onto the bench in the bathroom and watched in silent amazement as Georgie performed her magic.

Wish I could do that.

In minutes she had captured my running-amuck army of curls and like a general reviewing the troops, had ordered everyone into line. With a mouthful of pins, she wasn't talking for the moment. A rarity for Georgie.

So I asked, "Where are we going tonight?"

She mumbled something and poked me a little too hard with the next pin.

"Ow."

"F-stay f-still." Georgie fussed. She finished arranging the last of the pins and stood back to inspect her work. She smoothed a few stray soldiers back into formation and shook the can of hair spray, ready to attack with new weapons of mass destruction. I closed my eyes and held my breath as she let off the poison gas.

"Now for makeup."

"I don't like makeup." I had to stand my ground sometime, or she'd have me painted up like a French trollop.

"Just a little powder. Some mascara." She glared at my forehead, leaned a little closer and pouted her oh-so-perfect lips. "Don't you ever pluck your brows?"

"No, I don't. And don't you start." With crossed eyes, I glared at the maniacal tweezers she'd pulled

3

from her box of torture weapons.

Her lips twisted into a slight frown. "Well, okay. I guess the full look is in now."

Begrudgingly, I slipped into the heels she'd held out for me and stood. "Too tall," I said as I balanced my frame against the wall. "How about flats?"

Georgie put her hands on her hips and shook her head. "No way. You look fabulous. Tall's in."

Maybe. But where was the real Alyssa Manchester?

****

"And that's how the unreal Alyssa met the unreal Marcus." I took a sip of my passion fruit ice tea and stared at my very pregnant sister Sam across the table. Our lunch should arrive any moment. I was starving.

"Unreal? Did you know he was married that night?"

I shook my head and peeled the soft part of the bread out of my slice. "Georgie dragged me into the bar at the Vegas convention center. She'd heard venture capitalists hung out there. Marcus was having a scotch and the rest"—I buttered the piece and popped it in my mouth—"is history, as they say."

"Trawling for new investors?" Sam smirked.

"And fresh meat." I smoothed my napkin across my lap and studied the seafood salad the waitress placed in front of me. In the warm spring weather, sitting outside on the patio at our favorite restaurant was a treat after the long Northern California rainy season. I closed my eyes and held my face to the sunlight. The warmth felt good.

"Why didn't you leave?"

I swept my sandal-covered toe along the

restaurant's Mexican tiled floor. "Georgie was having fun. She'd met a guy. I sat at a table and had a lemon drop. It wasn't too bad."

"People watching?"

"Hardly." I pulled on one of my curls, then let it spring back into place on my forehead. "Georgie hid my glasses—wouldn't give them back."

Sam's smile broadened, knowing I'm blinder than a bat in daylight without my coke bottle specs.

"I couldn't see anything but flashing lights and the empty drink in front of me. I do remember I was thirsty. She hid my purse, too." I crossed my arms. "Called it a track bag."

"Oh, no. Alyssa without her monster purse?"

I tried to look insulted, but I don't think I pulled it off.

Sam chuckled and adjusted the bulk of her prenatal tummy.

I must have looked panicked.

She rubbed her seventh-month belly and smiled down at her bump. "She's kicking."

I glanced at the contortions moving under her T-shirt and gulped.

"It's okay. The baby does it all the time—" She grimaced and pressed on her lowest rib, arching her back as the baby bumped around inside. "—although she's much more active than Jojo was."

My mouth went dry, but I managed to say, "Is Joseph going to be back from training before the baby comes?"

"Oh, yeah, we have two months yet. He's back from Quantico in a few days."

I relaxed a little, sat back, and fiddled with the

paper straw in my ice tea, before taking another sip.

"So-o-o. This Marcus…" Sam rotated her wrist to suggest I continue my story.

"Oh, yeah." I tapped my fingers on the table and remembered where I'd left off. "Well, this guy comes over with two glasses of champagne and offered me one."

"And he was nice looking?"

"Gorgeous. Way too gorgeous."

****

The music pounded in my ears, so I barely heard the man's words above the din.

He leaned closer. "May I sit with you?" he asked.

He didn't look like a masher, so I offered him Georgie's seat. He set the glass of Champagne in front of me and tipped his own a little higher.

"Thank you," I said, although I couldn't hear the glasses clink when we touched them together.

I sipped mine. Nice. Better than the usual stuff you get at a bar. So I took another sip and smiled at the man.

"I'm Marcus," he shouted and touched his hand to his chest. Dressed in a tailored suit of fine gray wool with a blue shirt and distinctive silk tie, he could have been leading a boardroom meeting instead of picking up French trollops in a bar. But tech conventions mix business with pleasure.

"Just got here," he explained. "I had meetings all day and didn't have a chance to change."

Weird. It was like he'd read my thought.

The music blared into another heavy-metal beat. Maybe I cringed.

"Want to get out of here?" he shouted close to my

ear.

With a nod, I took a last sip of the Champagne. I waved to Georgie, dancing with some bald guy on the tiny dance floor.

She signaled thumbs up.

Don't know about that. I'd probably just dump the guy in the lobby and head to my room upstairs. I was attending three presentations on nano-technology tomorrow and needed to be at least partially awake.

The hush of the marble lobby was a relief after the blaring noise of the bar. I relaxed my shoulders and did my best to walk gracefully and not land on my tush. No matter how expensive, the five-inch heels pinched my toes.

He put his hand under my elbow and smiled down at me, all teeth and manners. "Why don't you take them off?"

"I beg your pardon?"

"Those shoes." He pointed to my feet and flashed me another smile. A nice, warm, want-to-get-to-know-you smile. "They can't be comfortable."

"Well, no. My friend lent them to me. The dress, too."

His gaze inched up from my stilettos to my thigh-high hem to my now burning face. I twitched, but tried to look cool. I wasn't used to this kind of inspection.

He took me by the arm. "Maybe we could sit in the coffee shop?"

There was that smile again. I swallowed and nodded, mumbling something too obvious to remember.

****

"You didn't sleep with him that night?" Sam lowered her voice and leaned forward the best she could with the bump in the way. Unfortunately, Alabama Kitchen was a tiny café in downtown Sereno. The older ladies at the next table glanced in our direction, and then tittered into their pastries.

I dropped my gaze to the half-eaten biscuit on my plate, and heat rose on my cheeks. I can never hide a blush.

"You did?"

"Shh."

I buttered said biscuit. "Never made it to my nano-tech seminars the next day either."

"Alyssa." Sam scolded. "On the first date?"

"No date. Just a Vegas Convention pick-up, if you want to call it that."

"Wow."

I let out a long sigh, added boysenberry jelly and bit into the confection. "It was the way he knew what I wanted. I just had to think something, and he knew instantly."

"Will you see him again?"

"He's been in China on business, but we have a date next weekend." A smile crept onto my lips.

****

"Marcus is back in town. He's picking me up at six." I spoke into my cell phone as I hurried down Sereno's main shopping street. "I have to find something to wear."

"For dinner?" Georgie asked.

"No. For dessert."

She giggled. "Good luck then."

I pushed my way into the lingerie shop and glanced around, feeling slightly confused. An airy scent of French perfume wafted over me.

The old college T-shirts I'd collected over the years didn't seem appropriate for my first big weekend away with Marcus. Neither did the granny gowns my mother insisted on giving me for Christmas.

I wanted Marcus to appreciate me. To think I was beautiful. He'd been travelling on business for most of the last month, and finally we had two days to spend together on the coast. He'd booked a suite at a five star hotel in Half Moon Bay, and I was dreaming of long walks on the beach. And a few other long things.

I touched the flimsy black lace on the mannequin and swallowed noisily. Maybe this was a mistake.

"*Bonjour.* May I help you, *Madame*?" The tiny woman with an endearing French accent appeared from behind the curtain.

I stared at the black bustier in front of me, complete with lacy garters and littered with little red roses in all the appropriate places.

"Um, no. I mean yes."

"Perhaps a more modest selection?" With a wave of her hand, she led me to the side wall and pulled a pale blue gown from her choices. "It has a robe, too." She smoothed the silk over her arm. "Something sexy, yet comfortable."

The way she pronounced *comforTA-ble* was so cute, I smiled.

The soft white lace on the robe had me drooling. Why was I suddenly into gooey creations that I wouldn't wear for five minutes?

"*Exactement, Madame.*"

"I'll take it."

****

Against the night sky, the waves pounded on the

shore, illuminated by the phosphorescent ocean. I turned and stepped into the suite and partially closed the French doors to our balcony. The bed, softly lit and turned back, waited in the background.

"Take it off," Marcus said, his voice already rough.

I grinned and modeled the gown, letting the silk swish softly over my legs. I touched the tiny satin rose at the breast of the gown and drew a hand along the lace of the revealing bodice. "This? You want me to take off this?"

He'd already unloaded his pockets of phone, wallet, and keys. Gaze capturing mine, he walked slowly across the room. He unbuttoned the second and third buttons of his shirt and grinned, a delicious wolf's grin that had my heart doing little pitter-pats. My breath left through the French doors.

When he shrugged the robe from my shoulders, the silk pooled on the floor, a quiet blue lake.

His hands smoothed down my back, warm, insistent. He kissed me softly, and then again, with more passion. My pulse was already pounding. Incredible heat flowed through my limbs. Wonderful shivers raced over my back.

I wound my arms around his neck, relishing his height. I had to stand on tiptoes to kiss his lips.

"I've missed you, babe," he whispered in my ear, nibbling on my lobe and down to my collar bone.

I froze.

He nestled his chin on the side of my neck, flicking his tongue with a light touch, tasting me. "You're so beautiful, babe."

I pulled back for a moment and looked up into his lovely gray eyes. Not light, not dark, just a gorgeous shade of gray-blue that had darkened since we'd begun to kiss. I swallowed hard and focused on the top button of his shirt. Damn. I snorted to myself. Babe? Shoulda known.

"I feel like Champagne," I said, working on a sincere tone and drawing little love circles on his chest. "I want to celebrate our weekend together."

He kissed my fingertips, like a real gentleman. "Of course. Let's order from room service."

I chewed on my lip for a moment, pretending concentration. "Could you go down to the bar and get it? It'll be so much quicker." I dropped my lashes. "That way we won't be…interrupted."

I felt his moment of hesitation, but then he smiled and walked to the door, grabbing just his room key before he left.

I listened for his footsteps and the swish of the elevator doors.

My heart pounding, I grabbed his phone and checked his final messages.

The last one, to someone named Susanne, said, *"Won't make it home tonight, babe. Meetings are running very late. Negotiations stalled. We will have to try again tomorrow for a deal. Kiss the kids for me and look for me on Sunday night."*

My eyes stung, and I hurried to the bathroom to change. I left the pool of blue silk where it was, stripped, and tossed out the gown. Stupid, I thought, glaring at myself in the mirror. Stupid, stupid, stupid.

I'd finished dressing by the time Marcus walked through the door, glasses and bottle in hand.

I zipped my overnight bag with vigor and stared at the floor.

He glanced at his phone on the bureau. His shoulders drooped as he set down the Champagne. "What gave me away?"

I gave a quick snort that he could hear and placed my glasses on my face. Body armor. "Babe? Really? How obvious do you have to be?"

He looked me square in the eye. "She doesn't care what I do," he offered as a flimsy excuse.

I wasn't buying the lie and crossed my arms.

"You liked it, didn't you?"

Too much, I thought to myself. Way too much. If I stood here five more minutes, I wouldn't leave. I grabbed my bag, my coat, and my pride, and walked to the door.

"Sorry, *Babe*," I said with emphasis. "I don't sleep with lying, cheating, scumbags. And I don't sleep with married men."

****

"Wow!" Sam shook her head. "But I don't understand how you knew he was married. So what if he called you Babe?"

"My friend Georgie—she told me years ago. If a guy calls you Babe all the time, or Sweetie, or Honey, he's using that pet name so he doesn't mix you up with his wife." I gritted my teeth, but one lousy tear dripped down my cheek and gave me away.

"He hurt you, didn't he?" She patted my hand. "I could sic Joe on him with a couple of his cop friends."

I laughed and brushed aside the tear. I knew she was joking, but it helped that she could see through my exterior shields.

"No. He's nothing. Who needs him?"

"Exactly." She sat back and smiled. "You have

your work and your friends. The right guy will come along."

After lunch, I gave Sam and her baby bump a hug and walked the six blocks back to work. I loped up the wooden stairs and crossed the covered porch. I dug around in my purse for my access card, swiped it across the light near the doorbell, and entered what had been a Victorian home on one of the side streets of Sereno.

Most of my company is situated in another Silicon Valley town. Big buildings full of cubicles and people. Big ventures and a big, colorful name.

But the real work is done in super-secret locations like this one, scattered across town. X sites, they're called. I'd been hired two years ago.

My first start-up had gone public three years ago, rewarding me with a nice round nest egg, but I didn't want to put my feet up and watch my money grow. While our scent robots were out saving the world, and the stock value was playing with the big boys, I still liked building things, solving puzzles, and working with super smart nerds like myself. I needed the challenge.

With a quick wave to the receptionist, a bulging-muscled guy in black, I accessed the next layer of security with a retinal scan.

My boss was a security freak, but after the last breach and the lawsuits that followed, no one questioned his obsessive routines anymore.

I sat at my computer, pressed the fingerprint reader and entered my codes to access the three remaining firewalls.

My team needed to finish the final step in our project by next Thursday, but the group was stymied.

We'd banged our heads against the whiteboard all morning, with nothing but old ideas to rehash.

I rested my chin in my hands and stared at the screen. Nothing. Not a coherent thought in my brain.

Did I really care whether we had a new subroutine to measure data input from our customers faster and more effectively than our competitors?

Meh.

I looked around the room. My two best engineers were huddled in the corner, looking as frustrated as I felt. In fact, my whole team was feeling the pressure. Deadlines did that. I walked to the kitchen and poked the button marked cappuccino on our monster caffeine machine. Better make it a double.

I leaned against the sink and shook a yellow packet of sweetener, waiting for the machine to finish dripping black, then white brew. Cup in hand, I grabbed a couple oatmeal cookies from the glass canister. My best programmer came around the corner and dug in the fridge for a cold drink.

"Got anything, Burke?"

"Morgan has an idea. We're trying to structure the code we'd need to make it work. We've designed a preliminary routing map if you want to take a look."

"Great."

"Need your help on the flow chart," Burke continued as he twisted open the top of the juice bottle. He pushed his wire rim glasses up his nose and blinked at me myopically.

"Let's get to it."

Chapter Two

My phone buzzed across my night stand. It was light, barely, and I turned over in my me-only bed and felt for the phone.

"Are you going to make it to Sunday brunch today?" My mother's voice reached down through layers of sleep and dragged me to consciousness.

"I'll be there. Always am," I said with my head still buried in my pillow. I cleared my throat again.

"Work late?"

I grunted something about three.

"Okay, we'll wait for you. We have important news to talk about today."

I blinked a couple times. Nothing was ever that important at our monthly Sunday brunch. The Manchester family—Mom, my older sister Samantha, her little guy Jojo, and her husband Joseph, if he wasn't on duty that day with Sereno PD—usually made going to my mom's house on the first Sunday of the month a done deal.

Sis lived with her family a few blocks away from Mom. Sometimes my little bro Alex drove down. He attended Berkeley Law and as a 2L, he always needed a free meal with a couple doggy bags to keep him going. Mom made plenty.

I arrived about one, still achy from fifty-two hours of writing code, but feeling better about the deadline that was now not quite so impossible to meet.

My guys would work today, and if we all put in the hours this week, we would have something for the senior execs to look at by the time Thursday came around.

I pushed through the door to my childhood home, plopped my purse on the tiled entry and shouted hello. Designed as a typical California two-story built in the sixties, it had the living room with its high pitched ceiling situated at the back of the house. The dining room and kitchen were placed to one side, and the family room hidden beyond.

Mom had redecorated a few years back so the place wasn't a total time warp. She'd done most of the work herself, and we'd scoured consignment stores for bargains. The eclectic mix of styles worked better than any designer could have pulled together for ten times the price.

Mid-tone hardwood and muted colors formed a backdrop for my mother's wide-ranging taste in art. I studied a new photographic print on the wall. Ansel Adams always did have a nice touch. Mom had good taste even if her funds were in short supply.

Mom returned my call from the kitchen. Samantha carried Jojo into the living room and smiled at me. "Here's Auntie 'lyssa, Jojo."

"Hey, baby boy. How's my buckaroo?" I held out my arms.

Jojo, at twenty months, is still shy with strangers, but knows me. He clapped his chunky little hands and held them over his head, to tell me he wanted to be up high. He weighs a ton—takes after his dad. As I hoisted him toward the ceiling, he giggled happily. I blew raspberries onto his fat belly, and he shrieked with laughter.

"Don't get him wound up, Alyssa," Sam said. "I want to put him down for his nap before we have dinner."

I nuzzled the sweet folds of my nephew's little neck. He smelled wonderful—applesauce, baby sweat, and soap.

Just like our mom, Samantha was the calm, disciplined mother. You know, meals prepared at just that certain time. Bedtime proceeded with a strict regimen of brushed teeth and washed faces. One book, just one, was read before Jojo was tucked into bed. That is, unless I had anything to do with it. Call me a parenting heretic.

Reluctantly, I handed the baby to his mother, but when Sam took Jojo, he whimpered. My heart melted a little around the edges. "Never mind, Jojo," I called up the stairs as Samantha headed for the still-in-use nursery. "We'll play after you have your nice nap."

"Hello, darling," Mom called from the dining room as she placed two bowls of veggies on the white table cloth. "I'm glad you made it." She adjusted the bowls until they were centered and then glanced up. "You look tired, dear."

I shrugged. "Work." Fortunately, Mom would never know about the hideous mistake I'd made with Marcus this past month.

She stared at me a moment longer, a slight frown buckling her brow. Then she brushed back her softly graying hair and turned toward the kitchen.

"Can I help?" I called through the pocket door.

Alex walked through the front entrance just then,

and I greeted him with open arms. He hugged me back. We tussled enough to measure each other's strength. It'd been a couple months since I'd seen my little brother.

"Stop that, you two." Mom returned to the dining room with an enormous plate of pot roast.

Although he was tall and dark like my sister, Alex's eyes were the same piercing blue as my father's. I forgave him for that and cuddled under his arm.

"Here let me help," Alex said and moved across to the dining room. He set down the large oval plate dead center of the table, adjusting the angle until it was perfectly lined up with the candlesticks.

Dinner was quiet, as always with the clink of glasses and the occasional grind of a knife against porcelain. Every Manchester knew eating was a solitary communion between you and the food on your plate. The meal was delicious as always, hearty and homey. Mom had even made popovers. Alex and I vied for the last one.

After the dishes were cleared—Alex's turn, but I loaded—we settled in the living room.

Mom sat primly in her pale blue wing chair, holding a large envelope with foreign stamps pasted across the top corner. She had a look in her eye that foretold something out of the ordinary. We usually ended up watching re-runs of Judge Judy. Guess not today.

My interest was piqued, and I could tell Sam was curious too. Alex arrived last, still drying his hands on a dish towel, and he shoved in next to me on the couch.

Mom cleared her throat and began. "I must have told you kids the story about Great-aunt Isabella."

We nodded in unison.

"How she left the family in 1938 to move to Paris and was never heard from again."

Another group nod.

"My grandparents did try to find her. They even hired a detective after the war, but Isabella had seemingly disappeared."

I tapped my finger against my knee, waiting for my mother to finish this introduction. She liked her moments of drama.

She cleared her throat with importance.

See?

"Well, we've received a letter."

"Is she still alive?" I asked. "She must be close to a hundred by now."

"Ninety-seven." Mom dropped her gaze and crossed herself. "But no, she died last month."

Mom picked up the envelope again. "This is a letter she left with a solicitor in London. He introduces himself as Paul St. James. Sometime back, Isabella requested he find her heirs. She left this package with him to be sent to the family after he received notification she had passed."

"Really loved us, didn't she?" Sam commented dryly, but then Jojo squeaked upstairs, and she was off to fetch him.

"I always thought it was exciting to have a mysterious, missing aunt," I said. "I could dream of stories about how she might have lived, where she'd gone, what she had done with her life."

Mom adjusted her position in her chair and stared across the coffee table at me. "Well, that's good perhaps, because she requires one of us to go to Paris and attend to her affairs. You, Alyssa, seem to be the obvious choice."

I blinked a couple times. Next to me, Alex chuckled and punched me in the shoulder. "Bingo, Sis. A chance to solve the mystery of Auntie Isabella."

"I can't go." I must have said this vehemently, because Jojo started fussing on the stairs.

Mom gave me a quiet once over and then proceeded to explain. "Well, Samantha can't go. She's pregnant again and has little Jojo to care for. And Alex will be at school for several more months before his summer break."

"What about you?"

"Me? Oh, no dear. I could never travel alone all that way. Besides, I don't speak French."

"And I do?"

"At least you took two years in high school," Sam pointed out.

I shot her a withering glance which she fended off with a graceful turn of her cheek.

Ignoring us, Mom continued. "The solicitor says someone needs to go within the week in order for us to claim the inheritance. You, Alyssa, are the one who must go."

"I have work. I have deadlines. I have—"

"Excuses." Sam chimed in.

Alex pounded me on the back. "Looks like today's your lucky day."

Mom handed me the envelope, and as things are done in the Manchester family, that was that.

I gave a short groan. How would I explain a trip to Paris to my boss? I opened the large manila envelope and read the short letter from Mr. St. James. A first class air ticket was included, but must be scheduled within the week.

"A week," I moaned. "I have to go within the week."

"It will do you good to get away for a bit." Mom rose and came to my side. She patted my shoulder in a loving yet firm you-don't-have-a-choice-Alyssa way. "Besides, you look like you could use a vacation, dear."

Still wondering how I'd explain this to my boss, I asked, "Have you ever been to Paris?"

Mom shook her head.

I tapped the plane ticket against my knee. Maybe I did need a break. It had been years since I'd had more than a couple days off.

"Just go." Mom smiled down at me. "Call it a family emergency."

****

Sam drove me to SFO five days later. I was so nervous; my stomach was jumping with more than cute little butterflies. Felt like seagulls, or maybe drones. I held my big black purse in my lap, the straps clenched to my chest.

Sam chuckled. "Relax, Alyssa."

"Easy for you to say." I chewed on my thumbnail. "You're not headed to a foreign country with no more than a few words of forgotten high school French."

She shrugged and down shifted as she pushed her minivan up the climb on 280 and passed the sculpture of *The Friar* on the hill above us.

Sam shot me a quick glance, and then returned her gaze to the wide curving highway that cut through open country of the Nor Cal peninsula. El Niño winter rains had turned the hillsides the most incredible shade of vibrant green. Scattered across the rolling landscape, big craggy oaks, black with last night's rain, still slumbered. Another week and the trees would leaf out, but for now, bright yellow mustard shaded the fields.

Sam shot me a pushy-broad look I recognized. "Be brave."

I gave her a rueful smile. "I don't have much choice."

We catapulted down the hills above SFO, and Sam parked in front of the International Terminal.

I sucked in a deep breath and opened the car door. "Ready or not, Paris, here I come."

No fog crept through the Golden Gate or hugged the mountains surrounding the bay this evening. My plane took off on time, and I must admit the private cubby in first class was very nice. Aunt Isabella must have been worth a few bucks to spring for this flight.

From my tiny window, I watched the computerized lights on the Bay Bridge trickle down into the dark water and then flash in rhythm along their way to Oakland. The Champagne was passed around, and I was off to Paris.

I must have slept, because I don't remember most of the night. The third glass of Champagne didn't hurt—or the feather duvet and lie-down-and-stretch-out-bed. Breakfast, then landing followed by immigrations and customs.

I stood in the center of Charles de Gaulle airport and blinked in surprise when a formally dressed gentleman approached me. He held up a sign with my name.

"*Bonjour, mademoiselle.* I 'ope you had a pleas*ant* flight?" The man's mustache wiggled as he spoke, like the little guy in the old French movies who could pop his mouth.

"Yes, I mean *oui*."

"*Très bien*. I am Monsieur André Folcher, Monsieur St. James' assistant in Paris. I will escort you to your new home."

"My home?"

"*Mais, oui*. Madame Sophie has given instructions that you must stay in her home while you are in Paris."

My forehead must have buckled in confusion. "Madame Sophie?"

"Ah, pardon, Sophie Delacroix is the name Madame Isabella Manchester took when she decided to remain in France. She is your great-aunt, *non*?"

"No, I mean yes, I mean *oui*."

"Never mind, your French will improve with practice, Mademoiselle." He grabbed my roller suitcase, turned on his heel and marched toward the *Sortie*.

I sighed and shouldered my bag to follow him. "Hope so."

The ride into Paris was quiet, the backseat of the Mercedes cushy. I watched for the Eiffel Tower, hoping to use it as someplace I could get my bearings. Too bad I never saw it.

Monsieur André concentrated on his driving, and only cussed once when a motorcyclist zoomed by and almost took off his mirror. I repeated the phrase a few times under my breath. Never hurts to have a cuss word or two in the local vernacular.

As we neared central Paris, the dingy, graffiti-infested buildings on the outskirts gave way to beautiful nineteenth-century architecture set on broad, tree-lined streets. Many buildings were faced with off-white stone and covered with frilly decorations that spoke of the Belle Époque—a real contrast to the sleek but utilitarian architecture of Silicon Valley.

I let out a long quiet sigh. *Alyssa, you are a long way from home.*

I could tell we were nearing the center of town. Off to the left, the Seine flowed between high embankments, and a long, glassed-in boat filled with tourists glided over the quiet waters.

Monsieur stopped across from a huge building, so French, so ornate, it could have been a wedding cake. On the opposite corner, a little café offered tables for people to sit outside. Jet lagged, I longed for a cappuccino.

Luggage in tow, Monsieur André walked past the café and opened a large door facing the street and the river. He signaled for me to enter. We went through another smaller door, and I stood on a winding set of steps.

Monsieur pushed a button, and the tiniest elevator I'd ever seen slowly descended inside a brass cage, with only room for me and my suitcase. Monsieur followed on the circular stairs. He opened the heavily carved wooden door on the fourth floor. With a graceful wave of his arm, he ushered me into a dark apartment. Only a little light seeped under the long curtains.

I stood in the entry hall, unsure what to do next.

"Mademoiselle. I am afraid the appar-te-ment has not been touched since Madame Sophie passed away. In her letter, she was most insistent that a member of her family be the only person to enter her home and look after her things. Here is the key." He placed the heavy, old fashioned key in my hand. *"Bonne chance."* With a quick nod of his head, he was through the door and had started down the first set of stairs.

I followed him out to the landing and put out my hand. "Wait. Monsieur. Please. What do I do?" My voice echoed down the small stairwell.

He turned and looked up. With a shrug, he said, "Your instructions should be on the table in the entry, Mademoiselle. This is how Madame wished it. She will explain all." With that, he was gone.

Chapter Three

I stood in the hallway for a moment longer, until I couldn't hear his footsteps anymore. I waited for another minute, hoping he would turn around and come back. No such luck. The wooden door banged below, and then the heavy metal one on the street closed.

I swallowed the sticky lump in my throat and pushed the apartment door open with one hand. I stepped into the entry. Light filtered through the kitchen window to my left and into the dim hallway. A cluttered hat rack stood to one side with an overflowing umbrella stand behind it.

The room directly ahead of me was almost dark. A few spears of light crept through holes in the curtains and settled in the room. My nose tickled at the smell of dust, ancient furniture, and old woman. I took a couple more steps into the darkened space and saw the outline of four big windows, each covered with heavy draperies. The windows wrapped around two sides of the room.

I found my courage somewhere and crossed the space. In the semi-darkness I managed to move through the jumble of furniture and finally arrive at the far left window.

I drew back the curtains and after choking on the dust I'd set free, stared in awe at the building across the square. The birthday cake.

Some view.

Then I turned around to face the apartment and let out a groan. It had once been a beautiful room, large in size, with a high, graceful ceiling. But even in the gloom, I could see the piles and piles of boxes stacked to the ceiling. Three deep, they covered the back wall of what must have been the dining space.

A jumble of long neglected furniture crowded the central area, with more boxes of every size leaning at tipsy angles on every horizontal surface.

A high, winged-back chair stood, lonely and worn, in front of the corner window. I moved toward it, going slowly around the piles of boxes so as not to knock anything over. Careful not to disturb any more dust than necessary, I opened those curtains too.

My heart did a flip. From the French-styled windows was a view of the Seine as it divided and flowed around an island midstream. I opened the old-fashioned window, leaned out over the small balcony and studied the busy road bustling below me. Peeling paint clung to window sashes. I chipped a little away with a finger and sighed, wondering what other maintenance skills I would need to learn.

I turned and inspected the disaster. "Aunt Isabella, what were you thinking?" I asked, for surely, her ghost still remained in this room. On a tiny table next to her chair, a pink china tea cup waited for someone to wash it. The tea had dried in concentric rings until it reached the bottom of the cup, leaving a dark brown circular stain.

A cold shiver chased up my spine. Was this where she'd died? I swallowed convulsively as I glanced around the dimly lit room.

I rubbed my arms against another set of shivers and stared through the window's filthy glass. No way was I staying here, instructions or not. "Sorry Aunt Isabella, I'll find myself a nice hotel and take the next flight home."

Curious, I made a quick inspection of the rest of the apartment before I left. The door to the next room, a small office, was nearly blocked with stacks of books, old magazines, and newspapers. I pushed it open enough to verify I'd never be able to reach the window at the far side.

Pile after pile of moldy books filled the bookcases to overflowing and were double and triple stacked against the shelves. Paintings and prints covered every square inch of the walls. Extras were then stacked on the floor like in some museum's storage room. Cobwebs hung from the light fixtures and spiders scrambled to safety, disturbed by the light.

The door to the bedroom—I guess it was the bedroom—was completely blocked. I wedged it open a few inches, enough to see that boxes and shopping bags stood at every angle on every piece of furniture. It didn't look like anything had been moved in half a century.

The room was covered in a layer of dust. Had to be years thick. Yuck. I sneezed and made my way back to the living room.

Whatever. Not my problem. I'd call what's-his-name in the morning and leave on the first available flight. No inheritance was worth this mess.

Ah, across the room, in the corner, a small bed was neatly made. After finding a working overhead light, I tiptoed my way through the piles of newspapers and stood beside the only uncovered spot in the entire apartment.

A lamp stood next to the bed. Bound in old red leather, a well-worn copy of *Les Misérables* occupied the table top. A pair of reading glasses sat on the open book, waiting for the return of their owner. My heart sank into my stomach. I closed the book and set it aside along with the remnant of a small white stone carved with the face of an angel.

I sat on the bed with a long sigh and picked up the old-fashioned wire-rimmed reading glasses. I looked out over the room and shook my head in disbelief. Poor Aunt Isabella. How could anyone live in such disaster? Then I remembered she had to be over ninety, maybe closer to one hundred.

I thought of my mother, alone now that my father had left us, and her children were all grown. Isabella had no children to watch over her and love her.

I was it. I was the one to take on the task of my aunt's final wishes. Why Isabella had never returned to us, never contacted us was still a mystery, but I had a job to do. Whatever money her estate provided, I could give to my mother to make her old age safe and comfortable. A teacher's pension was never that generous.

I let out a groan and rubbed my forehead, too jet lagged to be tired or hungry. *Might as well begin.* I hunted around the apartment, but couldn't find the letter Monsieur had spoken of. That wasn't too surprising. I'd keep looking.

I opened all the windows in the living room and sized up the job. No point in even starting with the other rooms until I had this one under control. I found rags and a bucket in the kitchen—don't even ask what that looked like—and began to move the boxes around to create some sort of order. At least most of the age-browned, crispy-edged boxes had labels. Bless Aunt Isabella's little pack-rat heart.

I peeked into a few of the open boxes. Some were filled with old clothing. I would go through those later. Others held books from long ago. The leather bindings were dusty and cracked with age. It looked like most of the titles were in French. Made sense, I guess. I noticed a whole bag of Victor Hugo novels, with several copies of *Les Misérables*. I really should read that classic one of these days.

I took down a particularly well bound copy of *A Moveable Feast* from the shelf and cautiously opened the leather cover to look at the front page. It was inscribed.

To my darling Sophie. Ernest Hemingway.

I blew out a breath. I'd better look through those stacks of books before I gave them away. I wondered how many others were signed first editions?

Jet lag fuzzies finally took hold late that afternoon. When I was too tired to do anything more, I took my purse and jacket and walked down the stairs to the little café situated on the corner below the apartment.

A drink, that's what I needed. Maybe two. I ordered wine and a salad, grateful the waiter had given me a menu translated into English. I didn't have the energy to look up food words in my travel guide. I guessed at soufflé.

I stared across the busy street and watched a couple of cop cars roar past with their European woo-woo sirens blaring.

My salad and soufflé arrived. The second glass of delicious Bordeaux relaxed my tired shoulders. I ate in silence, ignoring the British family across the way, although their little girl was super cute. My hunger taken care of, I grimaced at the thought of returning to the apartment above.

It was almost dark, maybe eight or nine o'clock. Too late to find a hotel room tonight. I gritted my teeth. I would leave the apartment first thing in the morning.

****

April 14: 3:25 pm.

Alyssa Manchester, cleared customs as a United States citizen at 1:45 p.m. today. Arrival of Mademoiselle Manchester to apartment under surveillance, escorted in by older gentleman.

Face rec software identifies him as André Folcher. Folcher left at 3:32 p.m.

No movement from Ms Manchester other than eating in brasserie Guinevere located on the first floor of the building at 7:45. Wine, Cheese soufflé and salad. No visitors or conversation with others. Left a large tip for the waiter. Lights switched on in apartment 4 at 8:34 p.m. Lights off at 9:16 p.m.

Surveillance ongoing.

****

I ignored morning as long as I could, until my craving for caffeine overcame my need to remain horizontal.

I groaned and put my feet to the floor. God. I detested jet lag. It had taken me hours to fall asleep last night. In desperation, I'd dragged a wooden screen from across the room to block my view of the piles of junk I'd have to face today. I'd drifted off about two.

With a longer groan, I lugged my body into wrinkled suitcase clothes and went in search of food. The café downstairs was open. I huddled at a table in the far corner, hoping the regular patrons would ignore me.

A woman with gleaming purple hair took my order and left me to my thoughts. The *café crème* was steaming. I had another to clear the fog along with a croissant. The butter was sweet and rich. I licked my fingers. France might be very bad for a girl's figure.

I paid *l'addition*—that means bill in French. I guessed I should see what needed to be done in the apartment, then go and find that hotel. Maybe the letter from Aunt Isabella would surface today.

I tromped back up the stairs and turned the key in the lock.

Double damn.

The elves hadn't come and cleared the place out. Still filthy. Still piled to the ceiling. Still mine to deal with. I would've let out a big sigh, but there was too much dust.

After I locked the door with the top lock in a collection of at least a dozen, I set my monster purse on the hall table and edged my way past the four-high piles of boxes to the window. I opened the filthy curtains and then the squeaky window. Fresh air. Nice.

Traffic noise from down below filled the room. I liked it better than the silence of the apartment. I felt more a part of the city even when the raucous police cars raced by with their wee-woo sirens blowing. There must be a police station close by.

I dodged through the junk and opened two more windows. I couldn't reach the fourth. It was stacked with boxes all marked *La Pin.*

"What the heck is *La Pin?*"

I searched my small travel dictionary with no success. I'd have to buy a more complete French/English dictionary, but not now. I was stalling. In a kitchen drawer, I found some large black plastic bags.

Get your ass in gear, Alyssa.

Two hours later I'd moved three huge piles of newspapers and magazines from the apartment to the dumpster around the back of the building. The front half of the living room looked almost livable.

I was hot and sweaty and would've loved a bath, but didn't have the heart to face the bathroom yet.

I'd found it hidden in the back corner of the apartment, but beyond poking my nose in the door, I didn't have the courage to enter. Moldy, grimy and piled with more boxes, it would need hours of attention. Maybe days.

The restaurant downstairs would provide my only facilities for now. I washed up the best I could in the kitchen sink and went to dinner. Hard work makes a girl hungry.

I looked up the words in my French phrase book. *Où sont les toilettes?* I repeated the phrase twelve times so I'd remember. Until I had the gumption to face mine, I would have to beg someone else's *toilettes.*

Over a glass of lovely Bordeaux, I considered moving to a hotel again. I might as well stay put, at least for now. If I found a room tonight, I might never return to the apartment.

****

By day three I was making real progress. I had my

sleeping area clean and comfortable. I'd bought new sheets, pillows and blankets at the BHV—the big department store right across the square. I'd made my bed and found a more effective lamp to position close by. Ten more bags of newspapers had ridden down the teensy elevator to the dumpster. I could only hope my neighbors didn't mind too much that I filled up their bins.

I'd gone through the stacks with care, but still no letter from Aunt Isabella. Hands on my hips, I blew my curly bangs off my damp forehead and studied the room. If I didn't find it in the next couple days, I'd need to call that lawyer.

Next: the kitchen. Maybe I should buy a gas mask first.

After scrubbing through the greasy muck of a pre-war kitchen, I needed a break.

****

On day five, I called Mom and filled her in on my progress. I heard Jojo in the background singing with Samantha, and my stomach dropped with sudden homesickness. We spoke for a moment, but they were off to preschool soon.

It was Sunday. A day of rest, right? After my coffee, I wandered across the bridge and into the square in front of Notre Dame. I had to *par-don* my way through the dense crowds of tourists until I found a place on the bench under the enormous statue of Charlemagne. The church bells rang, deep and rich, sending a chill up my spine.

Curious. Everyone in the crowd was fashionably dressed and carrying twigs of green bushes. I checked the calendar on my phone. Palm Sunday. Well, of course the French wouldn't have palms in Paris. I picked up a branch someone had left on the bench. The sprigs of boxwood were a good substitute.

I twirled the twig in my fingers and smiled. Mom had done her best to make us religious, but at least with me, it hadn't stuck. A church was a building, pretty, maybe even historic, but nothing more glorious than that.

I waited in the line that scrolled across the square and finally entered the church through tiny doors nestled inside the gigantic carved ones.

Inside Notre Dame, the towering Gothic arches rose above me into darkness. Ethereal blue light from the windows drew me forward. I stopped a moment to appreciate the artistry of the rose windows. People on their knees crowded the altar.

Perhaps God might exist in such a place. The organ began a hymn, and the choir raised their voices. "Alleluia."

I sat down in an old wooden pew to the side and did my best to say a prayer for Aunt Isabella.

I tapped the sprig against my palm. Had Isabella worshiped here? Did people know her at this church? My heart beat a little faster. I would come back in a day or two and investigate.

****

On Monday, I strolled across the square to the BHV department store and bought a French press and ground coffee. The following morning I made my own rich brew. I would hit the café for toast later or maybe indulge in one of those chocolate croissants I'd seen in the display case of the *pâtisserie* down Rue Victoria.

I opened my now sparkling corner window and

enjoyed the early morning view of the Seine. During the week, the crowds were different. No families pushing strollers hurried to see the tourist sites. Businessmen in suits and ties carried their briefcases and scurried across the street with their phones to their ears.

A few gaggles of teens followed their adult leaders toward the *Île de la Cité*. Easter break and the obligatory school trip. Not a visit to DC, like kids in the States did, but the history and highlights of Paris.

Armed with a second cup of coffee to bolster my courage, I ripped into the first box of La Pin and laughed when I unwrapped a small ceramic blue rabbit. I hurried to my newly purchased French dictionary and found the word.

Lapin. n. Rabbit.

I snickered. Of course.

I was halfway through the second box—yes, all rabbits—when a knock at the door startled me. Who even knew I was here?

I looked through the peep hole and then opened the door a crack. A very thin, very old man stood before me. A warm smile creased his ancient face.

"*Pardon, Madame. Je m'appelle Maximilian LaForet. J'habite là.*" He pointed to the identical door across the tiny hall.

I opened my door wider and put out my hand. "*Enchantée, Monsieur. Je m'appelle Alyssa.*" On my brief travels around the city, I'd heard someone greet a friend that way.

He began speaking in impossibly quick French. No way would I understand, so I showed my palms. "*Je ne comprends pas.*"

"Ah," he nodded. "I 'ope you are surviving within the apart-e-ment? *Oui?*" The friendly smile grew and lit his dark brown eyes.

I guess he figured we'd get along better if he spoke English, since I had already used up three quarters of my French vocab.

"It's been rather difficult. I have so much more to do before I can put the apartment on the market."

"You would sell such a flat? *Oh, Mon Dieu.*" His tisked his tongue against his teeth and shook his head. "Of course, it is worth very much money, but do you not wish to live in Paris? Is it not, how do you say, the perfect location?"

I loved the way he slurred the *tion* into *sssion*. I smiled at him broadly. "Please, would you like to come in? I have the kitchen in decent enough shape to offer you tea. Perhaps you would rather have a coffee?"

"*Merci, madame.* Or is it *mademoiselle?*" His wiry gray eyebrows rose. Was he flirting?

"It's *mademoiselle.*" I tapped my chest, and he bowed just slightly in an old-fashioned way.

He entered and glanced around the room, his gaze darting from space to space like a bird inspecting a new tree limb in search of possible predators.

I showed him to the green velvet couch I'd cleared the day before and went to the kitchen to put on the kettle.

When I returned, he was looking out the window toward the birthday cake or, as they say here, L'Hôtel de Ville. "You have a magnificent view, Miss Alyssa. A treasure, surely."

"Thank you. It is beautiful. Did you know my Aunt Isabella well?"

His forehead buckled, and he seemed confused for a moment, tapping his hand to his withered lips. "Is that what you called her?"

"Well, yes. Isabella Manchester. That was the name she was born with in America."

"Ah, yes. Isabella," he whispered, then shook his head. "Non, I only knew her as Sophie, Madame Sophie. She lived in this apartment longer than most people remembered. I moved here a few years ago, and she had been here many years already."

I set down a tray with sugar and milk, tea cups, and spoons on the large square trunk in the middle of the room. "So very strange," I said under my breath.

Monsieur cocked his head to the side.

"You see, our family lost track of Isabella before the war. Never heard from her again after France fell. In fact, most of the family thought she had been killed in the war."

"*Quelle dommage*. In all these years, you have never spoken to her?" His eyes brightened with the question.

"No. Her lawyer contacted us after her death." I poured tea from a Wedgwood teapot with a darling rabbit on the lid. I'd found it under a slew of ratty baskets on top of the kitchen cabinet.

I tapped my cup with a finger. "I wonder why she changed it? Her name, I mean."

Max shrugged his thin shoulders, then blew on his cup and took a quick sip.

"Did she ever mention her other name, her real name, to you?" I asked.

He stirred his tea and made no further comment.

I let out a sigh. "Sad, don't you think? She had

family in the States, and yet she lived here, all alone all these years."

Maximillian nodded with a brief frown and a shrug. He picked up and examined the little blue rabbit I'd found in the first La Pin box.

Then he glanced at the open cartons on the floor. "There are others?"

"Just a few." I closed my eyes for a moment and took off my glasses to polish them. A few thousand was closer to the count. "This morning I discovered six more boxes marked La Pin in the office. The place is more like a rabbit depository than an apartment."

"Humph," Max said with a teasing twinkle in his eye. "Perhaps ceramic rabbits multiply as fast as live ones?"

I offered him a second round of Earl Grey and a plate of Petit Beurre cookies. I wanted to fatten up the poor, old guy. Had he ever known a good meal? "Do you know why she liked them?"

Max shook his snow white head. "I know she was always looking for them. Every antique dealer in the area would call Madame Sophie if he found a little rabbit." He dropped his gaze to the tea pot. "But I'm not certain why they were impor-tant to her."

He gave his cup a wistful smile, folding the deep lines in his face. "Sometimes when she came home, she would show me her latest find. I do know the rabbits gave her great joy."

He rubbed his ear with a rheumatic finger. "In the end, it was what she cared about the most. She had no company. No friends."

"Just her and thousands of rabbits." With a sigh, I took another sip of my tea. "Poor Isabella."

Maximillian dug in the inside pocket of his well-worn jacket and pulled out a fine gold pocket watch. A tiny metal key hung from the fob. He clicked open the cover of the watch and glanced at the time. "Ah, mademoiselle, I must hurry."

A little disappointed, I forced my lips into a smile. Max was the first person I'd spoken to in days, and I realized how lonesome I'd been.

I put out my hand to help him rise. "Please come again, Monsieur. I have enjoyed our chat."

"I will do that. *Merci.*"

He creaked his way toward the door and turned to face me after I'd opened it for him. Then he smiled as if he'd had the most wonderful idea. "Do you like music?"

"Yes."

"I have tickets for a concert for *vendredi, sept heures.*"

"*Vendredi?*" I counted through the days of the week on my fingers until I came to Friday.

"Friday at seven?" See? I could speak French.

I smiled at Max and agreed to go with him. He seemed very pleased.

"Sainte Chappelle. I will knock at six." With that, he trundled across the hall and into his own dark apartment.

I leaned against my door frame until his door closed. Perhaps getting to know Max would be a good way to learn more about Isabella?

****

After my first visitor departed with an adorable bow, I set up a table in the office and lined rabbits up along the surface. Having at least something organized helped calm my inner need for order.

By dinner, I'd unpacked hundreds of greasy, dusty, hadn't-seen-daylight-in-decades rabbits and realized I'd need more room. I'd only unloaded the first layer of boxes and had two more to rummage through. I itched. I sneezed. I washed my hands. Still more bunnies bounced from their newspaper wrappings. I stopped to read the occasional headline or ad and noticed I was now into the sixties with my unpacking. Twenty more years to go. Hundreds of rabbits stared at me with expectant expressions. What now, Alyssa, they asked with twitchy noses and upturned ears.

Chapter Four

A few minutes after six on that Friday, Max knocked timidly at my door, and I opened it. He looked very different this evening from the first time I'd met him.

He wore a suit, very old, but at one time well-tailored and stylish. His shoulders no longer filled out the jacket. His white shirt was neatly pressed, his jaunty red tie carefully knotted. A beret, black and made of thick, soft-looking wool perched on his head. His dark eyes twinkled.

"Why Monsieur, you look very handsome."

He straightened with pride and crooked his arm, offering to escort me the three short steps to the elevator. "You also look lovely."

I was glad I'd dug out my one dress instead of wearing my usual jeans.

Surprisingly, when we reached the street, he walked quickly to the corner and the crosswalk. I had expected to assist him, but he didn't need my help. He may have leaned a little on his silver topped cane, but he still moved with confidence.

"Sainte Chappelle est là." He pointed in the general direction of the next bridge. I understood. We walked arm in arm through the evening crowd. The western clouds glowed with pastel colors, and somewhere, bells were ringing.

"Are you making progress with the apparte-ment, Mademoiselle?"

"Oh, please. Call me Alyssa."

He nodded in agreement. "Then I shall be Max."

I nodded. "And yes. The apartment is coming along, slowly." There was no point in complaining about the work still waiting for me.

"And you have found a few more *lapins*?"

I chuckled and met his gaze. He was teasing. "A few."

We waited in line for several minutes outside the gated entrance to Sainte Chappelle and were then escorted with a small group along the wide marble halls now used as a courthouse. Finally, we entered the small church.

Everyone hushed their voice as they crossed the threshold. I could see why. The tall, stained glass windows lining both sides of the room were stunning. Beyond stunning.

I must have dropped my chin to my belly button. The windows, each at least fifty feet in height, rose to an arched Gothic ceiling. Each one gleamed with gorgeous reds, and blues, and purples. The scenes depicted stories from the bible.

"C'est belle?" Max asked.

OMG. *C'est belle*, to the tenth power.

I stared, awestruck, as we were escorted to our seats near the front row. Max had sprung for the good tickets. Others had to sit much farther down the aisle from the small stage.

The musicians entered, bowed, and we all clapped politely. Six musicians stood on the dais, three violins, a viola, and a cello. An older man with long, brushed-back gray hair sat in front of an instrument that looked something like a piano. A harpsichord? He pulled off the Beethoven look nicely.

The first violinist counted the beat silently, and the musicians began the piece. I recognized the melody from somewhere, although I'm no authority on eighteenth-century music. Vivaldi, the poster outside had read. Sometimes Mom tuned to the classical station in the car. She always said it calmed her when she drove.

From the very first note, I was dumbfounded. The acoustics were incredible. Who knew a twelfth-century building could reverberate with such glorious sound.

The talent and the joy with which the musicians played had me enraptured. I couldn't take my eyes off the first violin. At times, his expressive face seemed almost bored, like he knew the music so well he didn't have to think about it. Then, in the next moment, he would grimace, working as if the music was the most difficult thing he'd ever done. His fingers moved so quickly, so lightly over the strings.

Sometimes the group played seriously, but just as often the musicians clowned and cavorted their way through the music, as if racing to the finish line, each hoping to win the prize. We, the audience raced with them, and at the end, we were shouting and standing and clapping in admiration. I'd never enjoyed any music so much.

I was surprised how many of the melodies I recognized. I guess I had Mom to thank. I may not remember the names or the dates of all the great composers, but the appreciation for their music was there.

I hummed one of the tunes as we left the building. "The concert was wonderful, Max," I said as we walked home through the moonlit darkness toward the Seine. "Thank you."

He patted my hand and looked at me with a far-off expression. I hadn't asked him about his life, his personal history yet, but from the look on his face, I wouldn't be surprised if he wasn't reliving another concert in another lifetime.

We walked past the gauntlet of tourist shops, and Max got a sly look on his face.

"I am not supposed to eat sweets anymore, but I have a dee-sire for a crêpe tonight." He stopped in front of a small street stand. "Would you care for one?"

I stared at the flat iron pan and shrugged. "I guess so."

"You have never had one then?" He spoke in quick French to the cook behind the glassed-in counter, and soon the smell of pancakes filled the air. The thin crêpes had chocolate, or lemon, or caramel rolled up inside. What's not to love?

My mouth started to water. "I think I might like these."

He handed me a chocolate filled one. I did.

I could have eaten three more, but didn't want to seem greedy on our first date.

Max and I linked arms and crossed the dark river. A brightly lit tourist boat slid past under the bridge, and a few happy tourists waved up at us. I waved back, feeling for a moment like somehow this was my home—my Paris.

"*À bientôt,*" Max called as we separated at our doors.

45

"*Merci,* Max. I had a wonderful evening."

****

Report to A. de Ville.

AM appeared at 6:05 in the company of elderly male neighbor. The two crossed Quai de Gesvres and Le Pont d'Arcole and were followed to Ste. Chappelle for the nightly Vivaldi concert, starting at 7 p.m. and ending at 8:49 p.m. Followed to local crêperie. Two chocolate crêpes ordered and consumed, then both returned to the apartment building. Light in apartment 4 came on at 9:14. No other movement.

Note: Surveillance isn't difficult with elderly escort and AM does not seem aware of tails. Identity of new suspect to follow.

****

Follow-up report.

Maximillian LaForet, age unknown. Possible alias. No records further back than 1995. Resident of building for the last six months.

****

Tired of sitting inside and with the sky so blue and the clouds so fluffy, I went out to hunt for a pâtisserie. A girl's gotta eat. I took a small box of my aunt's pictures and letters with me, items I'd sifted from the piles of newspapers in the apartment. Although I still hadn't found the mythical letter, I hoped these would reveal something about my aunt's mysterious life.

The process of culling cards and letters had slowed my cleaning efforts considerably. I'd chucked the first loads of newspapers without going through them. Then I'd noticed the piles were filled not only with the days and weeks of newspapers and magazines and years of junk mail, but also personal letters and pictures. The farther down in the piles I went, the older these memories became. As I sorted, I pulled out what looked interesting, leaving it to read later. I regretted my initial tossing and hoped said letter had not been lost.

Around the corner and down Rue Victoria, the aroma from an adorable tea shop slash bakery called to me. A handsome man stood at the doorway. He smiled and bowed just slightly, as if to encourage me to enter.

Why not? He certainly wasn't hard on the eyes, and the pastries in the display counter were TDF. Who knows, maybe he spoke a little English.

After I found a spot by the window, he handed me a translated menu, and I looked up into his large gray eyes. "How did you know I wasn't French?"

His gracious smile worked his whole face, and then he put out his hand in that dramatic way the French have. "Your hair. There is no such beautiful hair in all of France."

I blushed before I had a chance to draw a breath. Damn. "*Merci*." I choked out, remembering at least one word. I dropped my gaze to my menu.

"I have embarrassed you, *non*?"

"Yes, I mean no. Well, yes. I don't see my curls as all that attractive."

"I disagree. You are striking. And so tall. Are you a model?" He took a step closer. "You must be one of the American models who has come to Paris for the spring fashion show?"

I chuckled at the thought. Yeah, right. I'd trip on any runway a designer pointed me down.

"You laugh?"

"I'm sorry. I don't mean to be rude. I'm an electrical engineer from California."

He reached for the little metal chair across from me and sat at my table. With no one else in the café, I guess that was okay. Before I had a chance to pull away, he took my hand in his and studied my face intently. "*Elle est belle et intelligente.*"

I got the gist. He was hitting on me. I narrowed my eyes. I pretended to adjust my glasses and took a quick glance at his left hand. No ring, but that wasn't a definitive sign. I gritted my teeth and remembered Marcus.

I studied his face more intently. Easy, since he was still staring right at me. He had a nice nose, thin and French, with a good strong chin, darkened by a week old beard. I'd guess thirty-ish, but it's hard to tell with guys.

His dark brown hair combed back from his face had streaks of lighter brown through it, like he'd spent time at the beach. More natural than any hairdresser could muster.

The outdoorsy type?

His hair touched the top of his starched white shirt, and he'd wrapped a typical black apron around his trim waist. I'd noticed he was tall when I'd walked past him at the door.

He smiled again, showing me perfect pearly whites. Nice smile. It went up to his eyes.

"I am Anton."

I swallowed hard. "Alyssa," I said, trying and failing to control the heat on my cheeks.

****

Who knew a pastry chef could be so cute? Anton brought me some of the chocolate *macarons* he'd just finished making, and I thought I might fall over in ecstasy. My eyes must have rolled back in my head, because he laughed in appreciation as I reached for another.

"So good," I said with my mouth full. The chocolate cream in the middle had me happily humming to myself.

"I'm glad you like them," Anton said, his expression serious. "I make the croissants, too. Many cafés just bake from frozen pastries. We make ours from itch."

"From scratch?"

"Yes, yes. From scratch."

After two more *café au laits* and swearing his croissants were the best in all of Paris, no, maybe France, I rose to leave. I had to get back to the apartment and finish my day's allotment of garbage runs.

"L'addition, s'il vous plait," I said, euros in hand.

After handing over my change, Anton waved goodbye from the steps of the pâtisserie.

I slung my purse on my shoulder and walked back home with a little more spring in my step. I might try the *brioche* tomorrow. Anton had said it would be very fresh.

I tapped my key fob on the sensor and opened the first and then the second door to the building. I'd better take the stairs after that many *macarons*. I was only huffing a little by the time I made the fourth floor.

I glanced at Max's door. No light showed underneath, and I didn't want to disturb the poor guy. I opened my door and pushed in, but stopped in the entry hall.

From the very beginning, the one thing I'd sensed

in Isabella's apartment was the feeling of safety. Now, for some reason, the secure feeling had been disturbed. I stood still for a long moment, testing the air.

"Hello?" I called.

Now that was stupid. No one would answer me, I hoped. Even a dumb burglar would have more sense.

I closed the door and flipped a couple locks. When I stepped into the living room, I frowned. I could have sworn the curtains and window were closed when I left. Now a cool breeze flowed in from the river below. I rubbed the goose bumps on my arms.

Maybe I just hadn't been paying attention. Perhaps the windows weren't closed all the way, and the breeze blew them open. Feeling a cold shiver slither down my spine, I shut them quickly and turned the antique locks.

Just in case, I peeked around the corners and checked every dark space in the apartment.

"You see, silly. No boogey-man. Just your imagination."

I put down the box of letters I'd never had time to look at and climbed into the clothes I'd designated as grubbies. So much more work to do. Today I would tackle the bathroom.

Gross.

****

After Mademoiselle Manchester left the pâtisserie, I stripped off my apron and hurried to my office. Bruno lounged outside the entrance to our office building, and a smirk crossed his face when I approached. "From itch?" He shook his head and snorted at my ridiculous malaprop.

"A baker might not have perfect English," I pointed out, and Bruno shrugged.

"Bugs in place?"

"In and out. No problem."

****

Smelling of multiple cleansers and disinfectants, I finished the bathroom in record time. Chocolate really revs me up. I still had three boxes of antique bath powders to lug downstairs for tomorrow's trash, but I now had a bathroom even my mother would be proud of. And finally, I could take a decent bath. No more quick wash-ups in the kitchen sink. No more *Où sont les toilettes?*

I stood at my front window, surprised at how late it was. Across the square, the chandeliers inside L'Hôtel de Ville gleamed from the formal rooms, and the sky only had a few streaks of deep orange left to the west. The traffic cruised down the street.

I was too tired to go out, so I dined on toasted bread and jam, and French yogurt. I loved the little glass jars the yogurts come in. Maybe I'd take a few empty jars home, to remember my time here.

I wandered into my reclaimed bath. I had to admit, there was something romantic about a claw foot tub. This wasn't one of those faked-up jobs they sell now in posh bath boutiques in Sereno, but a real antique. Cast iron and porcelain, it would take at least three guys to lift it.

It was long enough to allow me to stretch out and used more hot water than I could dream of wasting in dried-up California. I turned on the old-fashioned taps and filled the tub to almost overflowing. Such decadence.

I'd saved one unopened box of bath salts date marked from this millennium.

Lavender. Thanks, Aunt Isabella.

I dumped in the whole box, and the aroma filled the large bathroom. I'd bought new towels yesterday at the BHV. No way to save what was left of the small, linen jobs I'd found in the cupboard. I'd demoted the best of them to cleaning rags and humanely disposed of the rest.

I sank down and let the heat send shivers of warmth up my spine. At home I dashed in and out of the shower in under five.

This was heaven.

I even poured in more super-hot, make-your-toes-scream water when the tub started to cool. After four, no almost five days of constant cleaning, and sorting, and lugging, and tossing, I deserved this luxury.

My thoughts wandered to Anton, the *pâtissier*. So cute. *Délicieux*, as the French would say.

Almost as yummy as his chocolate macarons.

What would it be like to gobble him up? I giggled but then let out a long, ultra-sincere sigh.

What would be the point? He was a French baker. I was a California engineer. Not much crossover there even though he did have a nice smile. And a nice body.

Another shiver strolled up my spine. I would be leaving soon, going back to my job in my X cubicle. It could be a week, maybe two until I could find a listing agent and put the apartment up for sale.

A week or two? With a cute French guy?

"Get a hold of yourself, Alyssa, girl. The last thing you need is another meaningless affair."

I wiggled my toes in the warm water and sighed again. But shouldn't every girl have one memorable night with a handsome Frenchman?

****

The next morning, while washing my tea cup in the kitchen sink, I happened to peek out the corner window and noticed Max sitting in a small patch of garden below. I leaned out for a better look.

The tiny open square was situated between the four interior walls of the apartment building. Although the space couldn't receive that much sun, Max sat on an iron bench reading a newspaper in a patch of bright light.

I wanted to ask him another question about Isabella, so I hurried down the steps and out into the courtyard to greet him.

He glanced up when the heavy metal door closed behind me.

"*Bonjour, Mademoiselle Alyssa. Comment allez-vous?*"

"*Très bien, Monsieur.*" I almost felt as if I should curtsey.

"Come. Sit with me. It is glorious morning, *non?*" He moved over, and there was just enough room on the bench for me to join him.

"Thank you, Max. I hadn't noticed this little garden until today."

"*Non?*" He glanced around the enclosed space. "It was Madame Sophie's favorite. She worked in her garden on sunny mornings."

I had a hard time imagining the old woman doing that kind of back-breaking work and must have squinted my eyes in confusion.

"She did what she could in those last few years. Last fall, she had a boy come to dig and carry the heavy trays of plants," Max explained.

I looked around the courtyard. It had probably once been a parking area, but now many of the paving stones had been removed to build a sumptuous garden. Neat rows of flowers and vegetables grew in the patch of sunlight.

A small fountain sat to one side near a large leafless bush that climbed the wall. Above, a few interior windows looked out over the space, and I spotted my kitchen window on the fourth floor.

"It's very pretty."

Max smiled with a far-away look. "She called it her masterpiece."

A few plants had no doubt arrived of their own volition, and I had a sudden itch to work in the soil. "Do you think anyone would mind if I did a little weeding?"

"*Mais non*," Max said, but his wiry gray eyebrows rose in surprise.

It wasn't like I didn't have enough to do, but somehow being out in the spring sunshine was invigorating after so many hours of dust. I searched the courtyard and found tools in a small shed tucked in a corner.

The ancient gardening gloves were too small for my hands, but I located a hand trowel and a rake. Since I was already wearing my grubbies, I set to work.

"I am sorry, Alyssa. I would join you," Max said from his bench. He rubbed his right leg with his arthritic hand. "Even if I could get down on the ground, I'd never get up again."

I laughed. "That's okay. Just enjoy your paper and the sunshine."

The warmth on my back felt wonderful, and soon I

had pulled the plants I was sure were weeds. How different could they be from California weeds? Dandelions, spurge, a little wild grass.

Mom had me out in the garden with her even when I was a young girl, helping her with her veggies and flowers. I'd pulled these weeds before, and soon I had a nice pile of the usual suspects.

I found a water hose and gave the garden a quick drink. It hadn't rained in several days, and a few of the daffodils looked thirsty. The clumps of purple tulips were almost ready to bloom. With another couple days of warmth and sunshine, we would have a real garden.

I rose and brushed off my knees. "I think I'll buy a few annuals to fill in the spaces." I fisted my hands on my hips. "Max, do you know a good place to buy some garden plants?"

"*Oui.* Cross the *pont* toward Notre Dame, and turn right on the first street beyond the quai."

I followed his directions in my head. "Those low green buildings?"

He nodded. "Ask for Madame Miriam. Her shop is across from where the orchids are sold. She will help you. Soon it will be time to plant the seeds of summer."

I was excited about planting more flowers. It seemed the least I could do for Isabella.

Chapter Five

"Captain, I have the latest report on LaForet."

Claire smoothed her long dark hair back over her shoulders and then stood at attention in front of my desk. Since none of my team wore uniforms, she could have been anyone's junior assistant.

As her superior, I wasn't supposed to notice her pretty face and youthful figure, but her good looks and quick mind had come in handy on several cases when the team needed a beautiful woman to work undercover.

"Good." I reached across my cluttered desk and took the file she offered. "Anything important?"

"We are still tracking his whereabouts before the Wall came down. Difficult with possible aliases involved. Interpol is doing a search and should get back to me in a few hours."

I grunted and speed-read the page. "Do we have a chance at digging into the KGB's data base?"

She shook her head. "Not likely. They do not consider our department top priority. It would take months to clear the paper work."

I rotated my chair to face the window and looked out over the square in front of Police Headquarters. Although our team had "evolved" over the years, from several hundred officers when my father headed the staff, to my little team of ten, we still had the same mission: to return treasure stolen by the Nazis more than seventy-five years ago to the rightful owners or their heirs.

I tapped my fingers together. Sure, the job sounded like something out of one of the ridiculous romance novels my mother read, but just a few years ago, a retired German had been caught hoarding hundreds of priceless oil paintings. Most of the art had been looted during the war and given up as lost. I had three of my team in Munich right now, working on the provenance of the stash.

My assistant stuck his head through the door. "She's on the move."

****

Anton was right. The brioche was very fresh, the butter like heaven, and the *confiture de fraises* to die for.

He smiled as I swallowed the last bite and licked the strawberry jam from my fingers. There were more customers today at the pâtisserie, but he'd found time to teach me about rolling my French r's.

"*Le beurrrrre*," he repeated.

I tried to find the place in the back of my throat, but ended up sounding like a choking lion.

"More breathy," he suggested.

I tried again.

"*Bon.* You will speak French in no time."

Doubt that. With only a few weeks to go, what I did learn would surely sift back into my brain, file labeled 'Unused Data.'

Sad. I liked listening to Anton speak to his French customers. He had such a subtle exuberance in the way he communicated. The words were staccato, never long and drawn out, like Americans spoke. More like a song, but I still hadn't mastered the tune.

Anton hurried off to assist two ancient *Grandes Dames* to their table, smiling generously and making their day with his smooth way. They were both blushing by the time he had them seated and their coffees ordered.

So smooth, I thought, smiling as I watched him walk away. I'd always had a weakness for a tight butt. Reluctantly, I turned to the box of pictures and letters I'd meant to sort yesterday.

The pile contained birthday cards, holiday letters and assorted thank-you notes for a present sent to a child. It seemed Aunt Isabella had several families in the United States with whom she kept in touch.

A flush of jealousy swept over me, and I pinched my lips together. Why would she stay in contact with these people, but never reach out to her real family?

By the time I'd sorted to the bottom of the pile, I'd even matched up a few families as the children grew through the years—a Bar Mitzvah invitation from someone in New Jersey, a funeral announcement from Florida. I'd never heard of any of these people.

I should make a list and see if Mom had ever known these families. Sorting through the jumble in my purse until I found a pen and a notebook, I began writing down the addresses. I'd contact these people when I returned home. Maybe they could explain why Isabella aka Sophie had changed her name. And why she had never returned to the United States.

"Anything interesting?"

I jumped at the sound of Anton's voice in my ear.

"Just some people my aunt seems to have known."

"Family perhaps?"

I must have stiffened, because he jumped back. "Pardon, Alyssa. I am too noisy?"

I chuckled. He did have the cutest little malaprops. "Nosy."

"Ah, *Oui*. No-o-osy." He touched the tip of my nose with his finger and shot me an apologetic smile.

I smiled back. "No. Nothing important." I dumped the last of the letters into the box and tucked it in my purse. "Most are in French or maybe German. I can't figure out more than a word or two on any of them."

"I read German," Anton said. "French of course and some Italian in a pinch."

"Really?"

"Of course. We live in a country surrounded by people who speak many languages. How would we get along, if we could not communicate with them?"

I thought about this for a moment.

"You speak Spanish, no?"

"Enough to order a margarita or *huevos rancheros*." I blushed, feeling a little stupid.

"*Oui*. America is so big, you do not need to speak other languages to survive."

He picked up my empty *café crème* to bring me a fresh cup. "If you need a translator, I would be glad to help," he called from behind the bar where the monster coffee machine gleamed and roared.

"Thanks."

"And please, take these macarons for your afternoon tea."

I peeked in the tiny box he'd pushed across the counter. Four different colors, four different flavors. Yum. "You've been busy."

A smile lit his eyes and warmed the back of my neck. "I love to bake. It is my passion." He handed me my café in a to-go cup.

I walked down the street and across the square to the apartment, thinking about taking a course in Spanish or maybe Chinese when I returned home. I climbed the four sets of stairs and went to work unwrapping *lapins*.

****

I'd cleared most of the office of magazines and sixty-three boxes of mostly eaten chocolates. Isabella had quite the sweet tooth. I'd peeked in several of the boxes and noticed dozens of half eaten pieces. She didn't like the coconut ones. That much I learned about her. Certainly not my fav, either. But why not toss the candies you wouldn't eat instead of keeping them?

I looked out over the room and wondered what experience had twisted her thoughts into saving every bit of string, wool, button, and cloth, and yes, half-eaten chocolate she'd ever touched.

With the last of the candy boxes in the dumpster, I had room to begin my rabbit inspection. I'd dragged in another long table and placed it next to the one on the wall of the office. More room for the warren.

I had a feeling Aunt Isabella not only loved these rabbits, but had an eye for a good antique when she saw one. I wasn't going to toss them when they might fund Jojo and his new sister's college education.

Of course, several mangy-looking stuffed bunnies had to be humanely disposed of, but don't worry, I saved the Steiff rabbits. Most of the other *lapins* were made of more durable materials—brass, glass, ceramic. Some had bright painted surfaces with flowers or graphic designs. Some were plain with just one color. A few had interesting faces or comic poses, including the first little blue bunny.

I'd found a few crystal ones. I'd almost tossed them, thinking they were tourist junk, until I noticed the name Lalique etched on the bottom of the largest one.

Done in frosted glass, one rabbit had a wonderful balance and feel in my hand. Maybe I'd take this little guy home, and keep him to remember Isabella.

I walked along the display I'd arranged, first sorted and organized by material, then height, then color. One thousand, six hundred and forty-eight rabbits.

So far.

The ones I'd become fond of sat in a little row on the window shelf. The selection had grown in the last hour. I stood back and shook my head. Did I share a few of Aunt Isabella's compulsive, keep-everything-you've-ever-touched genes?

I crossed my arms and sighed. I should locate a couple antique dealers and de-lapin this place.

"Sorry, Aunt Isabelle. I hope you took what you wanted with you."

****

The next morning, the bells of Notre Dame called to me from across the river. I put on something besides grubbies and crossed the bridge. It's only a couple blocks to the square. I shielded my eyes against the glare and studied the spires.

Had the great cathedral been Isabella's church? There were other smaller churches, but none seemed as close. Or as special.

I wandered inside and asked the lady behind the information desk if I could speak to a priest. She pointed toward the line of parishioners waiting to enter the modern confessional rooms at the side of the church.

"Uh, no. I need to find out if someone attended this parish."

The lady gave me a puzzled look. I was about to look up the words in my trusty travel dictionary when a woman said, "May I help translate?"

"Please." I told her what I needed and stressed that I wanted to speak with an elderly priest, if there was one available.

In a few minutes, I was led to the small building next door to the church. I waved and thanked my Good Samaritan on the way out.

Once inside, I asked the young man behind the counter to look up Isabella Manchester on his computer. He smiled helpfully, his dark eyes joining in. His dark hair was neatly trimmed, and he was formally dressed for a Tuesday morning in button down shirt and conservative tie. His official-looking name tag read Jordan.

After a few moments, he shook his head. "Sorry. No one by that name."

I turned to leave but then asked, "How about Sophie Delacroix?"

Jordan glanced up. "Madame Sophie? Yes. I know her. She's a very long-time member, but I haven't seen her in a while." After checking his screen again, he frowned. "And we haven't received her usual donation this month. She was always very prompt."

"She died recently."

"Oh." The boy looked flustered. "I'm so sorry." He quickly crossed himself.

"It's okay."

Jordan tapped his fingers on his desk for a moment and then looked up. "Father Horatio might have known her. He served as a priest here years ago. Way back during the war. He's retired now, but has come back to Paris for the Easter holiday. I believe he's in the study. Would you like to speak with him?"

"Yes, please," I said and waited on a hard chair in the tiny reception room while the boy tromped up the steep stairs.

"Would you like to come up?" the boy called from above. "Father Horatio struggles with the steps."

"Sure."

Jordan introduced us, and I shook Father Horatio's hand. His eyes, a piercing green, stared beyond my shoulder. He was emaciated with age, his white hair only fluff around his ears.

"I'm afraid," continued Father Horatio in English as I sat in the only other chair in the comfortable room, "I don't see very well anymore. Jordan said you were looking for information about Mademoiselle Delacroix?"

"Yes. I'm her great-niece. I came to Paris in order to settle her estate and am trying to find out a little more about her life here."

The old man's forehead wrinkled. "You don't sound French."

"No, I'm American."

"Huh. She never mentioned relatives in the States."

"Yes. The family lost track of Isa…uh…Sophie during the war. Did you know her then?"

He rubbed his hands together. "Yes. Madame Delacroix attended mass here when I was a young priest. I came to Notre Dame just before the war broke out. I left in the fifties for another calling. I knew her, not well, you understand, but I knew her during those years. I wouldn't know about her life after 1953. We didn't keep in touch."

"So you met her during the war?"

He nodded.

"What was she like?"

His face pinched into a wrinkled knot. "You must understand. The war was a very difficult time. People were hungry, afraid."

I waited quietly while the old man searched for a memory.

"I don't think she attended regularly before the Germans took possession of the city. At least I don't remember her."

"And after the Germans came?"

"After?" He rubbed his chin in thought. "I think she found solace in our cathedral. She sometimes asked for my blessing after she attended Matins. She never spoke to others. Never joined in the community. I often wondered if she was very lonely."

"What did she look like then?"

"Pretty. Too thin. But that wasn't surprising, given the times. Very dark hair. Very quiet."

"Dark hair?" I repeated to myself.

"There were stories after the war..."

I had risen to leave, but sat back down. "Yes?"

"Just that she had helped people. Fed people. Especially children. She had a large garden. Maybe had done...even more."

I narrowed my gaze at the old man. "More? More than what?"

He shrugged and waved an arthritic hand. "Only rumors."

I thanked Father and went downstairs. I gave a wave and a smile to Jordan as I passed.

"Was Father Horatio helpful?" he asked.

"Somewhat."

"I'll miss Madame Sophie," Jordan said with a brief frown. "She was a nice old lady."

I moved up closer. "She spoke to you?"

"*Oui.* Sometimes she would sit with me after church, over in the park. We talked about her garden. She still remembered all the names of flowers, even when she forgot what day of the week it was. I helped her carry things home sometimes. Funny though, she always called me François."

François? Odd. I chewed on my fingernail on the way out. I wasn't surprised Isabella was confused at times, but who was François?

Chapter Six

"Anton, do you know anyone in the antique business?" I'd finished my plate of crispy *pommes frites* and was sipping a second glass of mellow burgundy. Café Rulliard was quiet this late in the evening. Only one elderly couple sat outside enjoying their glasses of white wine.

Anton smiled and walked from the serving station to the table on my right, wiping it down with a soft rag. He pursed his lips in thought.

Anton worked varied shifts. I'd only been to the Café Rulliard once when he wasn't there. Even on that occasion, he'd shown up five minutes later on his bicycle, saying he'd been caught in traffic and late for his shift.

He finished wiping the table and sat down. Tapping his finger on his lips for a moment, he then shot me his wonderful French grin. "I will ask my mother. She knows much more about antiques than I do."

I rested my chin on my hand and stared into his fabulous gray eyes. "You've never mentioned your mother before."

"Non? She lives in the town of Port-Villez, north of Paris, near Normandy. I don't see her as much as she would like, but my sister, Gabrielle, and her husband live nearby."

"I have a sister too. Samantha. Her husband's a

cop, and they have a little boy."

My smile must have grown wistful, because Anton said, "You miss them?"

I did miss them, but I blinked back the burn of tears and shook my head. "Silly. I shouldn't complain. How many women get an all-expense paid trip to Paris, even if it does involve a whole lot of house cleaning?" My throat tightened, and I swallowed another sip of wine to give myself a moment. I waved my hand. "Besides, I'll be home in no time."

Anton handed me his handkerchief despite my brave-sounding statement, and I dabbed at my drips.

"It's good to miss your family. It means you love them."

Oh damn, there went the tears again. "I guess I'm tired. I've been rabbit hunting."

"*Comment*?"

"Aunt Isabella was quite the collector. That's why I need an antique dealer. It's been a huge job."

Anton pinched his lips together thoughtfully, and then nodded. "If you would like, I could help with your work. I have the afternoon off on Sunday."

"Yes, please." I squeezed my eyes shut. I took off my glasses to give myself a moment. My plea had come out slightly desperate, but I was tired and needed a friend.

He stood and flipped his towel over his shoulder. "Come for *petit déjeuner* that morning. I will have news by then about the dealer."

"Thanks, Anton."

"*Au revoir, ma petite*." He took my euros but then looked around the empty café and shouted something into the kitchen. "Come. I will walk you home."

It was dark now, past nine. We took the long way down Rue Victoria and walked out on the *Pont au Change* overlooking the Conciergerie. The just-risen moon, full and shining low on the Seine, looked like something out of a classic, Woody Allen movie. Perfect.

Conversation. Think of something to say, Alyssa. "What are all the locks on the bridges for?" I asked, suddenly nervous to be alone with this handsome man.

"They are lovers' locks."

I turned away and squeezed my eyes shut. Great, let's talk about love. I swear my blush glowed in the dark.

Anton didn't speak for a moment. I noticed we'd matched our strides, yet he respected my need for space.

His hands remained in the pockets of his coat—a dark blue pea coat with double buttons. "When two people marry," he finally continued, "or sometimes just fall in love, they come to this bridge and make a vow."

"Do they ever get taken off? The locks, that is?"

He shrugged one shoulder. "We all have heart breaks, *ma petite*."

He moved a little closer, and I could feel the heat of his body, sheltering me against the cold wind blowing down river. I reached out and tucked my hand into the curve of his arm.

He folded my fingers into his.

Nice. They fit together.

His hand was strong, his palm warm and firm for work.

Too bad we had just another few steps to my place. I would have liked to talk to him more, learned more about his family. Held his hand a little longer.

When the little man on the traffic light showed green, we hurried across the Quai de Gesvres. I pointed out where I lived.

With a quick bow, so French, he held open the door and closed it between us. "*Au revoir*." He waved with a smile and was gone.

Damn. No kiss. I turned away and let out a disappointed sigh.

I stomped up the curved steps—the first of four floors to my apartment, huffing under my breath. Maybe he didn't like me. Maybe he was just being polite to a pitiful foreigner. I clenched my jaw and groaned. Maybe he was flirting with me to improve my already lavish, American-style tipping.

Halfway to the second landing, I heard distant pounding on the outside door and stopped to listen. Anton called my name along with another series of loud rapping. I turned and went down the steps. Had I forgotten something?

Through the glass, Anton waved me forward, and I opened the outer door. It always took both hands to maneuver the lock and pull back the bulky door.

"You forgot something."

I glanced at both of his hands, but they were empty. Confused, I frowned at him. Maybe I just didn't understand his translation.

Then he reached toward me, and with the crook of his finger, he tipped up my chin and gave me a quick kiss on the lips.

My heart did a happy little calypso dance. I blinked, considered my next move and kissed him once in return.

When I stepped back, he opened his eyes and grinned at me. *"Au revoir, Alyssa."*

I rushed up the stairs three at a time, grinning.

Chapter Seven

"Did the FBI respond to our request?" I asked my sergeant as he entered my office.

"Yes, sir. Claire received the fax a few minutes ago." He ducked out again closing the door silently behind him.

I folded my hands behind my back and paced the fine, inlaid wooden floors of my office. I preferred to walk the wood instead of the Persian rug centering the room. The click of my heels helped me think.

I stopped at the far side of the room and stood in front of the portrait of my father, painted the year before he was killed in a car accident. I stared intently at his sober face, but he had no answers for me.

Sergeant Bruno LaStrange, my second in command, re-entered the room and silently closed the fifteen foot door behind him. Dressed in the nondescript clothes he used for undercover work, he looked the part of any middle-aged French workman. His well-worn face, dark eyes, and salt-and-pepper curly hair blended well into the populace of Paris. He could be anyone, anytime. He took off his worn cap and tucked it under his arm.

Impatient for the news, I turned to face him, and he gave me a quick salute.

He handed me a copy of the file but read his aloud:

"The United States census confirmed, Isabella Manchester, born, April 17th 1912, to James and Margaret Manchester. James, age 32. Born in Scotland. Emigrated in 1907 from England. Margaret Sullivan Manchester, at age 17 she emigrated from Scotland in 1908. Three children—two daughters and a son. They lived about fifty miles from St. Paul, but moved west to central California in 1945."

"Probably where she gets those wonderful—"

Bruno's left eyebrow rose at least a centimeter.

I cleared my throat and turned toward the window. "—blue eyes."

"Probably, sir." Bruno chuckled at my discomfort. When I turned back to glare at him, he tucked his hands behind his back and rocked back and forth on his toes, but wouldn't meet my gaze. "May I speak, sir?"

I waved a hand in his general direction.

"She is who she says she is, sir. Alyssa Manchester, born and raised in California. Parents divorced. Father remarried soon after—his much younger secretary. She has an older sister and a younger brother."

"We know all that."

Bruno didn't react to my frustrated tone. "She has worked for several high tech firms over the last five years, after graduating from the university I believe they refer to as Cal."

"The FBI did report she'd let her Top Secret military clearance expire after moving from one company to the next." Bruno scanned the document in his hand. "Yes. She worked on a military weapon for the U.S. Government during their problems with Afghanistan. Some sort of robotic device."

"Hardly pertinent."

"But interesting," Bruno defended his conclusion with a shake of his finger. "She is an intelligent woman, but has no idea what's in that apartment, if anything. Or why we're watching her. I think, perhaps…"

I sat at my desk and steepled my fingers under my chin. I knew what Bruno was leading up to. I had considered the same tactic myself.

"I think, perhaps sir," Bruno repeated, "we should be honest with her."

I puffed out a breath through my lips. "Are the bugs still operating?"

"Yes. The ones I installed last week are transmitting. No camera yet. Do you…?"

"No. Not unless something happens to raise our suspicion further."

"Jean Paul has carted off every box and bag of rubbish she has put in the dumpster, and inspected it thoroughly. Nothing of value has been found, although he claims the old magazines do have possible—"

I slammed my hand on my desk. "I'm not interested in making a few euros selling old magazines to a *bouquiniste*." I clamped my jaw and gritted my teeth to cut short my frustrated rant.

"Yes, sir. No, sir."

Bruno left, closing the door behind him.

I glanced at the picture of my father and ran my fingers through my hair now grown longer to fit my undercover persona. Would this treasure ever be recovered? The one my father had searched for his entire life?

I unlocked my bottom drawer and withdrew the small box I kept there. The finish of the finely inlaid wood was worn from generations of handling. I opened the box and stared at the picture inside, careful to hold it up to the light for just a moment.

Two women, dressed in the clothes of the '30s, sat in a gracious room. One woman was elderly, my great-great-grandmère, Angelina Marie de Ville. Her daughter sat to the left, with a child at her knee, my grandpère.

The boy, about five, was dressed in shorts and a little velvet jacket. His longish hair hung over his ears, combed with loving care. His face was turned toward his mother, not the camera. At the last moment, the willful little boy had moved and ruined the shot, leaving his face a blur.

An inlaid tea table occupied the background, and on it sat a barrel-topped wooden box, probably a tea caddy. No one in the family recognized or remembered it now.

I flipped the photograph over and examined the neat writing at the top of the card. In faded ink, the list included my grandfather's name, Henri, and was dated: *Octobre*, 1936. The photographer's address, faded and brown with age, had been stamped on the lower left. Under magnification, I could see the numbers, but no such place existed today. The street had been blown to bits by the Luftwaffe in 1940, and no records of the photographer remained. Another dead end.

I picked up the only other object in the box, a small key, and fisted my hand over it.

Damn this key. It had driven my father wild over the years. Would I be doomed to the same fate?

I measured it for the hundredth time in my hand. Made of brass, it had no value; no longer than the pad of my thumb, I was sure it held the secret.

I found the enlargement of the photograph on my computer and examined Angelina's necklace for the hundredth time. Even with the challenge of an aged black and white photograph, I could see the beauty and workmanship of the piece she wore. Father swore the Tsar himself had gifted it to our family generations before.

I twisted my lip. I don't know if I believed the old family legend, but the jewels alone were no doubt worth a bucket load of euros in today's market.

"Why, Angelina, did you take this photograph with you when you fled the Germans?" I tapped it gently on the back of my hand. "Why this photo? Why did it mean so much to you that you took it and left everything else behind? There must have been other photographs. Better ones."

I leaned back in my chair, took off my glasses and closed my eyes. I'd read the history of the war, heard the family legend from my father and grandfather dozens of times, but I'd found nothing to help me understand her reasoning.

As the Germans overran the Maginot line, French defenses fell into disarray. My grandfather remembered the booming of the canons and the low flying planes with swastikas painted on their wings. The family joined thousands of others, refugees on their way south.

His mother and grandmother had hidden him in the hedgerows or ditches, covering him with their bodies when the fighters flew over, strafing the refugees. He remembered the smell of the green grass as it exploded with gunfire around them.

The family, like so many others, had escaped with

the things they could carry and little else. They had lived—survived—in the south of France during the terrible war. The women took in washing to pay for the little available food that wasn't confiscated by the Germans.

Then Angelina suddenly died. Her heart. And there was no one to answer the questions. Why had she never told anyone about the secret of the photograph and the key? Was she afraid to speak of it? And where had she hidden the necklace?

I closed the box and returned it to the drawer my father had kept it in for fifty years. He had returned so many possessions to so many people. His life's work. I was proud of him. Artworks, jewels, even books of precious photographs stolen during the war by the rapacious Germans had been returned to their owners.

Yes. But so much irony.

And now, finally, I had a clue. In the thirties, Angelina had known a certain Madame S—no other name given. Before his death, father had located letters between the women. He'd sniffed out rumors that a certain Madame S had worked for the Résistance.

For years no proof materialized, but he finally located a family who swore this heroine had not only helped people escape, but had also protected their possessions when they'd left the country.

The trickle of stories had flowed into a stream.

Some of the displaced were Jews, running in fear of their lives. Others were refugees, afraid of being robbed as they headed south ahead of the German advance. Many had never returned.

I tapped my finger against my desk. Had Angelina hidden the necklace with this unknown woman?

Chapter Eight

"*Madame, puis-je parler avec vous?*"

I stopped outside the door to my building and hesitated before engaging the automatic lock.

The neatly coifed woman was well dressed, from the silk scarf artfully wrapped around her neck down to her gorgeous Italian heels. She drew her blond hair back from her face with a graceful, manicured hand.

"*Je suis désolée, Madame. Je ne parle pas français.*" At least I knew how to say that much.

"*Anglais?*"

I relaxed my shoulders and tucked my thumb under my purse. "Yes. Is there something I can help you with? I'm not a local, but I could try."

"That is very kind of you, but I'm not lost." She handed me her card, in French of course, and continued. "*Mon mari,* my husband, and I are real estate, um, brokers would be your word for it. We heard an apartment in this building might be coming up for sale soon."

I frowned. "How did you hear that?"

The lady blushed under her perfect makeup. "May I buy you a coffee?" She pointed to my café on the corner.

I shrugged. The bistro in our building was full of Saturday morning customers enjoying their pastries. I would be safe enough. Besides, what would a lady dressed in designer clothes be able to take from me? In worn jeans and faded shirt, I'd just dropped off another load of second-hand books at the church down the street.

We settled and ordered. I re-examined the card she'd handed me. I could pick out the word *maison*, meaning house, but there was nothing else, besides their names and a telephone number I could decipher.

Across the river, the bells of Notre Dame rang gloriously. Must be eleven. Not even the rush of traffic along the Quai could drown out their insistent call. I stopped for a moment to listen.

The woman smiled. "They are beautiful, non? It would be a great value to live within the sound of those bells."

I smiled at her. "What did you say your name was?"

"Dominique Simone. My husband Philippe and I have a small office on Rue Saint Antoine." She pointed east with a perfectly manicured nail.

I nodded. I'd ridden the 69 bus down that street toward the Bastille the other day. "Nice neighborhood."

"Yes. Our clients are very..." She looked up and seemed to be searching for the word.

"High class?"

"And rich." She covered her finely colored lips with her hand and smiled.

I liked her frankness and smiled too, then sipped my coffee.

I was still curious about her information gathering. "You didn't tell me how you knew..."

"Ah," she said sheepishly. "You will think this is a bit ghoulish, but we follow the obituaries." She drew a small slip of newspaper from her oversized, fashion-forward bag that probably cost more than my whole wardrobe and handed it to me. "Apartments of good quality are difficult to come by."

Madame Sophia Delacroix, estimated age 95, died in her sleep at Hospital Hôtel Dieu after being found unconscious at the bus stop near L'Hôtel de Ville. She was a long time resident of the Marais. No known survivors.

"I knew her, you see," Dominique explained.

I looked up in surprise.

"Not well, you understand. Everyone in the neighborhood knew of her. She was a bit of a character, the old dear. Every once in a while, she would wave *bonjour* as she hobbled by our office. She always went to the Tuesday market in the square behind St. Paul's.

"Sometimes she allowed my husband to carry her bags. She was a very proud woman, but my husband has a gentlemanly way about him. He could usually flirt with her enough that she would relent and let him help carry her purchases home."

"So you have been to her flat?"

"Oh, no. She would never allow anyone inside. She always left Philippe at the front door of the building with a very proper '*Merci beaucoup.*'"

I wasn't surprised. The health department would have been on Isabella's case in a second if she'd let anyone inside. I stirred my coffee with the tiny spoons the cafés in France always give you and thought about Isabella's long and lonely life.

"Was she a relative?"

I gave the woman a quick nod. "My aunt, well, great-aunt."

"Do you plan to live here permanently?" Dominique asked with a bird-like tip of her head.

"Oh no, I have work in California. I need to get back. And my family…"

She straightened her shoulders and smiled widely. "Then I am at your service. I can help you with everything you need. Cleaning people. Movers. Furniture and antiques dealers. When the flat has been prepared, we can help you get top price."

I tapped my spoon on the rim of my cup. "I appreciate—"

"Oh, dear. *Je suis désolée*. I have said too much." She knotted her hands in her lap. "You are still in mourning? Did you love the old dear very much?"

I shook my head regretfully. "No, I'm afraid she was even more distant with our family than she was with everyone else. Perhaps a little…" I tapped my finger against my temple.

"Yes. I thought so. Living alone can be difficult for the very elderly."

"Did you ever see her with other people? When she was walking by, I mean?"

Dominique pursed her lips prettily. "No. I don't remember anyone. Sometimes she would show me a new trinket she'd bought."

"A rabbit?"

She blinked in surprise. "Why, yes."

Dominique patted the top of my hand with her fingertips. "She did not seem unhappy, if that helps. She was always well dressed, active. There was a light in her eyes. *Vous comprenez*?"

"Yes. Well, I should get back to work." As I rose, the little metal cafe chair scratched against the sidewalk. "Thank you for the coffee."

In the way of any good salesperson, Dominique didn't want to give up. "Would you like to come to our office sometime? Perhaps meet my husband?"

"Maybe." I dropped my gaze and fiddled to find my keys in my purse. They'd slipped to the bottom. "Let me think about it."

And look you up on the Paris version of Yelp.

Dominique rose also. "Good, anytime. The hours are on the card. It was nice meeting you, Alyssa." She left a generous pile of euros in the tray, waved and was gone, walking briskly across the square of L'Hôtel de Ville, now awash in bright spring sunshine.

I spent the afternoon washing rabbits. Since most of the little critters were so dusty and grimy from years of grease and dust, they needed a good, soapy bath. After a lifetime of watching the antique show on public television, I knew not to wash off the 'patina,' on certain ones. Finally, most of them looked presentable.

I already had a few more favorites.

****

Later that afternoon, I walked past the wide open plaza to my café and waved to Anton when he opened the door for me. He seemed a little breathless but escorted me to my favorite table and brought me a hot chocolate.

Today was cooler than last week had been, with gray clouds whipping across the sky. I wrapped my hands around the mug and enjoyed the heat and the rich chocolate. It was so thick, it looked more like pudding than cocoa. Good thing I was doing the stairs several times a day.

After serving pastries to another guest, Anton

tucked his white towel into his apron strings and sat down next to me. "What have you been doing today, Mademoiselle?"

I took another sip of chocolate and grinned. "Washing rabbits."

"*Quelle dommage.*"

"*Oui, mais c'est fini et je suis heureuse.*"

Anton leaned back and looked me up and down with approval. "Your French is improving."

"I bought some tapes to listen to while I work. It gets pretty lonely, washing rabbits, you know."

"I would be glad to assist Mademoiselle."

I shook my head. "You don't want to do that, trust me. The apartment is still way beyond awful."

He shrugged his shoulders in the quick French way. "Tomorrow is my day off. You promised I could come and help, *s'il vous plaît.*"

I know my cheeks had turned bright red by this point. Damn my Scottish blood, but I did need an extra body to help move things around. Especially someone with a few good muscles. Some of the furniture was very heavy, and I didn't want to scratch the beautiful old wood floors. I stirred my fluffy whipped cream into my cocoa.

"I will bring macarons," Anton whispered to close the deal.

"Chocolate?"

"*Mais, oui.* It is your favorite, *n'est-ce pas?*"

Oh, yes it was. Especially filled with pistachio. "Okay, come around two. I should be decent by then. I could use help moving a few pieces of the antique furniture."

He grinned and pecked a little kiss on my hand.

I let out a sigh. So easy to please, so difficult to resist. Was I jumping back down another rabbit hole?

****

I hurried through the reception area to my office, and Bruno glanced up at me. He took off his ear phones and stuck up a thumb. "You're making progress."

I grunted something I was not willing to say aloud and signaled him to follow me. After he closed the door, I asked, "Did you find an antique dealer who will cooperate with us?"

Bruno handed me a finely crafted business card. "I've filled Monsieur Royer in on the situation."

When I opened my mouth to object, Bruno held up his hands to slow my reaction. "I have worked with this man before. He has excellent credentials and is very discreet. He will do as we ask."

"Good."

"Simpler if—"

My turn to hold up my palms. "I know. After tomorrow, after I finally walk into that damned apartment, I will know if we can trust her."

"Ah, but the question will then become, sir, can she trust you?"

****

The sky had cleared, and the black clouds had moved on. Since I had help coming tomorrow, I decided to treat myself to a little bus trip.

I caught the 69 bus across the street, and it trundled its way down the narrow alleyway past the graceful old buildings of the Marais district. The guide book said this area had once been a marsh.

When much of Paris was rebuilt by Napoleon III, this little area remained intact. Medieval walls of the old city still stood in sections. Some of the houses, leaning like they would topple any moment, had to be six hundred years old.

In the last twenty years, the Marais had been gentrified into a warren of crooked streets filled with posh stores, expensive apartments and trendy cafes.

We passed the monastery and St. Paul's church. I dug through my purse to find Dominique's card and checked the address on Rue Saint Antoine. The bus stopped down the block, just before the pedestrian zone.

I could have walked through the door and asked my questions, but I wanted to get a feel for their business, so I took a window table in the café across the street. I ordered a coffee and snooped.

The Rue Saint Antoine is a busy boulevard, full of noisy traffic and pedestrians. Several people stopped and looked at the sales listings taped to the carefully cleaned windows. Most moved on, but one couple went inside and chatted with Dominique. I watched her through the plate glass windows, sitting at a modern desk to one side of the office.

She spoke with animation and handed over several pages of information. The couple walked off hand in hand, looking very excited.

I finished my coffee and left a larger tip than I should. I still hadn't gotten used to *le service compris*, meaning you didn't have to leave further money. I'd read that French servers were paid better than American ones. Maybe I would ask Anton.

I smiled at the thought of seeing him tomorrow and getting to know him better. He was very sweet to offer to help. Maybe I could cook him dinner sometime.

I snickered at the thought and almost ran into a

skateboarder racing down the walkway. Get real, girl. You're a terrible cook. Anton was French, for goodness sake. Cooking probably ran in his blood. Baking certainly did if those macarons were any clue.

I sighed. Maybe I could take him to dinner, but someplace other than the Café Ruillard.

The bell over the agency door jingled as I entered the office. Dominique looked up and grinned, reacting as if I were her long lost sister. "Alyssa, I'm so glad you came by. But oh, dear, Philippe has gone out to buy us some *déjeuner*." She grabbed her phone from the desk. "Let me call him and have him bring something for you."

Before I could argue, she'd punched a few buttons on her phone and spoke in rapid French. I caught three words. One of them was my name.

"I will have him bring you a sandwich. *C'est bon*?"

"Thanks, but you needn't bother."

She waved her hand to disagree in that graceful Parisian way. "We will break bread. We will drink wine. We will get to know one another." She smiled happily. A few minutes later, a tall, balding gentleman rushed through the door holding several plastic bags.

Philippe, I presumed.

The fragrance of fresh bread and *charcuterie* wafted into the room. I was suddenly hungry.

He handed Dominique the bags and came forward to greet me. He had a strong handshake and a willing smile, important tools for a salesman. Although not a handsome man, he had interesting features: a strong nose, high forehead and bright blue eyes. He was dressed formally, white collared shirt and what my mother would call a George Bush tie.

"I am so glad to meet you," he said in meticulously pronounced English. "Dominique told me of your encounter."

By this point Dominique had set places for each of us at a small table farther back in the room, and was pouring glasses of white wine to go with the meal. "Here, please take this seat. It is the most comfortable," Philippe offered and pulled out my chair.

Go easy on the wine, girl, I thought as I unfolded my napkin, or you could sign away your life.

"This is our favorite place for lunch." Dominique continued, unwrapping the large meals. "Very American."

The sandwich did look familiar. Ham, cheese, mayo.

"It's called Soob-way."

I glanced up in surprise. "You mean Subway?"

"Is that how you say it?" Philippe asked, but he didn't seem annoyed by my correction.

"Do you have them in California?" Dominique chimed in.

"Nearly every block." But the sandwich was good, the bread fresh and soft, and I enjoyed something that tasted of home. Something familiar. I could have used a soda instead of the wine.

Dominique dabbed her napkin against her lips and cleared her throat. "Philippe, I told you Alyssa is the great-niece of Madame Sophie."

He nodded. "First of all, my sympathies to you and your family. I did not know your aunt well, but she and my wife were friendly. She was a *grande dame*. The last of a rare breed."

Dominque crossed herself and closed her eyes

briefly. "A survivor."

"I was told she had lived in the apartment even before the Germans came. We, of course, have looked at the public deeds. She held title as far back as the records go."

"There were many documents lost during the war," Dominique added.

"There shouldn't be a problem for me to sell it," I said. "I have the deed and a copy of the will from her lawyer in England."

Philippe put up his palms and shook his head. "No, no. There would be no problem. We can assist you with all of those details, and of course, we work with a very reputable property lawyer. That is not how all real estate transactions are made in France, but in your case, we would want you to have one."

"And a translator too, although one of the *notaires* we often use speaks perfect English." Dominique put her hand on her husband's arm. "Perhaps we are getting ahead of ourselves, dearest. Alyssa has not decided if she should sell the apartment. Perhaps she would prefer to remain in Paris. Or rent the apartment until her family can make a decision."

"I will be making the decision." I sipped my wine. "My family has entrusted me with the job." No need to explain how I'd drawn the proverbial short straw during Sunday brunch.

Philippe studied me more closely. "Would it be possible for us to see the apartment?"

I groaned at the thought. I had weeks of work left before it would be presentable enough to show anyone. Except Anton. "I'm afraid the apartment's not yet cleared. My aunt was a bit of a...packrat." I smiled at the couple and rose from my chair. "Thank you for the sandwich. I will let you know when I'm closer to being ready."

Dominique stood to take my hand. "*Bonne idée. Au revoir.*"

I pushed through the glass door. It was less than six blocks home. I could see the towers of L'Hôtel de Ville at the end of the street. I walked briskly down the wide sidewalk enjoying the cool spring air.

****

Bruno entered my office late the next afternoon, and I saw eagerness in his expression. "Mademoiselle Manchester went to a real estate agent's office. Claire followed her on the bus."

I rubbed my chin with concern. "Claire was careful? We can't spook Alyssa now that we are so close. It has taken years to get past that door."

"She was careful."

I frowned anyway.

"Stop worrying. Before long, anyone will be able to walk into the apartment. We won't need a warrant to look through the closets and under the bed. We can go in as prospective buyers."

I leaned back in my chair and nodded.

"Should I pull the bugs?"

"We have time."

****

I woke early Sunday morning to the sound of bells. It'd been warm yesterday, and I'd kept my window open all night to catch any hint of a cool breeze.

I dressed, wrapped a light, bright scarf around my neck and hustled across the bridge to the Marché aux Fleurs flower stalls.

The little green buildings down the street from Notre Dame looked like they'd been there for ages. Even this early on Sunday, the crowds had already gathered to shop, carrying their bags and baskets and their clever little roller bins. I purchased a purple blooming orchid for my kitchen table, a small bag of organic fertilizer, and some size-large gardening gloves.

I wandered through the displays and even stopped to pet the baby rabbits in the bird market. I pondered the tiny red-beaked wrens and the bright parakeets, but sighed when the hopeful sales lady greeted me with "*Bonjour.*"

If I wasn't going back to California so soon, it might be nice to have a little bird to keep me company. No matter how lonely I was, it would be silly to buy a creature that needed me for its survival.

"Alyssa?"

When I heard my name, I turned and recognized Philippe waving from across the street. He dodged between rows of parked motorcycles to greet me with two kisses, one on each cheek.

"Are you starting a garden?" he asked.

"Just filling in a bit on my aunt's project in the courtyard."

"Charming."

I glanced around him. "Where's Dominique?"

"She likes to sleep in on Sundays. I needed a few things for our small plot." He showed me trays of marigolds and herbs in his shopping bag. "May I walk you home?"

"Well, I was going to—"

"No please, I insist. Those are too bulky to carry all the way back to your apartment." He took my bag from me, offered me his arm, and led me across the boulevard.

Setting a brisk pace, we headed toward the bridge. "Perhaps while I'm here, I could take a look at the apartment?"

His smile was friendly, but something in his eyes sent a nervous twinge along my shoulders. More than curiosity. Perhaps a touch of avarice?

I pulled my arm back. "Can we make it another day, Philippe? I still have more shopping to do."

"Of course, of course." He bowed formally and handed me my small bag. "Forgive my impatience."

"No, no, you were only trying to help."

"See you soon then," he added, in high spirits. "Give Dominique a call. She's anxious to have you over for dinner."

"Thank you. I will."

I watched him saunter away and frowned. Pushy. That was the word. I rubbed my arms and turned back to my shopping.

I ended up with more seeds than plants. I chose a dozen varieties: zinnias tall and short, alyssum, sunflowers in three sizes and colors. And a packet of basil. The shopkeeper said it would grow very fast. I threw in a little lavender plant for fun.

At least Max could have some herbs for his salads this summer, and the birds would have seeds to eat in the fall.

****

The doorbell rang, and I pressed the button to allow Anton inside the stairwell. Right on time.

I peeked over the stair railing.

"Bonjour," he called as he rounded the last corner.

He smiled and held up some flowers.

"Thank you." I stuck my nose in the bunch of purple sweet peas. Their intense scent went straight to my brain. "Lovely."

"They are the flowers of spring, *non*?"

"Yes, and they smell wonderful. Come on in." He closed my door, and I dug around in the tiny kitchen for something resembling a vase. A few days before, I'd tossed all the old jars, burned pots and pans, along with the spices and the cans of food with expiration dates back into the nineties. Now I only had ground coffee and milk in the itty-bitty fridge.

I found a vase with a rabbit on it, of course, trimmed the stems and popped the flowers in with some cold water. I fluffed their frilly edges and turned to find Anton close behind me.

My heart beat a little too fast, so I dodged around him and placed the flowers on the bureau in the hallway. He followed me into the large living space.

Most of the room was cleared now. I still slept in here, and my single bed was neatly made in the corner. The shoji screen blocked it from view.

I studied the space objectively and grimaced. Pretty hopeless. The furniture was a horrible hodgepodge of styles and periods: chairs of unmatched sizes and heights, tables and lamps that didn't speak to one another in French, much less English. I still had piles of books in one corner. There hadn't been time to sort through those yet.

As Anton looked around the room, he scrubbed the light stubble on his chin. "Do you mind?" he asked, waving a hand at the mess.

"Have at." I crossed my arms and stepped out of

his way.

"Let's move this here," he suggested and lipped his fingers under the round table I'd shoved in the corner. I grabbed the other side, and we placed it in front of the far left window. He dragged a couple chairs, of almost the same size to the table. Voilà—an eating area with a view of birthday cake.

He shoved one of the many trunks against the wall between the windows and placed a large mirror on top. Another chest, something from India, I assumed from the elephants carved on the front, went on another wall. I piled some books on top, an ugly lamp, and a few of my special rabbits.

I dug out two of the oil paintings stacked in the corner of the office area. Anton lined them up and studied them intently. Two were of rabbits, well, duh, but their impressionistic style and soft pastel colors were quieting.

He hung one on the nail already in the wall, and it covered the shaded bit in the paint like it belonged there. The other, slightly smaller picture—an impressionistic vase of flowers—fit between the lovely French windows.

Anton dug around the office and lugged a large rug from a dark corner of the room.

"I didn't even know I had that," I said with a rise in my voice. I grimaced at the cobwebs gathered along the rolled edge, but Anton dusted them off.

He placed the red flower rug in the center of the room. Immediately, it added warmth and substance to the space. Then he set two old wing chairs by my favorite corner window. The sofa remained in it position, anchoring the room.

"Livable," he said with a satisfied nod.

I had to agree. "Want to see Isabella's rabbit collection?"

I waved him toward the spare room. We dodged boxes and picked our way through the mess into the still uncleared disaster. Isabella's collection now covered two tables I had squeezed in next to the long wall. I hadn't realized how long we'd worked until I had to turn on the overhead light.

Anton gave a low whistle. "*Beaucoup de lapins, ma chère.*"

"I think some of them may be valuable. I've been going on Ebay and several antique sites. Some have markings. Doulton, Wedgwood."

"This one is very nice." He'd picked up my favorite little Lalique bunny and thoroughly examined it. He turned to me and smiled, still holding my friend. "I remembered. I do have an acquaintance, well, more like a friend of a friend of my mother's. I spoke to him for you. He is willing to come by and tell you what to keep—what has value. He will appraise for you, but not buy."

"Can he come in a few days? By then I may have this room cleared."

Anton nodded and wandered from the room. I flipped off the light.

"I'll give him a call. He should be able to make time for you. And then, if you wish to sell, he can give you the names of some honest dealers."

I let out a little sigh, relieved at least this much of my challenge might be settled.

Anton seemed to be thinking about something, but then he placed the rabbit on the dresser in the entryway.

"I'm hungry. Come. Let me take you to my favorite place for dinner."

"I'm not dressed." I brushed off my dirty shirt.

"It will not matter."

****

The evening air was cool and felt like rain. I buttoned my coat, and once outside, tied a warm scarf around my neck. We walked past the bistro on the corner and waited for the light to cross the busy street running parallel to the Seine.

A girl jogged across with us, wearing warm-up gear with a bright green scarf wrapped strategically around her neck. Her headphones and tennis shoes matched her outfit.

"I'll never keep up," I said with a sigh as she passed us and continued down the walkway along the river front.

Anton looked at me quizzically, his brows drawn down into a V above his fine nose.

I waved my hand in the runner's direction. "French women…they always look so fashionable. Even out for a run, she looks like a page from one of those French glamour magazines."

Anton glanced over his shoulder and then chuckled. "French women work very hard to look beautiful. They are proud of the time they spend on their *toilette*. We Frenchmen, we appreciate this."

I groaned under my breath, feeling frumpy in my wrinkled shirt and worn-at-the-knees jeans.

"But sometimes beauty, when it is so simple, so easy to see, is even more magical."

I glanced in his direction. Was he looking at me? Talking about me? I blushed. Hopefully it was dark enough he wouldn't notice.

He leaned closer. "You do not like the compliment?"

I combed my fingers through my hair. "I'm not used to them. The men I work with don't really see me as a woman."

"A great shame."

Damn. My cheeks were flaming. I tipped my chin down as we walked into the pool of light of an old fashioned street lamp.

"It's necessary, too," I said. "In the States, men and women who work together don't compliment each other on their looks."

He puffed out his cheek and shook his head.

"It's actually against the law."

"Truly?"

Anton took my hand and then rounded his arm over my shoulder. He backed me against the stone balustrade of the bridge. His gaze met mine, and I caught my breath. "We do not work together, do we, Alyssa?"

I know he could hear my intake of breath.

His thumb trailed along my cheek. "You are a very beautiful woman, Alyssa. I am very attracted to you."

I gulped. It sounded so romantic, the way he said the words in his adorable French accent. My heart pounded in a delicious way.

His lips touched mine, not hesitantly, because there was nothing hesitant about Anton, but he waited for me to advance the kiss.

Hell, yes. I curled my arms around his back and pressed him closer. Warm, hard, he angled his mouth and deepened our kiss.

I came up for air and smiled into his eyes. "Nice."

"Very. You should look at yourself in the mirror sometime, *chérie*. You are a very beautiful, very special woman."

I swallowed hard, and had to push out the word. "*Merci*."

We walked—well, I floated—across the Seine to the river island called *Île de la Cité*. We ducked down a side street to avoid the mobs of tourists coming from Notre Dame.

Anton opened the door for me, and we stepped into an adorable little restaurant. A long bar filled the front room. Several Frenchmen stood sipping wine or aperitifs. A few perched on high stools. One raised his hand, and Anton responded in quick French. I didn't catch anything except a couple of "*Bons*."

He waved *au revoir* to the senior gentlemen in the group, and the waiter led us through a tiny corridor to the dining room. I swear, the ceiling in the hallway was so low, we both had to duck.

The dining room was small, maybe a dozen tables positioned around the walls of the low-ceilinged room. Ancient timbers crisscrossed the ceiling. The last of the vivid, evening twilight flowed in through the blurry, old glass windows.

The waitress pulled out the well-worn table to seat me in the booth. Anton took the chair across from me. The smell of fresh bread called my name. My mouth started to water.

We were alone for the moment, but more customers soon filled the tiny space. I slipped my glasses into my purse. Up this close, I could fake perfect vision.

A vivacious Asian woman arrived with our menus.

All in French. I must have looked helpless, because Anton grinned. "Do you trust me?"

I handed him my menu and listened as he ordered our meal. The waitress brought a bottle of wine and glasses. Anton held up his glass, filled with a red Bordeaux. "To a beautiful woman."

I clinked my glass to his.

Delicious.

He studied me in the candlelight. "Your eyes are very blue. I had not noticed before."

I tucked a curly hank of hair behind my ear, dropping my gaze to my silverware. "Yes. We all have blue eyes. My brother and sister, that is. Genetics."

He broke a chunk of baguette from the little basket and chewed thoughtfully. "From your mother's family? The color, I mean?"

I shrugged. "I suppose. My family's Scottish for more generations than we can count. Even after my family emigrated, they married Scots."

He tapped his fingers on the white table cloth for a moment and then smiled. The first course of the meal arrived, and we enjoyed the tiny *amuse bouche* of cold zucchini soup. Between the luscious cream and the herbs, and the little silver spoon to eat it with, I was in heaven.

"Is this a famous French restaurant?" I asked, tearing off my third piece of French bread and slathering it with the most incredible butter.

"No." Anton shook his head and then leaned in closer. "We don't share this restaurant with the tourists. It is a French national secret." He smirked, and I figured he was joking. Maybe.

Our entrée arrived, and I looked into Anton's

amused face. "Frog legs? Are you kidding?"

"They are the best in town." He picked up the first little pair and nibbled off the bits of meat. Fried in brown butter, they smelled wonderful. Fresh, salty. Like Mom's homemade Sunday chicken in miniature.

I closed my eyes and took a quick bite. Surprise. Itty-bitty chicken wings. The brown butter sauce was heavenly.

I was relieved when steak and frites arrived for the main course. Maybe one new food group— amphibian—was all Anton expected me to brave about.

But dessert. OMG.

Pistachio, Chantilly crème, and fresh raspberries had to be the best combination of flavors on God's green earth. If no one had been looking, I would have used my finger to clean the ramekin.

Café crème and luscious handmade chocolates ended the meal. By the time I ducked back through the little corridor, I was so content, I wanted to curl up on a couch and snooze.

Anton had other plans. He took my hand and led me past the cathedral, across the bridge, and down the steps toward the left bank of the river. "Before we go much farther, ma chérie, please put your glasses back on," he suggested nonchalantly.

"I don't really need them," I demurred.

He tucked his chin back and crossed his arms patiently.

"Oh, okay." I dug in my bag and replaced my specs. The fuzzy gray world cleared.

"You needn't be self-conscious about the glasses, Alyssa. I think they are attractive and fit your face, your personality."

"Total geek?"

A quick snort followed my comment. "A beautiful, exceptional woman."

****

The boats on the Seine mostly served the hordes of tourists. We walked down the quai, and Anton called over to a small, private boat docked on the left bank. A male voice responded, and a tiny man appeared from the little craft below us.

If ever a Frenchman had a French mustache, this was it. It even wiggled as he rushed through his words.

Anton helped me on board. The motor started, rumbling from the back of the craft.

We passed several of the big boats, but soon had a chunk of the Seine to ourselves. All the beautiful buildings were lit, accentuating their decorative structure. Like frosted wedding cakes, each was more elaborate than the last.

Slowly we cruised down the quiet river. I loved the façade of the Musée d'Orsay with its two big clock towers. I was saving up for at least a day there to immerse myself in its collection of Impressionist paintings.

Anton pointed out a few highlights, including the obelisk in the center of the Place de la Concorde. I'd walked past it a few times, but never realized it was three thousand years old.

"Did Napoleon steal it?" I asked.

Anton drew back and pretended to looked insulted. "It was a gift. A Frenchman, Jean-François Champollion, deciphered the way to read hieroglyphics, and the country of Egypt gave us this as a *cadeau*—a gift. Surely you have heard of the Rosetta Stone?"

Then the Eiffel Tower came into view. Lit a golden color, it shone in the night sky. Little elevators in the legs of the structure brought people to the decks higher and higher up. A search light turned from the top.

"Quelle heure est-il?" Anton asked our captain.

"Vingt-deux."

"Bon."

"Oh, look." I cried out in surprise, and pointed my finger like a five-year-old. I bounced in my seat like one, too. Reminding me of the biggest Christmas tree ever, the tower was sparkling, bright-white lights combined with the golden hue. It took my breath away.

Anton grinned at the spectacle, too. *"C'est ma favorite."*

"It's beautiful."

It was getting chilly, and Anton cuddled me under his shoulder. He smelled good, so I tucked my nose beneath his chin.

"C'est froid."

"What? My nose is cold?" I asked with a quiet chuckle.

"Oui."

"Tough. I like the way you smell."

"Oui?"

"Oh, yeah."

He bent toward me and kissed me. I combed my fingers through his hair, the soft ends curling around my fingers. I drew my palm to the back of his neck and over the soft beard of his cheek. We touched tongues for a moment and stopped after several short kisses.

I couldn't quite catch my breath, and as he tucked a daring hand under my coat to caress my breast, I moaned softly into his mouth. The kisses grew longer, deeper, and waves of heat flushed over me, wonderful on the cool evening.

Wonderful, period.

He sat back and smiled at me. I didn't want to stop, but it wasn't fair to continue when I was sure I would send him home tonight.

I chewed on my lip for a moment. Well, almost sure.

He drew his palm down the curve of my chin, and I giggled. What can I say? It tickled.

He snuggled me back into his arms and said, "Your nose is no longer cold."

Chapter Nine

After a few hot kisses at my door, I said goodnight and ran up the stairs before I lost what little willpower I still had. It was too soon to invite him in. I didn't know this guy yet, and I wasn't going to hook up with him until we'd had more time together. A lot more time.

That didn't mean he didn't set my little heart pounding and warm my insides with his touch.

My computer was blooping when I came through my door. I flipped a couple locks and hurried to answer the internet chat.

"Hey, sis. How goes Paris?" Samantha smiled and waved. The words didn't quite match with the movement of her lips, but it was good to hear from her anyway.

"Great." I scooted over the one chair that wasn't heaped with junk and sat down.

"Where have you been? I've been calling for hours. I thought you'd be home by now."

I dropped my gaze. I hadn't mentioned Anton to anyone back home. The last thing I needed was a lecture about men from my sister.

"Just out," I prevaricated.

"With whom?" Sam was really good at reading me, even seven thousand miles away.

"Well, I met this guy named Anton."

"French? Sounds interesting." Sam moved her head

102

in closer and rested her chin on her hands. "What does he do?"

"He works at the little café I go to sometimes." Every day.

"A waiter."

"Don't be a snob, Sam. He's a chef, a pâtissier. That's an important job in France."

"A baker?"

She was impossible. I pinched my lips together.

"I'm not being critical. I'm just translating."

"Yes, and he's nice. He's helping me with the apartment. You know what a mess this place is in."

Now she frowned, her special, I'm-the-big-sister-and-I-know-best frown. "You let him in the apartment? Alyssa—"

"Oh, my oven's beeping." I lied. "Gotta go." I clicked the red receiver on my screen before she had a chance to argue.

Feeling totally guilty, I stared at the computer screen for a moment, knowing she'd try back. I ignored the first call, but felt remorseful and answered on her second.

"Alyssa. I'm not trying to tell you how to live your life—"

"Then don't." I pouted at the screen.

She let out a long sigh. "Just be careful. You got your heart busted up before, and I don't want to see you hurt again."

Why was she always so right?

"Alyssa?"

"Yeah, okay. I know. I think I might be a little caught up in the romance of Paris thing."

She smiled at me, a gentle smile. "You always

were a sucker for *Casablanca.*" She hummed the famous tune.

I shook my head with a grin. "Don't worry, Sam." Get it? "I'll be fine. Maybe I'll take a step back."

"A step or two?"

Maybe.

I heard Jojo crying in the background. Sam looked over her shoulder and then back at me.

"Go ahead. We can talk later."

"Luvs ya, baby sista."

"Luvs ya, too, big sista."

The screen went blank. Suddenly, I felt lonelier than I had in days. My chest hurt, and I found it difficult to breathe.

I opened the windows looking out over the Seine and sat in the wing chair Anton had placed there. No matter how beautiful Paris was, no matter how nice Anton seemed, I missed my family. The bells of Notre Dame rang in the distance.

I might need a pastry in the morning, to go with my coffee.

Chapter Ten

I finally had time to plant the seeds I'd bought last Sunday. It was cooler this morning, so I hurried down to do the heavy work before the sun warmed the garden space too much. I found a small hand spade in a worn pail and began turning the soil. The space smelled of fresh grass and daffodils, and I drew in a deep breath of clean air.

"Dig deeply, Alyssa. Break up the soil with your fingers. Do you see, darling?" my mother had said encouragingly. I remembered the moment so clearly, even though I couldn't have been more than four or five.

Mom's hands were strong and brown from the sunshine. They crushed the dried clods of California clay easily. It was harder for me with my little fingers, but I tried.

"Good job, little one." Her words echoed in my memory. "You have a green thumb, you know. Remember the sunflowers you grew last summer?"

"They were bigger than me," I'd said.

I sat back on my heels and drew in a deep breath, recalling my mother's next words. "Alyssa. You're a big girl now. I need you to understand something."

I squinted at her, shielding my eyes with one hand in order to see her better against the bright sunlight. There were tears on her cheeks, and I swallowed hard, trying not to cry too.

"Your father has decided not to live with us anymore." She had a choke in her throat.

"Why?"

"It's better for him." Mama dropped her gaze to the ground and continued to dig the earth. "He thinks he'll be happier."

My heart beat big and hard in my chest. "Molly's mama got 'vorced last summer. Is that what daddy wants?"

"I don't know yet, darling."

I stood up, suddenly frightened and angry. Now my chest really hurt. I choked back a sob and threw down the little shovel I'd held in my hand. "But you love daddy. You said you loved him. I heard you."

"I know dear, I do love him. Sometimes love isn't enough."

A shadow crossed my eyes, and I glanced up to see Anton standing over me.

"Oh, Anton. How did you get in?" I sniffed and hurriedly took off my specs and brushed the wet streaks from my face with the back of my hand.

"Your neighbor, that old guy Max? He said you were out here."

"I-I was planting some seeds." I couldn't look at him. My face was hot, and I bit my lip to keep a sob from escaping. Damn. Why was I sitting in the garden crying over events from more than twenty years ago? Ridiculous.

Anton knelt beside me and touched my cheeks with his hand. His eyebrows drew down, and his lips formed a thin, worried line.

"I'm sorry," I said between hiccups.

"*Pourquoi, ma petite?*"

"I was remembering something...painful...from when I was a little kid."

"A difficult moment?"

I fiddled with the spade, cleaning the dirt from its sides. "The time my mother told me that my father was leaving us."

"Ah." He drew me to my feet and wrapped his arms around my back.

I rested my head against his shoulder and drew in a couple quick breaths to calm myself. "Silly. So long ago."

"But still difficult?"

"He left us to marry another woman. He abandoned us."

"Do you see him now?"

I shook my head. "Haven't spoken to him in five years."

"Ah." With that word and the gentle smile on his face, I knew he understood.

I smoothed my hair back from my face, brushed away the stupid tears, and forced a smile. "I wasn't expecting you."

"I had an hour. I thought you might like to go to lunch."

****

Later that afternoon, my phone buzzed and Dominique's name popped up on the screen. I ignored the call and let it go to voice mail.

She'd already called several times over the last week, asking to take a peek at the apartment, but each time I'd put her off.

Focused on the clearing process, I didn't want any

interruptions. Besides, I'd only cleared a path into the main bedroom and knew even a real estate agent would need a superior imagination to see the value in this place.

I owed it to Jojo and the rest of my family to maximize the value when I sold the apartment. If that meant another couple weeks of dust and garbage bags, so be it.

I tied my hair into a scarf and dug through the old clothes on the bed. I don't think Isabella had ever thrown out anything. As I sorted and folded and tossed decades of clothing, I began to understand why.

Chanel, Yves Saint Laurent, and other designer brands lay mixed in with the worn sweat shirts of the eighties and dowdy house dresses of faded gingham. Dust motes floated in the air. I sneezed loudly.

I picked out a gorgeous, silk sheath labeled Madeleine Vionnet I thought Samantha would like. I'd show it to her the next time we talked online. The soft blue color would go with her eyes. Amazing needlework. The collar had been embroidered with seed pearls and tiny silver beads.

On the top shelf of the wardrobe, I found a dozen hats spanning a half century of style. My favorite—an adorable straw cloche from the late thirties. It still had the Galeries Lafayette label hand-sewn inside. Although the blue silk ribbons had faded, my mother could replace those. The ladybug pin was perfect.

I modeled it in front of the bedroom mirror. Maybe I'd keep this one, but when I tried to think of a place I might wear a hat in super-casual California, I came up blank. At the least, it would make a great decoration. Something about its jaunty attitude made me smile.

I stood back and examined the piles. "You certainly were a clothes horse, Isabella."

I was going to need an expert in the field of antique fashions, too. I hung up what looked salvageable and tossed the rest in garbage bags. Ten to be exact, but when I'd finished hauling them down to the trash, and the room was nearly cleared, I realized the bed itself was a treasure.

I gave Dominique a call. "Do you know anything about antique furniture?"

"*Mais, oui.* A bit," she replied. "I have been to the Musée des Arts Décoratifs many times."

"Great idea."

"I could meet you there."

I thought about this for a moment. I didn't want anyone to know what was in the apartment, and Dominique was already too curious. "No. I think I'll go sometime soon and take a look around."

"We could meet for lunch at the museum restaurant. My treat."

I chewed on my fingernail a moment. "Sure," I finally said, giving in to her not so subtle persistence.

"Tomorrow?" She sounded so pleased, I couldn't put her off.

"One?"

"*D'accord.*"

I'd have time to wander through the museum first on my own.

****

For once there was no line in front of a museum. Even though the Decorative Arts collection is part of the Louvre complex and had the same gorgeous interiors, it didn't get the draw of the main art gallery.

Lucky me.

Audio guide in hand, I followed the well laid out corridors and started recognizing furniture pieces soon after I hit the Empire section. Yep. I had one of those side tables. The scroll work on the legs was identical. And those two upholstered chairs looked familiar too. I clicked a few pictures with my cell, careful to turn off the flash.

Up on the top floor under the rafters stood an exact copy of my newly uncovered bed. The sensuous lines, the gorgeous wood grain, the glorious inlay.

"Wow," I said under my breath.

The museum guard eyed me suspiciously and moved in my direction.

I held up my hands and smiled. "I won't touch it. Promise."

She returned my smile. "Isn't it beautiful?" she said, effortlessly switching to English.

Sure wish I could do that with French.

"The curved lines of the Art Nouveau period have always been my favorite," the guard said.

I walked around the enormous bed, studying the fine grain of the wood and the gorgeous workmanship of the carving. "So, if I could buy one of these, what would it cost me?"

She puffed out her cheeks in that cute French way. "If you could find one in perfect condition..." She waved her hand over her head.

"A hundred thousand euros?" I asked, thinking high.

"More."

"More?" I squeaked.

"But you see this bed was designed by Gallé. It is

signed, and this is the only known copy."

I turned away and grinned, but resisted a fist pump. Little did she know.

I took a few more pictures, but then realized I was late to meet Dominique.

"*Merci*," I said to the guard. Oh, boy. Merci, indeed. I knew I'd seen that signature someplace before. Jojo honey, you just won the jackpot.

My cheeks must have been flushed when I hurried into the restaurant and glanced around. The waiter pointed toward the sunny courtyard. From her table overlooking the gardens, Dominique gave a subtle wave. Of course, she was dressed and coifed impeccably.

"You look happy," she said after I sat down across from her.

"It's nice to get out." I wasn't telling anyone about the bed in Isabella's apartment, so I'd have to stall Dominique.

We ordered seafood salads and chatted about the museum. "I took a few pictures of rabbits," I said. "My aunt collected them, you know."

"Oh? Anything interesting?"

"One or two. But hers are probably copies," I lied. I was beginning to understand Isabella didn't buy copies. She bought the real thing.

I swallowed hard and took a sip of my hot tea. I mentioned the toy section of the museum and the adorable little Scharffenberger circus I'd seen there. "My grandmother had one of those toys when she was a little girl. She'd be thrilled to know there's a set in a museum."

When dessert arrived, Dominique folded her hands

under her chin and asked softly, "So, Alyssa, when will you be ready to show me this wonderful apartment?" There was a genuine twinkle of excitement in her eye.

"My gosh, this is wonderful," I said, digging deeper into my chocolate mousse topped with fresh raspberries. The creamy texture floated on my tongue and the flavor of dark chocolate cornered my senses.

She continued to smile.

****

After another morning of lugging down old paperback books to donate at the church on the corner, I decided to take an afternoon off and visit Monet's *Nymphs* at L'Orangerie.

The guide book I'd bought second hand at the English bookstore, Shakespeare and Co., said it was well worth the six euros entry. At this point, anything that wasn't old musty books would be an improvement.

I could've walked, but took my fav bus 69 through the just-wide-enough-to-pass stone entrance to the Louvre. I wandered around the glass Pyramid and down the side of the Tuileries garden. The banks of irises were in full bloom, shouting in every shade of purple. My friend Georgie loved irises, so I clicked off a few phone shots to send her.

On one of the little side ponds, several children played with rustic wooden sail boats. Running around the edge of the shallow pool, they pushed the toys with long sticks until the breeze caught the little sails.

I sat down on one of the garden chairs and clicked off a few pictures to show Jojo. Maybe I could find him a little boat to sail at home.

Finally, I reached the Neo-Classic building taking up one corner of the Place de La Concorde.

Long white halls led into the huge rooms of Monet's masterpiece. I studied the enormous paintings called the *Nymphs* for a long time, moving closer and then farther away, until I had the perspective I wanted. The room, built to Monet's plan, was very plain and white, topped with large, diffused skylights. Sitting on the low upholstered bench in the middle of the room, I noticed how the paintings changed when the light from above dimmed because of a small wandering cloud.

I liked the small, very dark painting best. The colors spoke to me—deep blues and soft greens and purples. I could imagine sitting in a boat on Monet's very quiet pond.

I imagined the moon had yet to rise, but the stars shed enough light as my vision adjusted. I could just make out the mass of trees in the distance and hear the swish of their long flowing branches as they brushed the cool, dark water. Somewhere beside me a bullfrog called for his mate.

He swam over to his lily pad and croaked, "Yup, yup."

I had to agree with him. It was a beautiful place.

The air was heavy, warm, and languid. Moisture lay thick on my skin. The lilies, resting in their leafy chairs reflected little pools of color in the dark blue landscape.

I smiled at my imagination, drawing my mind back into the museum space. Was that what Monet wanted me to feel?

Starting my walk home from the museum, I felt refreshed, as if I had spent a morning in Monet's garden.

I headed down the Rue du Rivoli, but the window

display at a famous pâtisserie suckered me inside. I left, nibbling on a second chocolate macaron. The cookie was good, I decided after popping the rest in my mouth, but second best to Anton's.

My feet were tired after wandering through the L'Orangerie. Maybe I would spring for a cab home. I caught the gaze of the driver in front of the Hotel Meurice, but didn't see the bicyclist barreling down the street. The rider hissed a warning, and I dodged back just in time not be knocked down.

That would have hurt.

Shaken and embarrassed, I waved the cabbie on and set out on foot. There were loads of people on the Rivoli, and the shops were full of tourists. I ducked through the crowd, but farther down the street, the crowds thinned to a few couples strolling in the late afternoon light.

An itchy feeling crawled up the back of my neck, and I turned to glance around. Was I still unnerved by the near miss with the bicyclist? No bikes were headed my way, but a man twenty yards behind me quickly turned down a side street.

I licked my suddenly dry lips and swallowed hard. Had I seen that man somewhere before? Hadn't he been walking through the L'Orangerie an hour ago?

He wasn't tall. Or short. Wasn't old. Or young. Handsome? No. But something about him set my teeth on edge. This odd sensation of being followed gave me the creeps.

I ducked into a store, and the salesclerk called a cheery, *"Bonjour."*

"Bonjour," I replied in my best French accent and pretended to be interested in a sweater on display.

When I glanced through the plate glass window, I spotted the man again, lounging at the bus stop across the street. He scratched the stubble on his chin and worked hard not to look at me. He flipped his gray scarf around his neck even though the afternoon was warm and windless.

I choked on the lump camping in my throat and almost forgot to say "*Au revoir,*" as I hurried out of the shop and down the street.

It was still daylight—not yet six o'clock. I was surrounded by people. I was in no danger. But my heart pounded so hard I could hear it in my ears.

A bus pulled up to the stop ahead of me. I made a run for it, jumping on board seconds before the door closed. I placed a two euro coin on the driver's pay stand and sank into a seat near the front, trying to regain my breath.

I clutched my bag to my chest and waited for my heart to slow. I was headed the wrong direction, but who cared? I'd grab a cab a couple of stops down the road.

Covering my face with my hand, I watched the gray man pull out his cell phone to make a call. He looked super annoyed.

****

By the time I made it back across Paris, evening had fallen, and the street lights glowed softly in a light mist. Tired, I took the little elevator to my floor. I'd never been so glad to be home. I unlocked, then closed my door and rested against its solid shape.

I hesitated. The light I usually kept on in the kitchen was turned off. Strange. As I reached for the switch, I tripped over something lying on the hallway floor.

Now I was totally spooked. A roar of terror echoed in my ears, but I managed not to scream. I turned on the light and moaned loudly at the devastation in my kitchen. My cute little, clean little kitchen had been ransacked.

Everything I'd purchased at the Monoprix and lugged home to the apartment over the last two weeks had been dumped on the floor. Flour, salt, milk. Even the eggs had been smashed.

I sank back against the wall, my heart pounding with alarm.

I stood very still for a few moments, goose bumps racing over my skin. Could someone still be here? I listened. Silence. Except for my pounding heart. And my rapid breathing.

I dropped my purse on the table and grabbed the one knife left in the drawer. I tiptoed forward and reached for the light switch on the living room wall. I let out a heart-felt, "Shit."

If anything, this room was worse than the kitchen. Every carefully placed piece of furniture had been either knocked over or smashed. The books on the bureau had been ripped apart, as if someone was searching for something inside them.

I hurried to the office and cried out as I looked inside. It looked like an IED had gone off here. Most of my rabbits lay in rubbled heaps on the floor.

I grabbed my Lalique bunny and held him to my chest. He was unharmed, but many of the larger ones were smashed beyond repair. It was as if someone had taken a hammer to them.

Should I call the cops? Face it. I didn't even know

how.

Feeling more and more like the Too-Dumb-To-Live-Blonde in a horror film, I continued through the apartment and stepped from the office into the adjoining bedroom. I released a breath. I'd only started cleaning this room today, and it looked pretty much the same. Fortunately, several old quilts covered most of the Gallé bed.

Then another cold chill slithered down my spine. Had I interrupted my visitor?

I thought of the man on the Rue de Rivoli and the phone call he'd made. A warning?

"Alyssa?" The whisper came from behind me, and I almost peed my pants. I whirled around and pointed the knife at the shadow of a man.

Max took an unsteady step backward, his wary gaze on my knife.

"Oh, Max. I'm sorry." I dropped the weapon to my side.

"What happened here?" he asked. "I heard noises when I came up in the elevator and was worried. You left your door open."

"I've had a break in." My voice shook.

He cursed in French and then German as he looked around the apartment. "Have you called the police?"

I shook my head.

"Why not?"

I shrugged my shoulders.

"Have you checked the bathroom?" he asked, pointing toward the en-suite.

Still wielding the butcher knife, I peeked around the screen into the bathroom and was overwhelmed by the sweet and sharp smells of lavender and peach. Even though Max stood beside me, I was more scared than ever, but other than a few dumped boxes of dusting powder, the room looked untouched.

I let out a grateful breath. Thank heavens for small blessings. At least I could take a bath before I cleaned up this mess.

Max took another look around, tisking as he walked through the rooms and muttering under his breath in a combination of harsh-sounding languages. He inspected the locks on the windows, although how anyone would climb four stories was beyond me.

I collapsed on my newly ripped sofa. "I should call the police."

He eased his old body down next to me. "Perhaps." He rubbed the wrinkles on his face with both hands. "Can you face a night of questions and intrusion?"

My shoulders sank, and I shook my head.

"I could help with the translations into French."

Disheartened, I looked around the room, and swallowed the sour lump in my throat. I pulled out my cell.

****

"Captain?"

I glanced up from reading Bruno's latest report.

Brows down, mouth pinched, Claire looked worried.

"What?" I demanded. "What's wrong?"

"Break-in—at Mademoiselle's apartment. The call was just relayed from the local prefecture. As you requested."

I'd already grabbed my coat and hurried past her.

"Sir." She handed me a white paper bag filled with macarons.

"What's this?"

"An excuse, sir."

****

The prefecture was just around the corner. Only a few minutes after my call, blue lights flashed in my windows. A fresh-faced policeman entered the apartment, looking more like a futuristic robot in his protective gear than a police officer. Max translated and Robo took the report.

In rudimentary English the cop assured me. "There hasn't been another break-in in this area in months."

"Great," I said with a sigh. "Why pick on me?"

Before the paperwork was signed, and the officer left, Anton poked his nose through the door, carrying a white paper bag.

"What are you doing here?" I asked.

"I was leaving the shop and noticed the police car parked outside your building. What's going on?" His eyes were wide with worry.

I explained and pointed to the destruction.

Anton set down the bag and put his arms around me. "You okay?"

I nodded, but my throat choked with tears. "Fine."

"Do you need me to stay awhile?"

I shook my head. "I'm fine." I wasn't, but I was unwilling to admit this to anyone.

I introduced Max, and the two nodded suspiciously at each other.

Reluctantly, Anton followed the officer out. "Lock your door."

I nodded.

Max gave me a wistful smile. "I am sorry. This old man is not much help."

"No, Max. You're a real friend. Thank you so much. I wouldn't have remembered any of my French by this point."

He patted my arm and slowly, painfully made his way to the hall. "I am next door, Alyssa. If you are afraid, call for me. I sleep very little these days."

I flipped four of the locks, then another hefty looking one for good measure, but I was the one who didn't sleep much. Nightmares of boogeymen haunted my dreams.

I felt age ten again, afraid of the dark. I finally got up and turned on even more lights. I put one of the unsmashed chairs against the door with a pot on top. At least if anyone broke in again, I'd hear about it.

****

"You look like hell, Alyssa," Anton said as he waved to me from the kitchen the next morning at Café Ruillard.

"Glad to see you too," I grumped and threw myself in the corner table away from the light of the windows. I'd hardly brushed my hair, just confined it to a messy bun. I hadn't changed from yesterday's clothes. I glanced in the advertising mirror hanging beside me on the wall and let out a long sigh. I did look like hell.

He brought two coffees to the table and sat down opposite me. "You didn't sleep, did you? I should have stayed."

I shook my head and slurped my coffee. Caffeine would have to get me through the day. "Don't you have to bake?"

"Macarons can wait. You cannot." He touched my arm protectively, and somehow I felt a little better.

I shrugged and slurped more coffee, hoping it

would clear the fog in my sleep-deprived brain. The cup rattled when I returned it to the saucer.

"You should have called me."

I dropped my gaze to the table. "It was late, and I only have the number here. Besides, I didn't want to bother you."

He rose quickly and went to the back of the restaurant. His voice echoed in the space in loud, punctuated French, and soon he returned without his apron. "We will go see what needs to be done. Eh?"

He put his hand out to help me rise, and we quickly walked back to my apartment. Although he never let go of my hand, he was silent, his face a mask. I couldn't read his thoughts. Was he worried? Angry? I didn't know him well enough to guess.

Once inside, we looked over the damaged room, the rumpled bed where I'd laid awake most of the night, the smashed antiques and ripped draperies.

I gulped back my fear. This was more than robbery. More than impersonal vandalism. There was anger here. Cold waves of confusion and fear rushed over me, and I shivered.

Anton draped his arm across my shoulder and pulled me closer. He felt sturdy, and I found a little courage.

"Do you want to wait outside?"

I clenched my teeth and shook my head.

He walked through the apartment without speaking, but the set of his shoulders was very easy to read. He was pissed. He looked into the office and tisked in his French way, with a puff of his cheeks. "Oh, *ma petite*. Your bunnies."

"He didn't get the Lalique one." I held up my

friend I'd rescued from the massacre and gave a half smile. "I didn't have the heart to see who else can be saved."

"*Je comprends*." He rubbed his chin for a moment in thought, and then turned to me. His expression softened. "I will speak to the authorities. My father, uh…my father knew some people in the police."

"Why didn't Robocop take fingerprints?"

He pursed his lips and slowly shook his head. "I am no detective, but I would say the chances are slim they would find any. Still, I will see what can be done as far as security. Did your aunt have insurance?"

I shook my head. "No idea. I guess I could call her lawyer." I looked around the room again and sighed. "I don't think insurance matters here. Most of her things weren't valuable." I clutched the little glass sculpture to my chest. At least the Gallé bed hadn't been harmed, although several of Isabella's antique chairs were now scrap. My stomach rolled over.

Anton pulled his phone from his back pocket and thumbed a quick number. "We should find you another place to stay."

"No. Really. If you can give me someone to call, maybe someone who speaks English, I'll be fine."

He firmed his lips into a thin line, but clicked off the phone and set it down. Turning me toward him, he moved his hands to my shoulders and bent to catch my gaze. "I don't want you here."

I pulled back from his grasp. Maybe it was the demanding tone in his voice, but I instantly focused my anger on him. I set my jaw and said, "I'm fine."

He read my reaction and stepped back. "I'm sorry. I'm just worried about you. We are friends, no?"

"I hope so."

"Do you want help with…" he spread out his hand to signify the disaster.

"Maybe with the broken things." I was suddenly so tired I didn't want to argue anymore. I walked over and sat on my little bed. All I wanted to do was curl up and wish my way home to California. Where did I put my ruby red shoes?

Anton stepped into the entryway and made a few calls. His voice was quiet.

Within the hour, my apartment was full of activity. Several people, including a couple of large, burly men, were hauling away broken chairs and lamps.

I wandered into the office. An elderly woman with her gray hair done in old-fashioned braids had just finished sweeping the room. All the salvageable *lapins* were again lined up on the table next to the wall.

"*Bonjour,*" she said with a quiet smile and kept working.

I returned the greeting and went over to arrange the rabbits again. They needed some sort of order. *I* needed some sort of order.

I concentrated on the process to calm my mind. It was soothing to think about their attributes. Material, height, color.

With a chuckle, Anton folded his arms and leaned against the doorframe. "You are a little A. C. D., Alyssa?"

I smiled at him. "You mean OCD? You bet." I placed the last red rabbit in order of height and stepped back to examine my work. "Most engineers are."

"My mother claims I am the opposite."

"That's okay. We all have our strengths. Although

I bet you are particular about your baking."

He shrugged. "One must always be particular about baking."

I tipped my head toward the burly guy walking down the hall with an armload of filled garbage bags. "Thanks for finding the cleaning crew. I don't think I could've faced doing this again."

"Do you want them to continue in the bedroom? They could help with the sorting."

I shook my head. "No, I need to do that."

He turned quickly, but I caught a pinched look on his face. Disappointment? I frowned but then followed him back into the living room. I had fewer pieces of furniture, but actually, the room looked quite nice. The dusty draperies, already in shreds, were piled on the floor.

In quick French, Anton must've told the woman to toss them, because she dragged the poor things across the room like so many dead bodies and ordered Burly Man Number One to take them away.

I walked slowly around the beautiful room. With the lovely, floor-to-ceiling windows opened and draperies gone, light filled the space. The trees outside were fully leafed out and softened the feeling of exposure. I moved to the first window and looked across the square at L'Hôtel de Ville.

The tourists on the street below took selfies by the fountains, and locals hurried to their appointments. I smiled and let out a long sigh. I felt more normal again. Safe.

Well, at least *safer*.

I crossed my arms and chuckled. "Guess I need to go shopping. Otherwise, I'll feel like the whole world is watching through these windows."

****

I enjoyed my shopping spree at the BHV. Being Thursday night, the shops were open late. Anton played my assistant and by the time I'd finished at the department store, I had three clerks following me. With Anton translating, I could explain what I wanted without my phrase book in hand.

"Americans call this retail therapy," I told him with a smile. I smugly handed over my charge card and didn't even look at the total. It was time I enjoyed a little of the money I'd rabbited away over the past five years. Suddenly my apartment seemed like the right place to spend some of the beaucoup bucks I'd earned working ninety hour weeks for most of my adult life.

I'd never cared about expensive clothes or designer handbags. I drove a five-year-old Prius. Paris was the first vacation, if you could call it that, I'd had in years. What else was money for?

Obviously you couldn't take it with you. Counting the number of *lapins* left behind, not even Isabella's bunnies had made it into heaven with her. Plus, I would have the investment returned to me when I sold the place.

I hesitated and pouted for a second, pushing my lips together in contemplation. Then I smiled to myself. *If* I sold the place.

Anton convinced two salespeople to help us carry the bags and boxes across the square. He could be pretty authoritative when he wanted his way. I watched him with gratitude as he juggled arm loads of plastic bags ahead of me, shouting at the helpers in staccato French.

He'd helped me pull back from last night's disaster and fear. I wasn't helpless or alone. I had a friend here. Maybe even a good friend.

I tipped our assistants more than I should have, and then we lumbered up the four flights of steps. The tiny elevator in the middle, packed to overflowing, rose with us.

Breathless and excited by the time we reached my floor, I pushed through the door, laughing. I couldn't wait to put away my new things and make this my home.

Anton dragged in the last bag. "What are you going to do with this?" he asked, holding up a box. As a last minute purchase, I'd included a kit to teach myself how to make macarons.

I shrugged. "Sometimes I crave chocolate macarons," I said with a giggle. "And you're not around."

He caught my meaning and stepped closer with a gleam in his eyes. "If you need to make macarons, I will come running." He kissed me lightly, drawing his hands down my arms. I responded, needing more warmth. My breath caught, and my heart raced. I grew warm and liquid as he drew me closer and pressed against me. I hadn't felt this swirl of warm excitement in a long time.

I knew he wanted me instantly. Could I trust him?

He caressed lovely soft kisses down my neck, and I arched into the shivers strolling over my skin. Nice.

I pulled my fingers through his fine, soft hair and circled my arms more tightly around his neck, returning his passionate kisses. He tasted nice. He smelled even better. Like chocolate and fresh coffee and something very male. I drew in his scent from the soft place behind his ear and nibbled to taste him.

"*Chérie?*" he said between kisses.

"Mmm?"

He touched my cheek with his hand, and I looked up.

His eyebrows furrowed.

I must have looked confused.

"We have a problem."

My heart sank, and I pulled away. "If you tell me you're married, I swear I will take one of my new kitchen knives and…"

His eyes grew wide, but then he laughed. "I promise. That is not the case. I have never been married."

I crossed my arms. "I've heard that lie before."

"*Je ne comprends pas.*"

"Never mind," I grumbled. The moment was spoiled, and I moved over to the window. "I should hang these drapes." I kept my back turned so he couldn't see the look of disappointment on my face. "And I need to—"

He took hold of my shoulders and then wrapped his hands around my waist, hugging me gently to him, front to back. "Our problem," he repeated quietly in my ear, "is that we have no place to make love. That is what you wish, no?"

My face flushed all the way to my curly hair follicles. Hoping he wouldn't notice, I continued to stare out the window. I opened my mouth but fumbled to find words.

"It is what I want," he whispered. "More than anything."

I must look like a beet by now. Frenchmen sure can get to the point.

He drew little circles on the back of my neck that drove me wild. I arched into him. "I do not want to take you to a hotel. That would not be the way to begin."

I shook my head.

"And my city apartment is not, well, it is not the most romantic of places."

I let out a long, regretful sigh as I studied my tiny single bed in the corner of the room. "We do have a problem then."

"May I take you away? Someplace romantic?"

I thought about this for...well, about three milliseconds and then turned in his arms. "That might be very nice." I played with the button on his shirt for a moment and then looked up into his lovely gray eyes. My sister's warning swam into my lusty thoughts. "Can we go in a week or two? When we know each other a little better?"

He brushed my hair back from my face and kissed me again, this time with a little more tongue. Again, I was thinking about packing my bags.

"You are special, *ma chérie*. I will wait, but not too long."

He tipped up my chin and kissed me firmly. "I had better return to work. The macarons do not bake themselves."

We separated, but I still held his hand as I walked him to the door. "I hope your boss isn't angry. You've been gone for hours."

"I am the boss, Alyssa."

My eyebrows rose in surprise.

"You did not know this?"

"Well, no."

He smiled enigmatically. "We have much to share with each other."

Chapter Eleven

My team jumped to attention as I slammed the door of my office.

Bruno looked the most contrite. "Sorry, Captain. I was following her, but she spotted me."

"I told you to watch her," I ground out. "I told you to keep her safe at all costs. *Merde...*" I drew in air through my nose and let it out slowly, then sat in my chair.

Bruno raised his palms. "I followed her the entire day. She spotted me. She's clever, observant. There wasn't budget to put another team on the apartment too."

I rubbed my forehead with my hand. "This is my fault. I should have moved more quickly."

"I disagree, sir."

I glanced up, surprised Claire had voiced an opinion. As the youngest member of the group, she rarely did more than listen.

I folded my arms. "Why?"

"Because, sir, if I may say, Alyssa doesn't entirely trust you." Claire pushed her long hair over her shoulder. "She has been recently disappointed in love."

Handing over several snapshots of a handsome older man, she continued. "Several months ago, Marcus Bradley seduced her and kept her in the dark about his marital status."

"Humpf. Explains the threat." Bruno snickered.

"You were listening, I suppose?"

He ducked his head. "Those were my orders."

I hated the idea of my lovemaking being on the official record. I would disable the devices the next time I went to Alyssa's apartment.

I tapped the photograph with one finger. "What's the status with this asshole?"

"We called our contact in Northern California," Claire continued. "As a favor, he followed Monsieur Bradley. The man has returned to his home and family. As far as we know from phone records, he has made no contact with Mademoiselle in several weeks, nor she with him. Certainly none since she arrived in Paris. We could contact the NSA for internet correspondence, but I'm sure Bruno could hack into her email."

I waved my hand. "No. Not now. After this last incident, I am convinced Alyssa is totally unaware of what we know."

"But someone's very aware," Bruno said darkly.

My throat closed, and I stared at the ceiling for a long moment. The room was silent. "*Oui,*" I finally concurred. "And we need to find out who."

****

The internet picture phone blooped at me, and I hurried across my apartment to open the program. Jojo's little face filled the screen. He waved when he saw me on his screen.

"'llysa, 'llysa. I slided down the slide." He grinned at me.

"Well, aren't you a big boy." I tapped a high five onto my computer screen.

"Big boy," he repeated.

Sam's face appeared behind her son's. "Are we disturbing you? He's been bugging me non-stop since we came home from the park."

"No. I'm happy to hear from you." I smiled and waved again at the little guy.

Sam squinted her eyes a little, moved in and studied my face. I pulled off my glasses and looked the other way as I polished them. "What's up?" she asked in her suspicious, big-sister tone.

Damn. I wasn't fast enough. "Nothing."

No way was I telling her about the break-in. She'd have me back in California even if she had to drag me onto the plane herself.

"Alyssa?"

"Sam. I'm a little tired. But everything's fine. Honest. Do you want to see what I've done with the place?"

I walked my laptop camera around the open living room and pointed out the improvements, including the curtains I'd almost finished hanging.

Samantha nodded when I returned us to my little work table. "You've been pushing too hard, Alyssa. You should get some help."

"I did have some people move a few things around," I said, remembering Burly Man Number One and Number Two fondly. "But I need to go through stuff. Everything's in an awful mess. The good things mixed with the total junk. It takes time."

"Just toss it."

"No, I can't," I said a bit too vehemently.

Sam tilted her head.

"There's valuable stuff mixed in with the garbage. Really, I'm okay, but I have to take my time."

She bought the excuse, so I continued.

"This could mean a lot for you and Joseph. Some of these antiques alone could pay for Jojo's college education. And for the next little ones, too. It could mean a worry-free retirement for Mom."

"Okay, okay. I get it. What about that guy? The cook?"

"The pastry chef who owns the pâtisserie?" I pointed out.

Sam shot me her big sister eye roll. "Well?"

I shrugged. "We're taking it slowly, Sam." At least I could be truthful about something.

She nodded, but turned her head to stare at me.

I put up my palm. "Scout's honor. No 'hanky-panky,' as Mom would say."

At least not much.

Not yet.

"When will you come home?"

"I haven't even listed the place yet. It's different here. Things don't move quickly in France. I may need to talk to my boss and extend my leave."

Sam smiled at me. "Well, take care of yourself. Mom asks about you every day."

"Why don't you have her call me?"

"Good idea. How about Sunday at dinner?"

"Let's wait and see. I may go out of town for a break."

****

Bruno pulled off his headset and gave me a skeptical look. "Sounds like she might take you up on your offer."

I rubbed my forehead and considered what to tell him. Although we had worked together for more than three years, Bruno had started his career as an investigator with my father back when I was still in school. I had counted on my sergeant's advice many times in the field, but we had never spoken of personal matters.

He leaned back in his chair. Bruno had raised two boys of his own. Could he give me advice on a matter of…love? I gulped at the use of the word and pushed the thought to the back of my mind.

I grabbed the chair next to his. "When we began this operation, I never suspected I would come to know Alyssa so well. My goal was to gain access to the apartment and determine if any treasure had been kept there."

Bruno scrubbed his chin and nodded.

Alyssa's determination and courage came to mind, along with images of her smile, her breasts and those long, luscious legs. I shifted in my seat and waited for my blood to cool.

Frowning, I brushed back the hair from my face. "Somehow it does not seem fair to take the relationship any further when I am not being honest."

"But you wonder how she will react when you tell her who you really are?"

"How did you know?"

"Captain, I've had to listen to the two of you over these last few weeks. You're a good undercover operative."

Restless, I rose and paced the wood floor. "You mean I can lie with the best of them?"

He put down his headphones. "But this is more, is it not?"

I arched my neck and rubbed the kink in my

shoulder. "Will you enjoy the 'I told you so' that is resting on your tongue?"

"No. I don't want to see the young woman hurt. Or you, for that matter, but she has done nothing to deserve our subterfuge."

I sank my hands into my pockets. "I don't know how to tell her, how to begin."

"Begin at the beginning."

****

"Hi Max," I called as I entered *mon petit jardin* early the next morning. With only a few hours of blue sky forecast for the next several days, I thought I'd better tend to my flowers before the rain arrived.

Max glanced up from his paper with surprise. I don't think he can hear very well. He smiled.

I pulled my hair into a quick pony tail and wrapped it with a curl. One thing about curly hair—I don't need a hair tie very often.

He leaned forward. "I have heard much thumping and banging in the last few days. *Ça va?*"

"I'm fine, Max. The apartment is shaping up."

I pulled on my work gloves, but then went to sit beside him. "You haven't seen anyone strange hanging around, have you?"

He shook his gray head slowly. "No. Other than the tall man who sometimes visits you."

I blushed. "That's Anton. He's a friend."

Max puffed his lips, as if unsure of my conclusion. Then he tapped his gnarled finger on his chin. "I do see the man who waits."

Even though we both sat in the sun, a cold chill crept up my spine. "What man?"

Max shrugged his thin shoulders. "He is difficult to

describe. Not old. Not young. Beard, yes and no. He wears a gray scarf sometimes."

I swallowed with difficulty. A scruffy man in a gray scarf?

"You would not see him, *ma petite,* but my window faces the bus stop. The last few days, he waits there, as if for the bus, but then he does not ride. He never rides."

Well, hell. I rubbed the goose bumps from the back of my neck and stood. I should tell Anton about the bus stop man. Even from Max's nondescript description, he had to be the same creep who followed me the other day.

Max frowned and patted my hand with his old, leathery one. "I'm sorry, Alyssa. I have upset you."

I feigned a bright smile. "No, Max. You're a good friend. I appreciate what you just told me. But why would anyone follow me?"

A French shrug was my only answer.

With a worried sigh, I gathered a few tools and knelt in the garden. Maybe an hour of sunshine, and soil, and green growing things could distract me.

I inspected my seedlings. I would have to thin them soon but would wait until after the rain. I dug up a few more pesky weeds and started working the wild, untouched area around the small fountain. It looked more like a bird bath, just a small marble pedestal with a wide bowl at the top. I doubt it had ever worked, because I couldn't find any source of power to operate a pump.

I glanced over at Max. With his chin on his chest, he was dozing in the warm sunlight. I smiled.

I pulled the long grass just going to seed and

loosened the paving stones to re-adjust them. After years of neglect, they'd tilted and sunk. Some were covered with soil. I brushed off each of the squares with my hands.

They were old, I could tell by the wear. But when I washed them with the garden hose, they glowed golden in the morning light.

I worked hard, lining the stones around the fountain as Isabella must have done and finally stood to inspect my work. When I took a step back, I almost tripped over something buried in the soil.

Turning around, I cleared the spot with my toe. There was definitely something there. Curious, I dug down with my little trowel and felt a smooth, tall shape sticking a few inches out of the dirt. Was it just a rock, or could it be a something else?

I hurried to the shed and found a large spade. Excavating this—whatever it was—was not hand trowel work.

I dug the dense soil.

"Are you digging to China?" Max asked. Had my grunting noises awakened him?

"Found something."

He stood, leaning on his cane and watching me finish the job. Finally, I unearthed a tall animal-shape covered in grime. It took all my strength to lug it closer to the water faucet, and as I washed it off with the hose, I laughed aloud. Of course.

"*Lapin*," I shouted to Max, wiping my sweaty face with a wet hand.

"*Le grand lapin*," Max agreed.

Cleaned off, he was a fine figure of a marble rabbit. Poised on two legs, his ears tipped forward as if listening for danger, he stood just over two feet tall. "How did Isabella ever get you home?" I wondered aloud.

Max walked around him once and then again, rubbing his stubbly white chin with one hand. "I remember a poem I learned as a boy." He straightened his old back, closed his eyes and recited the poem to me while standing in the warm morning sun.

"The rabbit has a charming face,
Its private life is a disgrace.
I really dare not name to you
The awful thing that rabbits do;
Things your paper never prints—
You only mention them in hints.
They have such lost, degraded souls
No wonder they inhabit holes;
When such depravity is found
It can only live underground."

I laughed out loud and clapped my hands together.

He gave a little bow, winking at me wickedly.

"I've never heard that poem before."

"It is before your time." He shrugged with palms and shoulders up. "A friend of mine used to recite it to me as part of my English lessons." His lips turned down, and for a moment, he looked very sad. Then he limped slowly back to his bench.

His eyes grew red and watery. He seemed to need someone to breathe along with him. I rose and moved over to sit beside him.

He patted my hand with a look of regret on his tired face. "It is always the wish of the young to live a long life, Alyssa. But when one does live that long life, and everyone you have known is no longer alive, the granted wish is not so sweet."

I stared at the shadowed walls of the little garden. How could I understand what he felt when I'd only lived twenty-eight years? I squeezed his hand. "I'm very glad we are friends, Max. You've made my time in Paris very special."

He nodded.

"May I ask you something personal?"

There went the shrug again.

"How did you receive your injury?" I indicated his leg and the cane.

In one way, I hated to intrude on Max's privacy, but in another, here was a man who'd lived through many years of history. Would he be willing to share those possibly painful experiences? I chewed my lip for a moment. Maybe this man's memories were a way to help me understand what Isabella had lived through.

"You may have guessed I fought in the war," he began, folding his paper and placing it on his lap. "Everyone in Europe was in the war, one way or another."

"Did you live in Paris then?"

"For part of the time. Before the war, I lived with my mother and brother near the Marais." He nodded his head in an easterly direction. "It was not so...*comment ça se dit?"* He waved his hand in a circle.

"Fancy?" I suggested.

"Yes, fancy. I was a young boy, maybe sixteen, but I had a group of older friends." There was that wicked smile again, but soon it faded into a rueful sigh. "I was their clown, *oui*? They would buy me wine and get me drunk for the sheer fun of it. It was a decadent time."

He dug in the inside pocket of his coat and drew

out a small round tin. After opening it, he offered me one of the hard candies and took one himself. He sucked on it and smiled.

The powerful flavor burst in my mouth. Mmm, citron, but I wasn't to be distracted. "What about your mother?"

He crunched on the candy and selected another before putting the tin away. "My father had been killed in the First World War. Many, many Frenchmen died then. My father died at Verdun. My mother worked so very hard to feed us. I was an ungrateful brat."

"What happened when the second war came? I've read about the Maginot line and how the Germans marched into Paris with almost no resistance."

"Have you?" He squinted his eyes and looked into the past. "In the very early years, I don't think I much cared about anything going on around me. I was out of school for the summer. I mostly thought about swimming in the Seine, and going for rides in my older friend's car. And getting drunk, of course.

"But my mother struggled. Even before the occupation, the price of food was very high. Soon there wasn't enough for everyone to eat. Later, the Germans rationed everything."

"Did you join the army?" I wasn't sure which one.

"I tried. I was too young—only seventeen—to fight with Franco in the Spanish war. I enlisted in the French army not long before Dunkirk. Then, for a while, there was no French army."

"And your mother?"

"Of course, my mother forbade me from taking up with the Germans. She hated them, you see. They had killed my father. I hated them, too.

"By the time I was twenty, the Resistance was stronger."

I pulled back in surprise. "The Resistance?"

"Oui. We worked in small teams, and we would cause trouble for the Germans. Steal food, if we could. Spy on them. It was...exciting. A game really."

He gave a phlegmy chuckle. "I had a friend, a very foolish friend, who would ride along behind the German trucks on his bicycle. When they weren't looking, he'd stick a poster of a naked Hitler on the back."

I drew in a quick breath and covered my lips to block my smirk. "Did they catch him?"

"No, he was too fast," he said with a chuckle.

He glanced at me with a faraway smile. "But I didn't understand. Not really. When the Germans first arrived in Paris, they seemed almost...friendly. I only understood when my friends started disappearing."

He hesitated, and I patted his shoulder. Finally, he swallowed hard and began again.

"As I said, we lived near the Marais, which was close to the Jewish district." He turned his head and looked at me as if I should already understand what he would say next.

I did. I'd wandered by the Deportation Memorial on the banks of the Seine and read about the round-up of the Jewish people in the city. The families, even children and old people, were imprisoned at the Vélodrome until they could be carted off to German work camps. Or worse.

He shook his head and let out another long, wet, old-man sigh. "We should have seen it coming. We should have stopped it, but the Germans were very good at manipulation, and they presented the Jewish people as the enemy of the state. When you hear something often enough, it's human nature to believe it's true. Fortunately, a few were not convinced."

He pulled on his oversized ear. "I lost two good friends. Their whole families just disappeared one morning. I never saw any of them again." He rubbed his gnarled hands together, and I immediately thought of Lady Macbeth.

"It wasn't your fault, Max. You were just a boy."

"Oh, yes. It was my fault. It was everyone's fault. We wear the blood of millions on our hands whether we dropped the gas canisters into the showers, or shot the bullets, or sat back and did nothing."

"But then you chose to help?"

"Yes. That is when I chose to fight." He looked very tired, and his shoulders sank.

"Max? Should you have a rest?"

He nodded, and as I helped him rise, he leaned heavily into me. I didn't want to leave him alone, so I helped him to the elevator, and then to his door.

He smiled weakly. "I would love to tell you more. Perhaps another time?"

"I would like that very much. Thank you for sharing." I patted him on the shoulder, and he slowly closed his door.

****

Feeling restless, I went back to the garden. The sun had shifted, and now most of the flower beds were in full light. Isabella had planned the space well. It received enough light from the south and west to thrive, even in this enclosed space. The warmth of the stone walls and the shelter from the wind helped the tender plants flourish.

I noticed a newly-leafed-out shrub against the far wall, now unfolding its blooms. Wisteria. The purple flowers were just beginning to show their color. I gently pulled down a branch and inhaled. Even now, the scent was delicious. In another couple weeks, the whole garden would be intoxicating.

I sighed. Would I be here then? Or back home? The work I'd done in California seemed so much less important now that I'd been away from the daily grind of Silicon Valley.

A few years back, when I'd worked at my first start-up, we'd built a scent detection system for the government. Now *that* had been important work. The system could find explosives more accurately than anything yet invented, except maybe a dog's nose.

Our invention had found bombs and IEDs. It had saved lives. I was proud of my work. Now, working for the big internet company, where everyone watched the stock price rise and fall each day instead of thinking about the benefits we could contribute, the work seemed—irrelevant. Especially when you looked at what people like Max and Isabella had survived.

I walked around the garden to my friend Monsieur Lapin and examined him more closely, now that he'd dried in the sunlight and breeze. I crossed my arms. "Are you a disgrace, Monsieur?"

He looked at me with unblinking eyes, as if to say, "Ah, Mademoiselle, if only you knew."

As I turned to go, something glinted into the corner of my eye. I leaned forward to examine my new immovable pet more closely, tipped him back, and looked into his partially opened mouth. There was something there.

My heart started to beat more quickly. Silly. It was probably just a shiny piece of quartz stuck in the back of the hollow.

I knelt down, but as much as I tried, I couldn't get my fingers in his mouth far enough to reach whatever was lodged there. Frustrated, I sat with crossed legs on the garden bricks and stared at the bunny, face to face.

"Monsieur Le Grand Lapin. You are not cooperating."

A deep male chuckle carried across the garden. "I had heard Americans were different, Alyssa, but talking to statues of rabbits is perhaps a little crazy."

Anton stood in the sunlight.

I rose to greet him, dusting off my filthy jeans and combing my hair back with my hands. It was its usual rat's nest.

"Hi," I said embarrassed. After all, here I was talking to stone rabbits.

He stepped toward me with a smile.

"I didn't know you were coming over. I would have…" I glanced down and blushed.

"I don't care, Alyssa. You always look beautiful to me. I like the way your hair glows around your face." He moved closer, and I could feel his heat.

"Sweet-talker."

With a laugh, he grabbed me and kissed me. I didn't resist. Laughing along with him, I wrapped my arms around his waist and drew circles on his back under his jacket. He had nice muscles. Strongly defined, but trim. Bet he looked gorgeous in boxers.

Or nothing.

He nibbled on my neck. Goosebumps rose and

followed his clever lips down to my shoulder. "Mmm, you taste like sunshine." He hummed in my ear.

"And sweat. I need to go clean up."

He stood back. "Can I watch?"

"No-o-o. That would find us facing our original problem."

He raised a single eyebrow.

"My rickety single bed, remember?"

He pursed his lips and kissed me again, long, and smooth, and sensual, teasing my bottom lip with his teeth until my breath came in short bursts. "Right now that does not seem such a problem," he whispered.

"What's up?" I asked between kisses.

"I thought we might have dinner together."

"Sure." Grinning, I pushed back and trotted across the square toward the back door. "Ring for me in an hour," I called over my shoulder.

I waved goodbye and ran up the stairs, full of sunshine and happiness, but stopped on the second floor landing. Why hadn't I asked Anton to help me with the secret of the rabbit? I took a few more steps and frowned at myself in the mirror in the hall. I trusted him, didn't I?

Of course, silly. I'd tell him as soon as I found out what was in there. No point in making a big deal about some shiny bit of rock, or a wad of old tinfoil. With a smile, I continued to my door. There should be no secrets between us.

Chapter Twelve

I remembered seeing a pair of tweezers in Isabella's sewing kit. I found them, and hurried down to the garden. I still needed time to get dressed before Anton arrived.

Damn. The tweezers didn't work. They were too short to reach my shiny little goal in the back of Monsieur Lapin's throat. I growled in frustration.

"Why won't you cooperate, you nasty old rabbit. I'm going to put you back in the ground if you don't choke that thing up."

Irritated, I pushed the statue by his ears, and he fell on his face in the soft soil. *Voila.* A shiny little brass key bounced onto the stones of the path.

"More like it," I told the bunny and set him upright. I brushed the clump of wet dirt off his nose Fortunately, he was no worse for the fall. I crossed my legs under me to examine my prize.

Humpf. Some prize. A little key—less than an inch long. No markings, just a few tiny teeth. I turned it over in my fingers and stared at it. Why would Isabella hide this key in that rabbit?

But had she? I looked for any marking or clue.

Who knows? Some former owner could have hidden it in Monsieur Lapin's mouth. A long-raised child could have slipped it in there decades ago. It could be a key to a diary, a locker. Or a tiny cupboard hiding somewhere in Paris. I twisted my mouth in contemplation, but then heard the bells of Notre Dame.

Rats. I needed to get ready. Anton would be here soon.

****

I managed to wash, dress, and be ready in record time. Thanks to years of California water shortages, I could take a shower in under three minutes. I slicked up my wet hair in a messy bun and slipped on the one black dress I owned. Even did the lipstick thing. It felt funny on my lips. I hadn't worn makeup in weeks.

Anton rang downstairs, and after locking my door, I hurried to meet him. He kissed me lightly and helped me into my coat.

"Should we go to the little restaurant on the Île or try a new place?" he asked after taking my hand.

"A new place. I feel like having an adventure."

"Hummm. Adventure."

L'Atlas looked like any French bistro on the outside, but inside, the small restaurant had been decorated with exquisite Moorish tiles. The smell of the Middle Eastern spices wafting from the kitchen was intoxicating.

Anton shook hands with the maître d' and spoke in quick French. We were led to an intimate table in the back, away from the crowd, and a bottle of Champagne was brought to the table.

"Are we celebrating?" I asked as we clinked glasses of pale bubbly.

"In a way." Anton sipped his wine and watched me closely.

"What?" I looked down. "Is my dress on backwards? Is my hair sticking straight up?"

"Relax, Alyssa. I was enjoying the view. You look lovely tonight."

My cheeks heated to a thousand degrees—centigrade. I was glad the room was in shadow. I still had trouble accepting the compliments Anton doled out so effortlessly. I dropped my gaze to the white tablecloth. "*Merci.*"

With patient gray eyes, Anton studied me for a long moment, then put down his glass and took my hand. "Why is it so difficult for you to see you are beautiful?"

I fiddled with my fork. "It's hard for me to trust your compliments."

"*Pourquoi?*"

I stared at the floor, the decorated ceiling, the wall over his shoulder, and finally blurted, "Because another man complimented me, flattered me, paid attention to me. He wasn't telling the truth." I took in a deep breath. "He was married. I was just another conquest, a plaything to him."

"You did not know he was married from the beginning?"

"No," I said a little too loudly and then pinched my lips together. "I would never—my mother was so hurt when my father left us for another woman. I'm certainly not interested in lying, cheating scumbags, handsome or otherwise."

Anton glanced at his hands and cleared his throat.

"Oh, no. Anton. I didn't mean…I didn't mean you were…" I flushed and shut up, choking on my size nine foot.

He faced his palms toward me. "*Je comprends.*"

Feeling as if I'd divulged a secret that had been

weighing heavily on me, I sat back and managed a smile. "So. On to happier news. What are we celebrating?"

"Uhh, I will tell you later," Anton said. "Our food arrives."

In a bustle of fragrant activity, our tagine of lamb was served. Sweet, savory, spicy, the smells of Morocco called. I was starving.

****

I didn't have the heart to follow Alyssa upstairs when she suggested coffee or a night cap. After kissing her goodnight, I made excuses and hurried down the street.

My phone buzzed in my pocket, and I jumped.

"As the Americans say, you are so busted," Claire chided.

"You listened?"

"*Oui.*"

"*Merde*," I hissed to myself and smacked my head with my hand. I'd forgotten the bug in Alyssa's monster purse.

"Why didn't you go upstairs for coffee?" my assistant asked.

"I did not have the courage."

"You will have to tell her soon."

How could I? I was her latest lying, cheating scumbag.

****

Morning brought a breath of courage, and I reluctantly arranged to meet Alyssa today. Noon. What is it the Americans say? High noon? The early morning rain had washed the air and the sky was a startling shade of blue.

Our rendezvous? Under the statue of Charlemagne in front of Notre Dame. It was a quick walk from my office and her apartment, and I needed neutral ground.

I glanced at the towering Gothic cathedral to my left and rubbed my hand over my bristled chin. Did I need sanctuary?

Alyssa was there, early of course, as all Americans are. I spotted her bright hair in the crowd before I could see her face. She had her back to me and was chatting happily with a family of tourists. Their small child smiled at her from his stroller, and she touched his hand.

I stopped and swallowed the lump in my throat. After today, she would probably never speak to me again.

I maneuvered through the throngs of tourists and called her name.

Alyssa turned and smiled. She waved *au revoir* to her acquaintances and hurried over to give me a hug.

"Hi," she said. Her eyes glowed, and the blush on her cheeks told of her pleasure.

I kissed her on both cheeks, then once on the mouth, a little longer, savoring her sweetness, her electrifying energy.

"I wanted to show you something," she said, her face alight with excitement. "It could be no big deal, but somehow I have a feeling it's important."

She tugged me by the hand, and we walked over to the garden behind the church. We found a bench in the shade, and she held out her hand. Resting in her palm was a small brass key. Identical to *my* brass key.

My eyes must have widened to the size of poached eggs. I know I stopped breathing. "Where...where did you get that?" I finally choked out.

"See? I knew it was important." She squeezed my arm and bounced up and down on the bench beside me, hardly able to contain her excitement.

"Tell me," she insisted. "You know more than you're saying. I feel it. I'm not stupid, Anton. I see the looks you give me, like you're hiding secrets you're busting to tell me."

I glanced at her sideways and an uncomfortable itch scooted over my neck. I rubbed it hard with my hand. The truth would still be difficult for her to accept.

"*Chérie.*" I licked my lips. "Can you wait here for me?" I kissed her cheek. "I will return in a few minutes."

****

When I showed Anton the key, he'd looked like he was going to explode. His eyes went as round as Frisbees, and his face turned a funny shade of pistachio.

I pulled his hand as he stood to leave. "Can't I come with you?" Wherever he was headed, it would be faster if I went with him. Whatever he had to show me, I could see it sooner if I was beside him.

"No," he shouted and started to trot away.

I rose and called his name, but the bells of the cathedral began to chime. Damn. I'd never be able to shout over those bells.

I hurried after him, but lost him in the crowd on the Marché Aux Fleurs bridge. Had he headed toward the Île Saint Louis or back toward the right bank? I stood on my toes and looked over the heads of the crowd, but every third man wore a blue pea coat. Anton had blended in with the crowd very effectively.

I crossed the footbridge and wandered a short

distance down the narrow street of the Île St. Louis. The antique stores and lovely shops were open, and the cafés bustled with lunchtime patrons, sitting on the little rattan chairs and watching the world go by. They ate their *déjeuner* and drank a glass of wine. I searched the street, but no Anton.

My curiosity raging, I headed back to the park bench. I didn't want to miss his return, but was stuck behind a gaggle of Asian tourists crossing the bridge.

A beautiful woman with long dark hair and ivory skin walked briskly ahead of me.

I sighed. Oh, to be so tiny, to be so petite. I felt a little—well, a not-so-little twinge of jealousy. To have such silky, long hair.

From my vantage point, I watched her cross the bridge.

Anton appeared out of the crowd. The beautiful woman walked up to Anton, my Anton, and gave him a quick kiss on both cheeks.

My heart stopped.

She spoke to him, teased him a little and handed him something.

He leaned against the bridge railing and spoke to her, his shoulders relaxed.

My feet wouldn't move forward, but my heart was racing in a really uncomfortable this-is-going-to-be-bad kinda way. At first, I thought, a friend. Please, just be a friend.

I blinked my eyes and stepped forward through the crowd. Wanting, but not wanting to be closer. Wanting, but not wanting to see what was going on. Dread, then anger, then furious jealousy pushed my pulse and breathing to painful levels.

Anton faced the opposite way. He didn't see me, but the woman did. She stopped speaking and put her hand on his sleeve. She wore a wedding ring. I felt sick.

He met my gaze. "Alyssa."

I turned and ran. He shouted my name, but I didn't stop. The last thing I wanted to hear was another pack of lies.

****

I slammed both entry doors on my way to the tiny elevator and would have slammed that if there had been any way to accomplish it.

My cheeks were wet. Damn. I rubbed them hard with the back of my hand. I would not cry over another liar. I would not. But I did.

I cooled off slightly on the slow ride to my floor. Hissing air through my clenched teeth, I managed to close my apartment door without shaking the foundations of the building.

I leaned against the old wood and cursed inside my head. Flipping locks one after the next soothed some of the anger. It didn't touch the hurt and humiliation.

"How do you manage, Alyssa? How?" I shouted at the mirror in the hall. "Two in a row? Girl, you are one stupid sucker."

I flung my oversized purse on the hall table. Being the truly awful day it was, I missed. My two-ton monster that contained my life dropped off the edge, clunked against a Chinese vase full of fake flowers, and knocked the damn thing over. I couldn't catch it before it smashed against the hall tree and broke.

Busted. Several large shards clattered across the floor.

"What a klutz!" I picked up a large chunk of

porcelain and slammed it onto the floor, adding to the disaster. With a furious growl, I kicked the debris out of the way and went in search of the broom.

The white and blue vase was—had been—almost three feet tall, wide at the bottom but with a narrow neck. I had no idea if the thing was a repro or not. Now it was trash. With a huge I'm-feeling-very-sorry-for-myself sigh, I pitched the dusty, silk flowers and picked up the shattered pieces off the floor. I tossed the first few in my nearby trash can.

After sweeping the hall, I righted the remaining shards, and noticed a dark object taped to the bottom of the vase. My heart beat a little faster. Avoiding the sharp edges, I reached inside and pulled it out. This was certainly my day for mysteries.

I ripped off the old tape and cloth, and unwrapped a small book. I thumbed open the dark green, leather-bound journal and read the first page.

This Journal belongs to Isabella Marie Manchester.

Holy shit. My heart was beating like a…like a terrified rabbit's.

Below, I heard pounding on the entry door and Anton shouted my name through my half open window. My phone buzzed once and then again. I clicked the power off. I didn't want to talk to *him.* Not now. Maybe not ever. Married men were off limits. Now and forever.

I left the rest of the broken shards where they were and headed for the couch. Had I found the answers to some of my questions? With nervous fingers, I turned the page.

March 4, 1938

My mother always says, "Begin at the beginning."

A journal is a place to put your deepest thoughts, the ideas you cannot share with anyone, the feelings in your heart of love and hate. And yes, sometimes fear.

Written in a different shade of blue ink, these last few words must have been added later. Boiling with curiosity, I curled my toes under me and settled down to read. I ignored the insistent buzzing on my intercom. Go to hell, Anton.

Chapter Thirteen

March 5, 1938

I begin this journal in the glorious spring of 1938.

Last May, I turned twenty-two. I moved to the beautiful city of Paris six months ago.

I can't explain to my parents why I need to be here. They certainly don't understand. I'm not sure I understand myself. I only know I must be away from the strict confines of their life. I can't discover who I am in dreary Minnesota.

I'd always heard Paris was a magical place. I read all of Hemingway's stories in college—over and over again. He was a great fan of the city.

Great painters like Degas and Monet found inspiration here too. Look at the Jeu de Paume Museum in the Tuileries, overflowing with their art. Much of it was inspired by the streets I walk.

And then there's Victor Hugo. I've read his wonderful novel, *Les Miserables,* twice since I arrived. He is my hero.

****

March 10, 1938

Father said he won't send more money. Mother demanded I board the next boat home. She wrote of the Nazi threat, but no one here seems very worried about a silly war.

I'm sorry. I can't. I won't go home. Not yet. There

are too many things to see, and experience, and taste. Too many people to meet. Too much to learn.

I know I'm being defiant, but I will use my small inheritance from Aunt Ali Jo to keep me another few months in this glorious place. My rent's cheap, and my friends buy the wine. What else do I need?

****

May 14, 1938

Today is my birthday. I am twenty-three. To celebrate the day, my new friends, Sophie and François, took me to visit the Eiffel Tower. They have always lived in Paris and have probably visited the sights many times, but they both seemed to enjoy playing tourist guide for their pet American.

We stood at the base of the huge tower, and I glanced down at my travel guide to read from the pages aloud. "Outside the United States, the Eiffel Tower is the tallest structure in the world. The total height of the tower is 984 feet."

Leaning back, I looked up through the metal structure. It made me dizzy. I've never seen anything like it. It's enormous. Even the bolts holding the iron beams together are enormous.

François led me toward the staircase inside one of the tower's four square feet. "Let's climb to the top," he called, his mischievous grin lighting his face.

"I'm afraid." I pulled my arm back. "What if we fall?"

He scoffed at my fear, pulling me up the first few metal steps.

Reluctantly, I followed him. Sophie laughed as we climbed higher and higher above the city. The wind blew my hair and whipped my skirt. I clung tightly to the banister as we scaled the open metal staircase. We were all gasping by the time we reached the first landing. It had to be two hundred feet up and gave me the chills to look down.

"Beautiful." Sophie sighed, pointing to the Arc du Triomphe in the distance. On the hill in the distance was a huge white church.

"Sacré Coeur," said François when I pointed it out. "It's newer than most churches in Paris."

I still clung to the railing, but when I looked out over the horizon, I felt steadier. "You can see the whole city."

"They were supposed to tear the Tower down after the Exposition," Sophie said when she caught her breath.

I turned to my new friend. Her dark hair had escaped its usual bun and fluttered in the breeze around her pretty face. The cold had brightened her cheeks.

"Why would they do that?" I flung out my arms. "It's fabulous."

"People think so now, but not everyone did when it was built."

"So why did they keep it?"

"The radio tower—" François pointed up. "—very useful for the military."

****

May 20, 1938

My French has improved so much in the last few months. Forced to survive in a different language, I've found I often dream in it.

The other night when we went to the Comédie-Française, I could even laugh at most of the jokes. The actor made fun of Mr. Hitler. He strutted around the stage like a puppet—all straight arms and legs. I even understood the ridiculous things he shouted.

We went for a drink after the show at the Hôtel du Louvre across the square. To everyone's amusement, François imitated the actor. "Heil, Hitler," he shouted. He was a little drunk.

"Heil, François," we shouted back.

He enjoyed being the center of attention. He's so handsome with his flashing dark eyes and dark hair. Although only seventeen and years younger than the rest of us, we keep him around as our personal joker.

For some reason, Sophie didn't laugh much tonight. She has been very serious of late, begging off at the last moment when we want to go out to have fun.

I studied her beautiful but somber face. Maybe she has a lover and hasn't had the courage to tell us yet.

****

May 28, 1938

Today I met the most handsome man. His name is Rainier, and he is very tall. I love the color of his clear blue eyes; they remind me of the sky. He has a wonderful smile and a fast motor car. He just moved to Paris from Alsace. I heard the difference in his French accent when he first spoke to us. Sophie said I have a good ear for languages.

I'd joined Sophie and François in the Bois de Boulogne for a Sunday picnic. We were sitting in the shade when Rainier came up and introduced himself to everyone, but he kept looking at me with those divine blue eyes. I couldn't help but look back. I know my cheeks blushed. I could feel the heat.

Dressed elegantly in a light blue suit of fine wool, he wore his dark blond hair neatly brushed back from his handsome face. So sophisticated.

Rainier said he worked for his father's company in Alsace, but had been assigned to an important new position in Paris.

We invited him to join us, and he bought a bottle of good Champagne to share. Later in the afternoon, the band started playing, and he asked me to dance. I was glad they didn't play a jitterbug, but a slow fox trot.

Rainier's eyes met mine, and he took me in his arms. I loved dancing with him.

****

June 5, 1938

Rainier invited all of us, Sophie, François and me, to take a ride in his motor car, and we drove out to Coucy-Le-Château. It took most of the morning to get there. The air was so fresh, we put the top down. After all the rainy days this week, it was wonderful to enjoy some sunny weather.

We walked through the ruins of the medieval castle, and Sophie found a piece of stone carving left from the church. Rainier held my hand to help me over the rough places. François threw rocks in the small stream nearby.

"What happened here?" I asked Sophie as she held out her treasure.

She pursed her lips into a frown and stared out over the devastation. "Several battles in the World War were fought in this village."

I rubbed my fingers over the worn face of Sophie's little stone cherub. "Such a shame," I complained to Rainier. "Why couldn't that stupid war go around the beautiful old things?"

He chuckled and shook his head.

The town still had a section of its old walls and gates. I stopped to take a picture with my Brownie. An ancient wisteria had grown over the old rock walls. If only I could capture the beautiful purple of the flowers.

We found a little market in the center of town to buy a picnic lunch and drove up the mountain into the forest. The cool air felt exquisite. Rainier parked the car at an overlook, and we admired the pretty village nestled in the green valley.

Rainier and I fed each other strawberries, so sweet, and ate cheese so fresh I thought I'd gone to heaven. Then Rainier kissed me.

Our first kiss. June 5, 1938.

My pulse raced when he drew his fingers through my hair. He said he liked the golden color.

Sophie and François were in the back seat, but they pretended not to look.

On the way home François puffed out his chest. "I'm going to join the Spanish Liberation Army to fight with Franco."

I hid my smile so as not to hurt his feelings. François is such a little boy at times.

When Rainier laughed, François sulked the rest the way home. Poor boy. He was only trying to impress me.

He has a crush on me, but I'm much too old for him. He's only seventeen but such a sweetheart. I hope he finds someone new to love.

After we dropped off my friends, Rainier drove me home through the narrow streets of the Left Bank.

"You should be kinder to François," I scolded.

Rainier took my hand. When he kissed it, little waves of heat rippled to my heart. "For you, darling, I will be very, very kind to all your friends."

****

May 27, 1938

It's so hot right now, I have to leave my windows open at night. The breeze has left Paris. I can't sleep.

On Saturday, I begged Rainier to drive me out to Chartres. We could have taken the train, but I wanted to feel the cool wind of the countryside on my face.

Of course, I wanted to see the cathedral and the historic old town, but mostly I wanted to be alone with Rainier.

When we walked into the beautiful Gothic church, I guess my religious upbringing bloomed in my heart. The colors of the stained glass windows, especially the blue of the Virgin Mary, took my breath away. I crossed myself when Rainier wasn't watching. The church was almost seven hundred years old. Nothing in America is that old.

We drank Champagne at a romantic café with a view of the church. A whole bottle. I have a taste for foie gras and Rainier ordered it for me. The creamy texture slid across my tongue. I closed my eyes in appreciation, and Rainier laughed.

We walked down by the river to admire the adorable timbered houses and the fast flowing river. I wanted Rainier to kiss me again. Not just a little peck, but a long, heat-your-blood kiss.

Coming back up the steps, he put his arms around me and kissed me, holding me close. I kissed him and giggled when he nibbled on my neck. Goosebumps raced down my back, and I struggled to find air.

He combed his fingers through my hair. "So beautiful," he said. "So perfect. Like golden floss." He studied my face for a long time, and I started to blush. "And green eyes, too. Perfection."

I dropped my gaze. "I'm not used to compliments."

He widened his eyes and looked surprised, then pleased. "Beautiful and modest."

He kissed me once more, pressing his hands against my back and sliding them down, moving me against him. A swirl of heat and desire rose through me, leaving me breathless when we drew apart. He wanted me.

I wanted him.

****

June 9, 1938

François wrote me a poem. It's terrible, but so very sweet.

It's about a little boy rabbit who runs away to war, because the little girl rabbit he loves won't marry him. Subtle, François.

But I kissed him on the cheek after I read it and told him it was lovely. He turned red when I touched him and forgot his proper French. Rainier said he speaks like a gutter rat.

François brought me a present too, a little blue rabbit with the cutest face. I wonder if he stole it?

****

June 11, 1938

Today I walked across the river to visit Sophie. She has the most wonderful apartment right by the Seine. Her father worked for the government until a few years ago, and she has lived there since she was very small.

The building is right across the square from L'Hôtel de Ville, near the Marais. Even though the Marais is falling to ruins, I think the district is wonderful. The narrow streets and tumbledown houses are so romantic.

Sophie had her windows open, and I heard the bells of Notre Dame across the river.

François arrived with flowers (he probably stole them too) and little cakes his mother baked for tea. I kissed him on both cheeks, and he blushed a deep red all the way to his ears.

Usually Sophie's a very happy woman, always laughing, always ready for an adventure. Even though I'm almost four years younger, she has been a wonderful friend. Today, I noticed she was most upset and asked her why.

"An old family friend has decided to emigrate to America," she said quietly. "I will miss her."

I consoled her while we sipped our tea. I knew why her friend was leaving. She's Jewish. Even though no one says anything, many Jewish people are afraid to stay in France.

"Many of my friends have left too," François complained. "One family went to Palestine, two others to Canada."

François lived with his mother and brother in the Marais too, right next to the Jewish quarter.

"It's very difficult to obtain a visa to the United States." Sophie nibbled a biscuit. "My friend had family in New York to sponsor her."

I set down my cup and looked out at her wonderful water view. A tug boat pushed a barge of coal down the river. "I don't understand why everyone's so mean to the poor Jews."

"It's an old problem."

"The movie I saw last week said terrible things

about them," François added. "And sometimes there are hideous cartoons in the newspaper."

Sophie's brows drew down, and she folded her arms.

After staring into the distance for a long moment, I sighed. "It must be terrible to have someone hate you—someone who doesn't even know you."

****

August 13, 1938

My mother wrote me the most horrible letter. She called me names and told me I was foolish and sinful to disobey Father. I cried all afternoon and didn't even want to go to dinner with Rainier.

"Put the damn letter in the fire," he growled.

I almost did, but then at the last moment, I changed my mind and saved it. I'll put it in my journal. I'll show Mother this stupid letter someday when all this war talk is over, and we are finally at peace. I'll show her I was right to stay in Paris.

Chapter Fourteen

I'd read the first ten pages of the journal before the phone rang again. No way was I stopping now. I ignored the ringing of the doorbell and my phone, and the man attached to the other end of the call.

Then the next and the next.

Pretty soon there was a knock at the door.

"How did you get past the concierge?" I yelled through my door.

"Alyssa, please. Just listen…"

"Go away," I shouted. "I don't want to hear your excuses. Your lies."

"Please. Let me explain."

"No," I yelled. "I saw the ring on her finger."

"Claire is not my wife. I swear."

"Yeah. Right." I locked one more deadbolt to emphasize my disgust.

It was quiet for a few moments. I sat down on the couch, crossing my arms with fury. "Creep," I hissed. "Thinks he can come over here and lie his way out of this." I added a few choice cuss words I usually don't say. Or need.

The silence lengthened.

Had he gone away? I swallowed the sudden sense of loss and sat still for another long minute. Would he knock again, or call?

Maybe I'd check. I tucked the journal under the

couch cushion, tiptoed to the door, and put my eye to the peep hole. Nothing. No one. He'd left.

"Good," I said, but the empty space inside me widened and grew painful.

I flipped the locks on the door and called out. "Anton?"

"Yes, Alyssa," he answered softly.

I jumped about a foot and let out a high pitched squeak.

"Will you listen now?" He'd been sitting on the step and rose slowly to face me.

Still disgusted, I exhaled loudly through my nose. "She's not your wife?"

"She's not my wife, never has been, never will be."

"Swear?"

He put up his palm and climbed the last step to the landing.

I allowed him to pass, and he took a moment to notice the shattered vase as he walked in. "Valuable?"

I shot him a half-hearted shrug. "Could've been. Now it's junk." I didn't mention the journal.

He sat down in the living room and rubbed his hands over his face, as if he was suddenly very tired.

I took the chair across from him and waited. Ankles touching, hands clasped, I raised my eyebrows in anticipation. This better be good.

His turn to explain. Maybe I'd listen. I tucked my feet under the chair.

He held out his hand. "I went to get this. Well, actually Claire brought it to me from my office."

"From the pâtisserie?"

"No, my office."

He didn't explain. I didn't ask.

I put my hand out, and he dropped a small key into the middle of my palm. It was warm from his touch. I studied it and then dug the key I'd found in the rabbit's mouth out of my pocket.

I matched them up. Same rounded top. Same color of old, unpolished brass, same size and weight but a different cut. Similar, but a different key to a different lock.

He sat back on the sofa, but was far from relaxed. "Where did you find yours?" he asked.

"You first."

"The key belongs to my family—goes back to the time of the war. My great-great-grandmother had it when she died. My father kept it. Before he died, he gave it to me."

I wiggled my nose and considered his statement.

"Your turn."

"A rabbit."

His eyebrows lowered, and he glanced around the room. "You have a lot of rabbits."

"Mmm, true. This one I found in the garden."

"Ah, the large one you were talking to?"

I nodded. "The key was hidden in his mouth."

For a moment he was silent, tapping his finger on his knee.

"So you think these are some sort of clue?"

"Yes."

"To what?" I still wasn't sure I trusted him and narrowed my gaze to watch him. How many times does a girl get burned before she stops putting her hand on the tea kettle?

"It's a very long story. One I cannot share with you quite yet. Can you trust me for a little while?"

I shot him a sharp sideways glance.

"Not so much?"

"Trust is earned, Anton."

"You are correct." He pushed his hands on his thighs and stood with a regretful sigh. "May I come again tomorrow? By then I will be able to divulge more information."

"Whatever." I rubbed my fingers against my temple. "Anton, I've seen another key."

"Where?"

I blew out a breath with my lips. Damned if I could remember.

"Think about it, *ma petite.* I will return."

I watched Anton cross the street and hurry toward Notre Dame. I frowned. Why wasn't he headed toward the bakery? I crossed my arms, feeling suspicious. And what was this about this office of his? More mysteries to be solved. I turned and faced the sunny room.

Isabella's journal called to me from under the cushions. Might as well find out what was happening in 1938. Anton would explain himself, someday.

Chapter Fifteen

October 1, 1938

See, I told Mother everything would be all right. Chamberlain said so. Rainier said so. Even Monsieur Daladier, of the French government who signed the agreement with the Germans said so.

There will be no war. I'm so relieved.

Rainier took me dancing, and we drank Champagne to celebrate.

****

October 14, 1938

I smoothed my new dress down over my thighs and fluffed my curls. Rainier is due any moment, and I must admit I am very nervous to see him tonight. I stared at myself in the mirror. My heart is beating so fast, I didn't even need to pinch my cheeks to make them blush.

Rainier wants to take me to bed. When he told me at dinner last week, I must have turned as red as my lipstick. He says he cares for me and doesn't understand why I am holding off the "inevitable."

Why am I afraid? I do love him. He is wonderful to me, but my mother's words harp at my soul. I will be sinning, I know.

****

October 16, 1938

I'm no longer a virgin. I can't speak of the first

time. Rainier told me to relax, but that was impossible.

Now that I understand his needs, I can pretend to enjoy our lovemaking. I want to please Rainier.

****

October 19, 1938

I knocked on Sophie's door and when she invited me in, her first words were, "So it has happened."

"What has happened?" I asked with a hopefully innocent face.

She narrowed her dark eyes at me.

I dodged her gaze, but blushed so deeply there was no hope of carrying off a lie.

"Was he good to you?"

"Yes," I said quickly. "Of course. Rainier loves me."

"Did he protect you?"

"Sophie…"

"Isabella. Your mother's not here, and you have no other woman to ask about such things. Did he use a condom?"

I nodded. "He doesn't want me to become pregnant."

"Good." She walked into the kitchen and began to prepare our tea. The water ran. The cups were arranged.

I followed her and pulled the bottle of milk from the ice box. "Sophie?" I hesitated, not knowing how to put my question into words. "How should, I mean, I don't know what…" I dropped my chin and swallowed hard.

Her expression softened. "Let's make our tea and then we will talk."

****

November 9, 1938

We'd met for petit dejeuner this morning at our favorite little bistro on the Île St. Louis. The St. Regis has the very best pastries in the entire district, and we partake whenever we can save enough centimes.

Sophie gave an angry huff and put down the morning newspaper. Still frowning, she sipped her coffee.

I was spreading strawberry *confiture* on my second croissant. Sophie hadn't touched her plate. "What's wrong?" I asked between crunchy bites.

"Haven't you heard what happened in Germany? The newspapers called it Kristallnacht."

"Night of crystal?"

"Night of Broken Glass." Sophie spoke German almost as well as she spoke French.

"The poor Jews in Germany have had such a hard time." She pinched her lips together in anger. "For years they've been persecuted. Now those Nazi hoodlums robbed their homes and smashed their shops."

"Why?"

Sophie shot me a disgusted look but then closed her eyes for a moment. "You're such an American, Isabella."

I straightened my shoulders. "Well, yes. I'm proud to be American. Just as you're proud to be French."

She dropped her chin. "No, I mean, you've been so sheltered in your precious Minnesota. You don't understand the persecution these people have suffered for thousands of years."

I put down my pastry and licked my sticky fingers. "I know about religious persecution, but I don't believe in it. Americans believe in Freedom of Religion. It doesn't always work, but Father and Mother brought me up to be open minded."

She gave me a French shrug and sipped her coffee.

I ate her croissant.

****

I closed the journal and rested my eyes for a moment, surprised by how drawn I was to Isabella's story. I rubbed my fingers over the soft green leather, still subtle after all these years.

Isabella was rash at times, but also so innocent and unworldly. But was she any more innocent than many people of the time? Or maybe just blinded? It was easy to see her mistakes from my vantage point seven decades in the future.

But why had Isabella eventually taken Sophie's name? I still didn't understand.

I heated water for a cup of tea, reading more while the water boiled. Anton left a message, but I didn't respond.

Chapter Sixteen

January 2, 1939

My friends have come up with the most exciting new game. We're going to see who can break the most Holy Commandments this year.

It sounds wicked, I know, but we won't do anything too bad. It's just a game, after all.

Rainier thought of it first, but I insisted on the time limit. Who knows where we'll be in another year? If inflation in Paris goes any higher, I'll have to tuck my tail and run home. I can't bear the thought of the bleak winters in Minnesota after all this time in Paris.

As we drank beer in Sophie's apartment and listened to music on the radio, we set out the rules of the Sinner's Challenge.

"We need to have a witness to our sins," François insisted.

"I agree." I said. "It's not a sin, if no one catches you."

****

January 4, 1939

I started the game this morning by not keeping the Lord's Day holy. I listened to the bells of Saint Sulpice across the park from my apartment and went back to bed. Even when the bells of the little Presbyterian Church down the street joined in, I ignored the call. I've never missed Sunday mass, and it seemed so decadent to lie in bed.

Rainier must tick that box, too. He stayed with me last night, and we made love again instead of going to communion.

When I came back to bed, he pulled my nightgown over my head and teased my breasts with his tongue.

"Father would have a fit." I giggled.

"Don't tell him." Rainier rolled on top of me and took my mouth with his, kissing me, touching me. I loved the pressure of his big, strong body over mine. I arched into him, feeling the lovely heat of his sex. His hand found my breast. I moaned.

****

March 10, 1939

'Thou shalt not steal.' came next on the Sinner's Challenge.

For the fun of it, the four of us would do the deed together. Sophie insisted Galeries Lafayette should be the location of our transgressions. As it was the most famous department store in Paris, she loved to shop there. I couldn't afford the prices, but it was the perfect place to steal our small prizes.

Trying our best to look innocent, we wandered around the store and decided what each of us would steal. François chose for Sophie, and Rainier for me. Sophie and I teamed up to challenge the men.

I stood in the central hall of the store. Looking up at the gallery of floors rimmed by beautiful balusters, and felt breathless. Above the top level, soft light flowed through the ceiling decorated with stained glass.

For my prize, Rainier led me to the jewelry department. He pointed out a silver necklace with a cross.

I cringed at the thought and pulled him aside. "A game is one thing, but stealing from God seems so—"

"Sacrilegious?" He grinned.

I swallowed hard and approached the jewelry counter. My heart was beating like a small rabbit hunted by dogs, and I almost darted away. I pulled in a breath to calm myself, but my hands still shook as I pointed out the necklace to the salesman. He glanced at me suspiciously.

François and Sophie watched from the next counter, spritzing each other with perfumes and laughing.

I fingered the necklace and forced a smile. When I looked up at the Grande Galerie, I felt as if five floors of shop-keepers were watching my heinous crime.

At the last moment, Rainier called the salesman over to ask about an expensive watch. I slipped the necklace into my purse and ducked into the crowd. My face was so hot, I had to hide in the notions department until my heart stopped dancing in my chest. I took off my hat and coat so I wouldn't be so recognizable.

As slick as François was, he almost got caught stealing his trinket.

Sophie and I pointed out a silk necktie as his quarry, mostly because he doesn't own one. François had other ideas. He went straight to the counter where they sold Lalique, the famous French crystal. Most of the expensive pieces were locked in a case, but one little rabbit sat on the counter, forgotten by the distracted salesman.

At the very moment François grabbed the rabbit, Rainier started coughing right behind him. I covered my mouth with my hand, terrified the salesman would hear my gasp.

François glared at Rainier, but managed to slip the crystal bunny into his coat pocket and make off with his prize.

"You're next, Sophie," François teased. "What will be your little crime?"

"Shhh," I hissed. "Someone could hear us."

Sophie ignored our wrangling and calmly walked up to the salesman at the hat counter. She pointed out an adorable straw hat on the display shelf. Jaunty red and white ribbons decorated the wide brim with the cutest little enamel ladybug pinned on the side.

"As you wish, Madame." The salesman handed it to her with great ceremony. "This is our latest style. It's featured in the latest issue of *Marie Claire*."

Sophie sat at the nearby dressing table and placed the hat on her head. She cocked it to one side and admired her reflection in the mirror. Then she grinned. "I'll take it."

Pleased, the salesman went behind the counter to look for the box. Sophie walked away *avec chapeau*.

I was so nervous I couldn't stop giggling. Sophie shushed me and dragged me outside. She bought me a cup of tea at the little café down the street.

We'd already chosen a small cellarette made of mahogany for Rainier to steal. He'd been acting so smug, we thought he needed the challenge. When we returned to the store, he was walking toward us and had his coat draped over a large object. The door man bowed and opened the glass door for him. We walked slowly, sedately down the street.

With a cheeky grin, he showed us the box, but Rainier had stolen the coat, too.

On the way home, François gave me his stolen bunny. I gave him a kiss on the cheek.

****

Ladybug pin? I jumped up and hurried into the bedroom. My favorite straw hat lay on the dresser and yes, there was the little pin. The ribbons had been changed, but this was the stolen hat. Sophie's stolen hat.

I walked back through the office and spotted my favorite bunny sitting on the window ledge. Well, damn. It had to be. The bunny was stolen too. I guess I had a thing for hot property.

Chapter Seventeen

March 13, 1939

Two sins down, eight to go.

Sophie volunteered to keep the tally and says she will buy a bottle of champagne for the winner for next New Year. Imagine. 1940.

I'd cashed in the ticket Father had wired for the trip home and used the money for rent. I don't think I'll receive any more letters from mother.

In her last note, she said I'd dishonored the Manchester name. Does that count as disobeying my father and mother? That gives me three sins in the tally.

****

April 14, 1939

I don't have time to write. I'm so tired. The money father sent lasted only a few months. After paying May and June's rent with my small inheritance, I may have to take a job in order to buy food.

****

April 17, 1939

Sophie suggested I move in with her, and I may need to accept her generous offer. She has an extra bedroom. It's tiny with only a day bed and space for one small chair, but it's free.

I should be grateful, but I've adored having my own apartment with its beautiful view of the Luxembourg Garden. I'd miss this place if I had to leave.

So I'm tutoring students in English at the college. The job pays poorly, but it's better than waiting tables. Thankfully, the Sorbonne is close enough to my apartment for me to walk. There are fewer and fewer classes being taught at the college these days, but fortunately for me, people still seem to want to learn English.

****

April 19, 1939

Waiting for my next student in the small square near the school, I shivered in the cold drizzle. The wind whipped through the narrow streets.

I didn't have enough money to buy a warm coffee. My mouth watered at the smells wafting from the bakery across the alley. I dug in my pockets and purse, but only found a few centimes and an old handkerchief. I'd have to drop in on Sophie tonight, if I hoped to eat dinner.

I glanced at the discarded newspaper on the bench next to me. Although slightly damp from the morning shower, I picked it up and looked over the front page. The war news and battles are listed by country and have grown longer and more depressing in the last months.

Some days it seems as if the whole city is bound up in the fear of war. People walk around with their chins lowered and their shoulders hunched against the terrible news.

Then on other days, there is be nothing in the paper about the troubles. People smile and say *bonjour* when you greet them. On those days, we pretend everything is fine.

****

April 22, 1939

Rainier has been so kind. He took me to dinner Thursday night and stayed the weekend. Before he left on Sunday, he gave me five francs. I was too hungry to be proud. I will eat this week.

I love when he visits me. I don't dare write down the things we do, but when he kisses me and holds me close to him, I feel happy. Safe. I don't understand why Sophie suddenly doesn't like him.

****

May 10, 1939

Sometimes I'm so lonely. It has rained for weeks, and I've only seen Rainier once. He said his work was very difficult and became angry when I pouted at him. He promised things will be better by the end of the summer.

****

May 18, 1939

François finally celebrated his eighteenth birthday. The next day, he left Paris to join the International Brigade of the Spanish Republican Army. Sophie and I kissed him good-bye when he boarded the train to fight with Franco. He looked very handsome in his uniform and his red peaked cap.

Poor François. Within weeks, the war was over. Franco had won, but François hadn't even made it to the front lines—only sat in a Spanish town and drank cheap wine, waiting for orders.

Somehow though, François seemed different when he returned. His skin had darkened in the Spanish sun, but there was a look in his eye that wasn't there before. He watches me when he doesn't think I'm looking. I can feel his gaze on me, whenever he's close.

He grew a mustache while he was in Spain. Rainier laughed and called it a stubby pencil line. I think it looks nice on his face, but it tickles when I kiss his cheek.

Rainier says François can't come with us anymore when we go for drives in the country. Sophie's still invited sometimes. She enjoys riding in the back seat. With the top down, she holds onto her hat and lets the breeze blow in her hair. Her laugh is so infectious, we all laugh with her.

****

June 13, 1939

François is a ghoul. He wanted to attend the execution of poor Mr. Weidman, but I refused to go.

Sophie and I had walked past the Place de la Concorde the other day and watched the workmen build the guillotine. The shiny silver blade at the top of the tall tower sent a cold shiver down my spine.

Sophie pulled me away. It was a sunny day in June, but I couldn't stop trembling. She bought me hot chocolate at Angelina's, and finally the warmth returned to my hands. Even though Mr. Weidman was convicted of mass murder, the guillotine seems a horrible way to die.

****

August 10, 1939

A Celebration!

Tonight our little group dressed in our finest and went out to have drinks and a late meal at Café de la Paix. Sophie wore her new stolen hat, and she lent me her best silk dress. The blue one. I insisted François be invited and Rainier relented.

The maître d' led us through the sumptuous interior

of the restaurant to a table by the window. After we ordered Champagne, Sophie and I watched the women leaving the Opera in their glamorous gowns. We picked our favorites.

Rainier had offered to treat for the meal, because his father's cloth company had received a huge order, and Rainier had organized the deal. In addition to good Champagne, he ordered foie gras, and beef, and chocolate soufflé with Chantilly cream for dessert. A feast.

Since I've been subsisting on day-old bread, hard cheese, and sour green apples off the tree in the garden, I was grateful for the change.

It was a hot night and the Champagne was cold. I felt a little tipsy after my third glass. Rainier and I danced to the jazz band that plays there on Fridays.

After dinner we argued about how to break the commandment 'Thou shalt not honor other gods.'

"We could jitterbug in front of the statue of Zeus at the Louvre," Sophie suggested.

"*Non, non.*" François waved his hand in the middle of the table. "I have a better idea."

I giggled. François can be very clever at times. I give him free English lessons, and he has learned a great deal. His accent has improved. He said being able to speak English will be important when the war comes.

François stood, his glass in hand. "We should toast the god of wine."

"Who's the god of wine?" I whispered to Sophie.

"Bacchus," she whispered back.

"That's him. Bacchus will be our new deity," François shouted across the room.

Rainier, in a benevolent mood, put the Champagne

bottle on the bar. Each of us bowed, or curtsied, as the case may be, and took a drink right from the bottle.

More than a little drunk, François spilled some on his shirt.

"I will tick off the boxes in my little book," Sophie announced.

****

August 12, 1939

This week has been awful. The heat was oppressive, and the air over Paris was filthy with dust and soot. When I hurried to work through the busy streets of the Left Bank, I could hardly breathe.

Most of my original pupils have left school. Many have left Paris. François found me a new student, and the three of us met this morning at the café across the river from Notre Dame.

When I arrived, I found them sitting in the outdoor patio. François rose and introduced me to Albert. I shook hands with the pale, underfed student and sat down across from them.

"Honestly, I don't know what I would do without you, François." I accepted the *café au lait* he'd ordered me. "I would starve if you didn't keep finding me students."

When I patted his hand across the table, François blushed and shrugged his shoulders. He touched his mustache, which has grown in nicely. It makes him look older. He's quite handsome now that he has reached his full height and his shoulders have filled out.

****

Early evening, August 14, 1939

"You have to credit me with another sin," I told Sophie.

It was a lovely warm evening. We were walking home from the picture show to her apartment near the Rue de Victoria.

I'd moved into her apartment a week ago. Even with my teaching jobs and my newest endeavor, selling the vegetables we grow in Sophie's little garden, I couldn't pay the rent.

The franc has fallen so low a barrelful of notes wouldn't pay the rent, so my dear friend took pity on me. I promised to pay her what I could, and we'll share the cost of the lights when the electricity is on. With the strikes, you never know. I think she was pleased to have company.

She laughed. "What sin?"

"Well, I have disobeyed my parents more times than I can count."

She nodded solemnly. "Are you sure you shouldn't *obey* your parents and go home, Isabella?"

"I don't know. I love Paris." I swung my arms out wide. Because I was a little drunk, I almost stumbled on the cobblestones in the street.

She caught me. We laughed together and walked on, arm in arm.

"We all love Paris." Sophie said, "But America's your home. When the Germans come…"

I wagged my finger at her. "If the Germans come…"

Her face grew serious, and I could almost imagine I saw a flash of fear. She stopped in the middle of the street and said with a very somber tone, "*When* the Germans come, Isabella, it will be difficult for the French, but we will survive. It may be even more difficult for an American."

"America is neutral," I insisted.

She pulled me to the curb, although there was no traffic. "They won't be for long."

****

August 15, 1939

I have a secret question. I haven't had the courage to say the words aloud, but they tumble around in my heart most of the time.

If I asked Father's permission to come home, would he forgive me and take me back?

I haven't spoken to my friends about my secret, but I think about going home nearly every day.

Suddenly, I miss Minnesota. I miss the long summer evenings with fireflies fluttering over the lawn. I miss my parents and my sisters. I even miss the snowy evenings when my family gathers for prayers.

I haven't heard from them in months. The silence is terrible, much worse than the reprimands, cruel words, and harsh letters.

I'm sorry, Mama. It's difficult to say, but you were right.

I don't know why I had to be so stubborn. I miss you.

Where will I find the courage and humility to write to you?

****

August 20, 1939

"Paris is no fun anymore," I complained to François at the café this morning. "Between the strikes, and demonstrations, and now the government curfew…"

He looked up from the newspaper he was reading. "Everyone must be off the streets by ten p.m.," he read aloud from the front page.

"It's not even dark then," I moaned.

François pulled a face and folded his paper. "The clubs are ordered to close early, and the shows will cancel many of their performances. Even the Opera will be forced to change their schedule."

I rested my chin on my palm and pouted. "Rainier promised to take me to the new movie, *The Wizard of Oz*."

"You can go to an early show."

That evening, Rainier finally made good on his promise, and we went to see the American film. My favorite character was the Cowardly Lion. I giggled at the terrible translations on the subtitles, but it was nice to listen to English for a change. Can you imagine? Color in film?

****

September 1, 1939

Sophie rushed through the door, her hair flying and her face a mask of fear. "You need to go home, Isabella."

"I don't have enough money." I looked up from my desk by the window. "Even with the translation work François found me, I only have fifty francs saved. It costs three times that much to cross the Atlantic, even in third class."

Sophie paced the room as she removed her coat and hat. "Sell something."

"What? I don't even own a watch anymore. I gave it to Monsieur La Bac in exchange for a pound of meat last week."

She pinched her lips together, hissing a frustrated sound. "Then I'll lend you the rest."

I shook my head and argued. She crossed her arms and pleaded. Finally I gave in, and to be honest, I felt a rush of relief. Home. And it's not even cold in Minnesota this time of year.

The next morning, we put on our best hats and went to the American Embassy to find the simplest way to purchase my passage. To our dismay, we discovered all the ships leaving France for the next month were fully booked. It would be seven weeks before I could obtain even the lowliest berth.

Many passenger ships had already been converted to transport carriers. Others were hiding out in the New York harbor.

"Cowards," I exclaimed. "I need to go home."

As we walked into the courtyard of the Embassy, I threw open my arms in dismay. "What do I do now?" The honking of an occasional cab on the nearby Place de la Concorde interrupted the stillness.

"London?" Sophie suggested, as she pulled on her gloves.

I twisted my handkerchief in my hand. "I could probably travel to London, but would that be any better than Paris? And I'd be all alone there. At least here I have friends and someplace to live." My throat tightened, and I squeezed my eyes shut to keep from tearing up.

We sat on the small bench beside a water fountain. Sophie reached her arm over my shoulder and gave me a hug. Her face took on a determined expression. "We'll think of something."

Later, we walked home, and the streets seemed very quiet, as if all Parisians were hiding in their homes. With no petrol to be had at any price, no one drove a car anymore. Most people rode bicycles if they were lucky enough to have owned one before this horrible war.

I sent a telegram to Rainier but haven't heard from him. He will come to me. I know he will, but I have chewed my fingernails to the quick. He will come to me.

****

Poor Isabella. I swallowed the last of my cold tea, rose and stretched. The crescent moon had risen while I'd been reading. Only a glimmer of dark twilight hovered on the western horizon.

I rubbed my tight shoulders and tried to imagine the terror of being trapped in a city faced with war, with no way home. And Isabella didn't have a computer to pop onto and say hello to her family. Letters took weeks, maybe longer.

A chill coursed down my spine. And why was Sophie so scared? I made a pot of coffee to stay awake. Even though my eyes were tired from reading the cramped handwriting, I returned to the journal.

Chapter Eighteen

September 15, 1939

World War. That's what the newspaper boys shout. After the German invasion of Poland, Britain and France have declared war on the Nazis.

I can't stop worrying and have nearly paced a hole in the red flowers of Sophie's best rug.

It only took two days for the German Luftwaffe to smash the Polish air force—a few weeks to control the entire country. The newsreel at the picture show called the German advance a Blitzkrieg. I trembled as I watched the tanks roll over the Polish army like so many children's toys.

I held Rainier's hand tightly and closed my eyes when the big cannons blasted the villages. The film showed scenes of the poor refugees walking along muddy roads in ragged clothes. Where will they go? How will they take care of their children?

Even after we left the theatre, I still felt shaken. My heart beat rapidly. The summer weather had held, but I was cold and shivered in my light dress. "What will we do?" I asked Rainier.

Rainier lit a cigarette and drew in deeply. He seemed very calm. "About what?" he asked, his face expressionless.

"About the war."

After drawing on his cigarette a few more times, he

crushed it under his toe. Smiling, he swung his arm over my shoulder. "Don't worry, darling. Wait and see. America will wait this war out, and as long as they remain neutral, you have nothing to fear."

"But when the Germans invade France, won't you have to fight?"

Rainier pinched his mouth and looked the other way. He never wanted to talk about the war.

We'd walked to the cinema, so we headed down the Rue de Rivoli toward Sophie's apartment. She was out of town this weekend, visiting her father in St. Lô. We had the apartment to ourselves. A rare event.

Hand in hand, we walked past the Pont Royal and along the river in silence. A pall of fear hung over me. With his work and the curfew, it had been weeks since I'd seen Rainier. I didn't want to disappoint him on our one night together. Maybe a glass of wine would settle my nerves.

I slipped the key in the door and turned the old knob. "I should go home to Minnesota." I whispered more to myself than him. I hadn't mentioned my decision to leave Paris.

"Why?"

"I'm frightened."

After closing the door, he came up behind me and kissed the back of my neck. His hands moved up from my waist and caressed my breasts lightly through my thin dress. My blood heated, and for the moment the war seemed very far away.

Turning in his arms, I smiled up into his handsome face. I pulled my fingers through his blond hair and caressed the muscles of his strong neck.

He kissed me gently and stroked my cheek with his

thumb. "Don't worry, darling, I'll always take care of you."

****

October 15, 1939
Still no berths to be had at any price.

Chapter Nineteen

November, 27, 1939

Last night we gathered at Sophie's apartment to play cards. It had snowed, and the streets were beautiful, so white, and clean, and quiet. Rainier had contributed the coal for the fire. I don't know where he found it. No one asked. Black market be damned, we were warm tonight.

After another hand of cards which Rainier won (I think he cheats), Sophie stood and cleared her throat. She held up her glass. "Isabella is now the leader in our Sinner's Challenge."

François hooted with pleasure, and Sophie turned to smile at me. Rainier raised his glass to toast my success.

I couldn't believe it. I was the leader with our game? My cheeks grew hot, and I covered my face to hide the blush.

Somehow the silly challenge didn't seem as important as it did a year ago, but with the war moving closer, I guess Sophie decided we needed a distraction.

"What commandment are you going to break next, Isabella?" François asked, leaning one arm over the back of his chair.

Rainier glared sideways at the boy, and I'm sure I caught a sneer on his lips.

I glanced between them. Honestly, if Sophie and I

didn't like François as a friend, I don't think Rainier would have anything to do with him.

"So tell us, dear Sophie, what's left for our little sinner?" Rainier asked.

Sophie pulled out her notebook and checked the list. "Well, we all need to lie about something. That might be fun."

I peeked over her shoulder and studied the list alongside her. "There's still 'Taking the Lord's name in vain.' "

"I should be ahead then, I always do that," François insisted.

I put my hands on my hips. "Oh *Mon Dieu* doesn't count."

Sophie disagreed with me and gave everyone a tick. She flipped through her pages again.

She tapped her pencil stub against the page. "The covets will be a challenge."

"Not really," I pointed out. "I've always coveted your ring, Sophie. The sapphire's gorgeous, so blue."

She smiled fondly at her one good jewel and held it out in the lamp light. "It was my mother's. God rest her soul." She crossed herself twice.

"So you see," I continued. "That's why I could never have it. It's too special. You would never give the ring to anyone."

"Another sin for you," François said. He jumped up and filled everyone's glass with the last of the beer.

"To Isabella." Rainier raised a toast. "Our little sinner."

****

March 5, 1940
Sophie has been sneaking out at night.

I heard her last evening, after midnight, when she closed the front door. At the time, I thought perhaps she was restless and left for a breath of fresh air in the courtyard. It'd been a desperately cold winter, but the shelter of the garden made it a refuge when the dreaded curfew was in place.

When I awoke in the morning, she hadn't returned, and I was in a panic. Had she been arrested—caught wandering the streets by the police?

I paced the living room and waited for her to return. I chewed two fingernails to nubs and started on my thumbnail.

It was dangerous to defy the curfew. The police patrolled the streets and would arrest anyone, no matter what good reason they might have.

Finally, she returned later that morning. She tried to tiptoe past me where I slept on the settee, but I heard her steps. I rose on one elbow. "Where have you been?"

She dodged my gaze and refused to answer.

I gritted my teeth. Sophie could be so stubborn.

****

March 6, 1940

Sophie ordered three new locks for the front door. I don't think I will feel any safer.

****

March 8, 1940

"Why so gloomy, my Bella?" François asked.

I turned from my perch at the window and sighed. "I'm homesick for Paris. The old Paris."

He pinched his lips together. "We need to lift your spirits." He searched Sophie's book shelf and placed his favorite recording on her old wind-up Victrola.

Anything was better than being this blue, so I

turned on the machine and set the needle on the record. The music began. Ray Ventura's scratchy voice sang "We'll hang out our washing on the Siegfried Line."

We sang along, and from the kitchen, Sophie joined in. François and I pushed back the big rug. After that, we turned on the radio and danced the Lindy Hop until I was breathless and laughing.

Later that evening after François went home, Sophie and I sipped our tea and toasted stale bread over the small fire. No one threw out the crusts anymore.

"The last time I saw Rainier, he promised to take me to see Maurice Chevalier at the Casino de Paris," I told her.

"I hope there isn't too much of a line." She crunched her last bite of toast. "The reviews in the paper have been wonderful."

"You're invited to come along."

"I love the way Monsieur sings." She put her hands together and cooed. "My father took me to see him years ago. He has such a romantic voice."

I set down my tea cup. "Josephine Baker is scheduled to perform with him."

Sophie settled back against her chair and her face took on a dreamy expression. "I haven't seen her in more than two years. She's such a wonderful performer—so unique looking with her lovely dark skin and dark eyes."

"The show's so popular, Rainier hasn't been able to buy tickets. He said he will, for me, even though he doesn't seem to like her very much."

"Why ever not?" Sophie asked. "What did he say?"

I shrugged. "It's not so much what he said, but the expression on his face when I mentioned her."

I picked up our empty tea cups and headed to the kitchen.

"Do we have time to work on your blue silk dress tonight?" I called over the running water.

Sophie set her best teapot, the cute one with the rabbit, on the counter to wash. "I stopped at the Tabac and looked at the latest fashions in *Marie Claire*. I think if we raise the hem a few inches and do a few tucks in the sleeves, it will look more like the new styles." She smiled. "Maybe we could use the trimmings to spruce up my straw hat."

****

March 20, 1940

A third class berth on the Bordeaux is available. Sophie bought the ticket. Somehow, I will repay her. I sail at the end of May.

****

April 10, 1940

Rainier promised to bring me chocolates when he returned from his next trip to Alsace. I don't mind the meatless days too much or even going without liquor most of the time, but no chocolates from Debauve and Gallais? They've been closed for a month now. I'm desperate.

François agreed. He has an even worse sweet tooth than I do.

One afternoon we dug through Sophie's last box of sweets and ate the ones she'd left behind. I even sucked the chocolate off the coconut ones. I detest coconut but may be forced to eat those if Rainier doesn't show up soon. Ugh.

****

May 8, 1940

Damn. Sophie did it again, and she'd promised she wouldn't frighten me with her after-curfew wanderings. Very late last night, she'd crept out of the apartment. I heard the door close and watched from the window as she hurried down the street. The moon had set early. The city was very dark.

Why was she going out at two in the morning?

Staying close to the buildings, she'd hurried down the block toward the BHV. On the corner, several people emerged from a vestibule.

Three, maybe four dark shadows huddled together. Dressed in dark clothing, even from a distance they seemed nervous. After Sophie joined them, they hurried into the alley just beyond the Rue Victoria.

I couldn't sleep and paced the living room rug most of the night. I counted the red flowers around the edge a hundred times.

Worried, yes. And angry too. No, furious. And to be honest, I felt left out. Didn't Sophie trust me? What could be so important that she defied the government curfew on a moonless night?

She returned a few minutes after dawn, exhausted and filthy.

I met her at the door. "Are you crazy? What do you think you're doing?" I hissed as she entered. She closed and locked the three new locks.

She widened her eyes and smiled, trying to look innocent. "I've been down in the garden."

"Liar. I heard you leave last night," I continued. "You met those people. What were you doing out after curfew?"

She shook her head, and her shoulders sagged. "Isabella. You mustn't ask me these questions. It'd be too dangerous…for both of us."

Even though she'd just arrived home, she picked up her basket and headed down the stairs. She wanted to avoid me, but I followed her into her garden and crossed my arms to wait while she gathered a few spring vegetables. I breathed deeply to calm my anger, but I would have my answers.

The hens clucked from the pen, so I let them out to peck for bugs. We have six chickens now; three are laying. I checked the nesting box and found a small green egg. If only we had a rooster.

When Sophie had filled her basket with tiny tomatoes and some early peas, she turned and looked up at me again. She rose and moved closer, looking cautiously around the courtyard. "Isabella. Do you trust me?" Her voice was barely a whisper.

"Of course." I lowered my voice, too. "You're my best friend."

"And soon you will sail back to America."

I dropped my gaze to the ground, feeling like a deserter. I only had a few days before I'd board the S.S. Bordeaux. "Yes, but we'll still be friends. I'll write to you, and you can write to me. I'll worry about all of you until this awful war's over."

She smiled, shooed a hen off the bench, and sat down in the patch of sunshine that wandered across the courtyard.

I was hungry, so I took one of the tomatoes and popped it in my mouth. It was small, but exploded with sweet flavor. Sophie offered me another.

"No, we should save them for dinner. François brought us a little cheese. Today's a meatless day, but we can have a fine salad with those peas and our egg."

She turned the bright red tomato over and over in her hand and stared at it for a long time. Worry lines were etched across her brow. I'd never noticed them before, but in the sunlight, I could see the little creases quite clearly.

Then she blinked back tears and sucked in a noisy breath. "Such terrible things are happening, Isabella. I can't sit back and grow tomatoes and wait for others to stand up against this...evil. So many people have no one to defend them."

I patted her shoulder. She leaned into me, looking even more exhausted.

I, too, had heard of the beatings and the arrests. The disappearances. Everyone had. An undercurrent of whispers flowed through the city, like a river of fear. "Can I help?"

"No." She shook her head and almost laughed. "I have enough to worry about without you running around in the night, working against the government."

"Sophie." I lowered my voice to a silent whisper. "Are you in...the Résistance?"

She quickly glanced away.

"You're a spy?"

"Shhhh."

"Is François?"

She put a finger to her pinched lips, even though there was no one else in the garden, and the courtyard windows above us were all closed to the cool morning.

Panic rose in my throat, and I squeezed her arm tightly. "You can't be serious. You could be arrested. Or shot."

Sophie's face flashed fear and then resignation. "That's why I can't speak of this. That's why you must

200

go home."

My heart constricted into a frightened fist, and I swallowed hard. I opened my mouth to object.

"I have to do this, Isabella, but I don't want to endanger anyone else."

"And François?"

"François knows the risk." She gave me a little half smile. "He's clever. And very fast."

****

May 10, 1940

François pounded on our door early this morning. It took me a few minutes to undo all of Sophie's new locks. She'd added two more since last week.

"The Nazis invaded Belgium and Luxemburg," he shouted as soon as I let him in. "The Netherlands too."

"France will be next," Sophie said.

I can't write more. I'm too frightened.

****

May 14, 1940

Today is my twenty-fifth birthday. François wanted to celebrate, but now is not the time for cakes and presents. Maybe next year, if we are still alive.

He showed up with a gift anyway—an enormous marble rabbit. I don't know where he found it, but we put him in the garden, and I gave François a kiss on the lips. He held me a little too long and a funny feeling stirred in my heart. I stepped away, feeling heat on my face.

He turned and left the garden without another word.

****

I set the open journal on my knees and sighed. Ah, the rabbit. A present from François, whoever he was.

The statue had been in the garden a very long time. I stretched out my shoulders and neck and returned to the journal.

Chapter Twenty

May 17, 1940

Last evening we listened on the radio. Reynaud, our new president, admitted the Germans have pushed through south of the Meuse River. My heart battered against my ribs, and François held my hand.

Sophie looked very pale. She left at midnight and hasn't returned. All of Paris is heading south. The streets are full of refugees carrying what they can. Our city will be deserted. I have nowhere to go until the Bordeaux sails, and Sophie and François don't want to leave. We will stay in Paris and face down the Germans. Lord help us.

****

May 22, 1940

François signed up for the French military reserves months ago but was sent home after the non-aggression pact was signed. A few days ago, he was called up again. As he boarded the train at Gard du Nord last night, I kissed him goodbye.

He held me tightly for a long time, like he didn't want to let me go. My heart twisted when he waved from the window along with all the other recruits. There were tears in my eyes. And in his.

****

May 23, 1940

François isn't allowed to tell us where he's

stationed. Censorship is extremely strict right now, but in his first short letter, he said he's being fed well. He will send a picture in uniform as soon as he can.

Sophie continues her secretive forays.

I don't ask anymore, but I sleep fitfully when she is away.

One morning, a few days ago, I walked into her room, and I must have surprised her. She quickly tucked a small package into a trunk I'd never seen before and closed the massive lid.

Although her door was partially open, she glanced up at me with a guilty look. I started to back out with a quick, "Pardon," but she called to me. "Isabella? Come in for a moment, will you?"

"I'm sorry, Sophie. I didn't—"

"It's fine, darling." She patted the place on her little settee, signaling I should sit next to her. "I know you leave soon."

"Hopefully. Who knows what will happen with this ship?"

Sophie thinned her lips into a tight line. "Events are happening very quickly now. I need you to understand a few things, just in case."

I tipped my head to the side and stared at her.

She chewed on her lip for a moment and then pulled the box she'd just hidden out of the trunk.

"What's in it?" I asked, leaning forward.

"Before I show you, you must promise me something."

"If I can."

"Promise never to tell anyone about this."

"Not François?"

"No, he can't know. It's too dangerous."

Her steely expression tipped my stomach. "Rainier?"

She shook her head emphatically. "No one." She squeezed my arm tightly. "Promise?"

"Swear."

She relaxed and opened the small wooden box with an arched top. When she held up the stunning jeweled necklace, I gasped. I reached forward, but then pulled my hand back, afraid to touch something so lovely and precious.

"Where did you get this?" I kept my voice low, even though there was no one else in the apartment.

Sophie displayed the necklace on her hand. It was made of gold with huge red stones, rubies, I'd guess. The diamonds sparkled in the light, but the delicate filigree workmanship in the shape of flowers was exquisite. I touched it with care. "It looks like something royalty might wear."

"That's the story," Sophie replied. "The necklace isn't mine, of course. I'm keeping it for someone. An old friend."

"Why?"

"People are afraid." She shrugged and returned the jewels to the box. "Some are leaving the country because of persecution."

"The Jewish people?"

She gave a sad nod. "And others, too. They're afraid they'll be robbed as they travel south to safety."

"You're a good friend."

"So this is what you need to know." She held up a small key, made of simple brass and no longer than my thumb.

I looked at her questioningly as she dropped the

key into the small box.

"If...if something were to happen to me"—she swallowed hard—"I might need your help."

She looked so sad, I teared up. I took her hand. "Of course, but nothing will happen. You told me yourself, the French will be fine."

"Yes, I did." She straightened her shoulders and smiled more openly. "If someone comes to the apartment someday, and they have a key like this one, then you are to find the box with the exact matching key and return their possessions."

"When will they come?"

"I have no idea. Sooner...later."

"The pairs of keys are all different," she continued. "Each person has a matching one to the one in their box. They should be able to describe what sort of box they have left too, but some may not be able to. It's the key that will tell you. Isabella, do you understand?"

I nodded. "But I leave in a few weeks."

"Yes, but I wanted someone to know."

My curiosity rattled around in my brain. "Sophie? How many boxes...I mean...how many people..."

She smiled a secretive smile and showed me the trunk.

I gasped. It was filled to the very top with boxes of all sorts.

"There are more," she said. "Let me show you."

Chapter Twenty-One

Ho—ly shit!

I dug the little key out of the pocket of my jeans and examined it closely. It had to be the same kind Isabella had written about in her diary. My heart was beating so quickly, I had to take a few deep breaths to slow it down to a comfortable rate. I rose and paced the room, chewing on my fingernail.

Should I call Anton? Should I tell him what I'd learned in Isabella's journal?

I folded my arms across my chest. No. I didn't trust him. I knew his key probably matched a key in Sophie's trunk, but still, he'd lied before. What were his real motives?

I stopped short and looked around the room with new curiosity. Where was that trunk?

Over the next two hours, I slowly searched every room. None of the containers, dressers or trunks contained boxes full of treasures. I dug through every single one. There were boat-loads of rabbits, but no royal jewels. No precious mementos.

After another circuit of the place, I flopped back on the sofa, exhausted and frustrated. I stared at the little green journal I'd left open on the coffee table.

I quickly scanned the final pages of the diary. First, I'd read the rest of Isabella's story. Perhaps she'd described where Sophie had hidden the trunk. Or perhaps she'd sold everything after the war and bought rabbits with the proceeds.

I would finish the journal and then make my move.

****

May 24, 1940

"We regret to inform you. Stop. S.S. Bordeaux seized by German Command. Stop. Sailing postponed indefinitely."

My throat filled with tears, and I choked out a frightened sob. Holding the telegram in my hand, I paced the flowered rug.

What should I do now? I couldn't go home. I couldn't stay here. I'm even afraid to write in this journal.

Everywhere there are secrets and lies. It will be ages before another letter arrives from François, and I've only seen Rainier once in the last three weeks. Does he love me anymore?

He has grown more secretive than Sophie.

****

May 26, 1940

"DeGaulle's an idiot." Rainier folded the newspaper and tossed it in the dustbin.

"Wait," I called. "Don't waste that newspaper. I can wrap the garbage in it all week."

He grunted something about poverty, but I ignored him. I was too happy.

Without warning, Rainier had knocked at the door last night, grinning and bearing more food than I'd seen in a month.

And now I was cooking bacon. Real bacon. I don't know where he got it, but with our eggs, we would have an actual breakfast this morning.

Oh, it smelled delicious. My mouth watered, and my stomach tumbled with hunger. I'd even used the very last of my butter ration to cook them. The yolks were deep orange, and the whites were crisping in the fat to a lovely golden brown.

"I wish we had bread," I said to him as he leaned on the counter.

"Greedy girl," he laughed and kissed my neck. "I'll bring more food next week."

"Promise?"

"Sure. Maybe some fresh meat, too."

My throat tickled in an uncomfortable, guilty way. Many people in our building were scrounging for food. Many children had nothing but a bit of bread to eat and had grown thin in the last few months.

And here Rainier had brought me a feast.

He cuddled my head under his chin. He was so strong, so tall. My heart started to race, and my skin warmed at his touch. His hands roamed over my body, heating my blood. He nibbled my neck and shoulders with soft nips and licks.

"So what have you girls been up to—you and Sophie?"

I flipped our breakfast onto two plates. "Not much, darling. With the curfew and the shortages, we mostly stand in lines to find enough to eat." My face heated with my lies, so I turned away.

"Anyone come to visit?"

"No one special. A friend brought her grandson over for a visit. I don't know where Sophie got the flour, but she had baked a cake. You should have seen the little boy's eyes when he tasted it." I laughed and pulled out of his arms.

I hated lying to Rainier, but Sophie had made me promise. In the last two weeks, several more people had dropped off small packages and taken away a tiny brass key. I'd even met Sophie's old family friend, Angelina, who was leaving tomorrow with her family.

I picked up our plates and headed for the dining room. "We're planting a larger garden to help feed everyone in the building. Would you like to help? We could use someone strong to move the paving stones."

"Sure, darling." He smiled and pulled out my chair. "Whatever you need."

I gave him a swift hug around the neck. "Thank you. We're going to plant a very big crop of beans and tomatoes."

"Such resourceful friends I have."

I dipped my spoon in the soft egg yolk and savored the richness.

Sophie had promised she'd be home tomorrow, so Rainier and I had the whole day to spend together.

I didn't ask—she wouldn't tell me anyway, but I no longer believed she was visiting her father. I saved some bacon and one of the eggs to make her a proper meal whenever she returned.

****

June 3, 1940

After more than a year of tense waiting, the 'phony war' had now started. The German army marched across Belgium and Luxembourg, and then the Netherlands.

Now they march across the north of France. The newspapers can't lie about it anymore, and the French government can't pretend everything will be fine.

It won't be fine.

Sophie has been missing for several days.

I couldn't sleep last night, so I finally tossed back the covers and padded into the kitchen. I made tea and sat by the window until the sun rose.

When the eastern sky had lightened to a depressing gray dawn, I dressed and hurried down to the Tabac around the corner to buy a paper.

What was happening on the shores of Dunkirk? Along with hundreds of thousands of English and Dutch forces, many of our French troops have been trapped by the rampaging German divisions. With our army's backs to the sea, there is little the people of Paris can do but pray.

I went to Notre Dame yesterday, got down on my knees, and said a long prayer for François. I don't know where he is. We haven't had another letter from him.

As I hurried through the cold mist, my heart felt heavy. It thudded slowly, painfully in my constricted chest. I couldn't draw a full breath.

Could François be trapped with the others? Or captured? Or dead?

I blinked a few times to clear the tears. What would we do without François to make us laugh? To entertain us with stories of his adventures? I twisted my hands together. I've never known a person who'd died.

The thought terrified me, and I swallowed again with difficulty, trying to dislodge the lump that lived in my throat. Maybe if I promised God not to sin anymore, François would be safe.

I crossed the quiet street, but a long line of people already stood outside the Tabac. I waited in the cold, and after handing over my centimes, I read the headline in *Le Matin:*

La Magnifique Resistance de Dunkerque.

Shivering, I stopped in a vestibule and scanned the story.

Thank God for the British. They'd sent every ship, boat, anything that could float to rescue the men. Everyone who owned even so much as a little sail boat was right now crossing the channel to save the armies. For several days the French troops had held back the Nazi onslaught while the evacuation continued.

How brave the English people were. I don't understand why the French don't like them much. Right now, I loved them more than I could say. And Churchill had come back for the French troops.

I'll go to Notre Dame again today and pray the English will save my François.

****

Midnight, June 3, 1940

I will never forget this day.

At first, when I heard the planes, I didn't understand what was happening. I was visiting with a neighbor in the little square down the street called La Tour St. Jacques. The ancient medieval tower in the center of the small park is the only remnant of a church that once stood there.

An iron fence circled the perimeter of the grassy area. Children often play in the shelter of the bright green trees trimmed in the funny, French way—all squared off and standing like soldiers in a row.

The low roaring hum grew louder. Closer. Interrupting the quiet.

I sheltered my eyes against the morning brightness and looked up. Everyone stopped and craned their necks to see what the noise was, and why it seemed so close. The elderly couple on the park bench stopped their conversation. The children in the playground stopped their game.

I didn't see the bomb drop but heard the deafening explosion as it hit a house across the street. Fire and dust flew into the air.

Shouts, screams. Then another bomb exploded.

We ran for the Metro station across the street. A young mother, struggling with her two children, dashed toward safety. I picked up her older child and ran beside her. We hurried down the stairs.

Another explosion ripped through the air, this one closer. Dust blinded me, and I choked. Heat flashed across my face. More screams.

"Hush," I shouted at the hysterical woman on the steps behind me. "Be quiet. You'll frighten the children."

The little boy in my arms whimpered and reached for his mama. I hummed a song to him about a rabbit and jostled him as we moved with the crowd. We ran down the next flight of steps, deeper into the Metro's labyrinth of underground passages. Finally, we reached the deepest part, three levels down.

"You're safe here," I said to the mother as I handed over her child.

A Metro train rushed into the station, squealed to a stop, but didn't leave. A few passengers joined us on the platform, but others, still sitting on the train, looked around curiously, wondering why they weren't moving on.

My heart was pounding so hard, I could hear the rapid beats in my ears, even over the din of voices and train engines. Then everyone hushed.

We stood, listening. Listening for the dull blast of the bombs going off. Listening to the sirens now wailing on the streets above.

The lights flickered off and then returned. Soon the station filled with people, and the tunnel reeked of sweat and fear.

Bile rose in my throat. I needed air, or I'd be sick. I covered my mouth with my hand and pushed through the crowd. I climbed a few steps and then a few more, until I reached the first floor. Brilliant sunlight flowed down the steps, and a cool breeze touched my face. I drew a clean breath. My stomach stopped heaving.

I glanced through the wrought iron bars of the stairway and saw an old man limping across the park. He stopped for a moment and looked up again as if he'd heard a noise.

A plane, a smaller one this time, appeared above the square, dodging the Tour by a few feet.

"Hurry," I shouted. The man was closer now, and I recognized him. Monsieur La Bac. I often bought cheese from him at his little fromagerie across the square and sometimes milk for the children in our building, if he had any.

He tried to hurry, but one of his legs was crippled from wounds in the old war. He limped forward, depending on his cane to steady him.

The plane flew over him and disappeared beyond the rooftops. I let out a long sigh and started up the steps to help him.

He waved for me to stay where I was. "Je suis bien," he called with a smile.

The plane must have circled back over the city. This time it came in low. Its engines roared; its sleek silver skin glinted in the light.

Monsieur turned and put his hand to his brow.

The bullets dug into the grass and through the yellow and gold flower beds. The roses exploded in a cascade of red. Monsieur fell. I screamed and looked away.

The plane flew on. There were swastikas painted on its wings.

I dream of that plane. I watch it dodge the Tour, cringe at its deafening engines. I sicken at the smell of roses.

****

June 7, 1940

Sophie insisted we stand in line at the American Embassy today. I held out little hope of booking passage on even so much as a garbage scow, but we managed to find one ticket on the Champlain. Three weeks.

I didn't know what would happen by then. Would there be more bombers?

****

June 9, 1940

The cannons boom in the distance every day now. Paris has become a ghost town—to use the American expression.

Sophie returned a few days ago, and tonight she and I listened to the radio. The French government announced they would leave Paris after all, "for imperative military reasons." They would resettle in Vichy.

"At least they have a way out." Sophie sounded disgusted.

I couldn't get warm, even when Sophie made tea

and poured a little of her good whiskey in it.

She went out that night. Again.

Late the next day, when she returned from wherever she'd been, she looked even more haggard.

I'd gathered what I could from the garden in the morning and made soup with a bone the butcher had sold me for a few precious francs. I was glad I could offer her a warm meal.

She sipped the broth and dunked in a piece of hard baguette.

"I heard from François," she said after she finished the bowl and seemed a little revived.

I grabbed her hand. "Where is he?"

She gave me that don't-ask-because-I-won't-tell-you look.

"He wasn't captured then?"

"He was but managed to escape one night with a few friends. The Germans have taken so many prisoners, they don't know what to do with them. I don't think even the Nazis were prepared for how fast this war progressed."

I must have looked frightened, because my heart was pounding. She patted my hand. "François is fine. He'll need to stay hidden for a while until things get sorted out. There are people who will help him."

She pushed at the crumbs on the table cloth and licked her fingers. "Have you heard from Rainier?"

"No. I'm worried." I combed my fingers through my hair. "With the Germans so close and the bombings, it's impossible to know where he is, or if he's safe."

Sophie took her bowl to the kitchen and rinsed it with care. We'd lost most of our china when a bomb struck in the next block and toppled our china cabinet.

We lived in darkness. The shutters remained closed on the windows to protect us, but this made the rooms very stuffy. Yesterday we taped the glass and hung quilts to black out the light at night.

Sophie placed her bowl in the drainer, then turned to me and leaned against the sink. "Isabella…we need to talk. About Rainier—"

There was a knock at the door. When I peeked through the viewer, I shouted with happiness. "François."

With shaking fingers, I undid the locks. François hurried in and shut the door, then grinned and put his arms around me to hug me close.

I hugged him back and kissed him on both cheeks. "What are you doing here?"

Sophie entered the hall and grimaced.

"I know, I know, dear Sophie." François threw his hands in the air as if to surrender. "I shouldn't have come, but I had to say good bye to our darling Isabella. She will leave soon, *non*?"

"I hope so. I'm booked for July third on the Champlain."

He stared at the floor and at his worn out shoes.

It seemed odd to be going home after all this time. Home to quiet streets. No bombs. No refugees. No hunger. The war would feel very far away in dreary, old Minnesota.

I licked my lips nervously. "François. We've been so worried."

Dressed in ordinary clothes, he reminded me of the little boy I'd watched mature over the last few years.

"I wish…" I closed my eyes for a moment. "I wish you could come with me, both of you, to America."

He kissed me lightly on my cheek, but then looked more seriously at Sophie. "Have you told her yet?"

Sophie shook her head. "Not yet."

"What?" I asked, full of curiosity. "Is it good news?"

Sophie didn't look at me, but quickly said, "Just that François brought us some wine. Didn't you, François?"

"Of course, Sophie."

I glanced between them, but remained silent. What secret were my friends keeping from me now?

****

June 10, 1940

Twenty miles, then ten. The German tanks advanced toward Paris. Refugees flooded through the streets ahead of them.

I wouldn't go out the day the government lined up the city buses on the Champs-Élysées, but the newspaper splashed the photographs across the front page. Diagonally set, the buses were supposed to stop the Germans.

"Can you believe this?" I asked Sophie at breakfast. We were lucky to have bread and coffee today. I winced at the bitterness of the brew.

"Chicory," Sophie explained. Then she glanced over at the paper and twisted her lips in dismay. "Desperation."

****

I turned the last page of the journal. The final entry was written on the back cover in a shaky hand. I squinted to read the cramped words.

June 11, 1940

France is crushed. Even the buses have been

moved. Paris has been declared an "open city."

What does that mean, Monsieur Wegand, now that the government and the rest of the military have deserted us?

I can't sleep. I can't eat. I'm too angry to write in this journal. We are truly Les Misérables.

****

I closed the journal and sat for a long while, listening to the evening traffic roar down the boulevard. Isabella had captured the fear she'd felt in a way I'd never experienced. I wandered into the hall and examined the locks lined up the side of the door. No wonder there were so many.

I now understood Isabella's habit of hoarding everything, even half-eaten chocolates, in the event those dreadful times happened again. Although the diagnosis hadn't been invented back then, she'd suffered from a kind of post-traumatic stress, and it had scarred her for life.

But where were the treasures she wrote of? And what had happened to the real Sophie? Or the real Isabella? Which woman had died in the hospital a few weeks ago?

Who had kept the secrets all these years? There had to be more to the story. I glanced slowly around my apartment. Where was the next journal?

Chapter Twenty-Two

After a restless night, I began my quest to find Isabella's second journal. I started with the trunks in the living room, searching for hidden drawers or cubbies where she might have stashed a small book. Isabella feared the Germans for a good reason. At that time, what she'd written would have gotten her and her friends shot.

The morning passed quickly with no luck for my efforts. I'd gone through every cabinet in the living room, and the desk in the small bedroom where Isabella had lived with Sophie. I'd pulled drawers out to look on the bottoms and checked behind the pictures still hanging on the walls.

I'd already emptied every *lapin* box and found no journals hiding inside.

Hot, sweaty, and more than a little frustrated, I searched the tall cabinets in the large bedroom and even crawled around on my hands and knees checking the floor boards under the living room rug in case any were loose.

I plopped down on my favorite chair by the window and admitted defeat. For now.

I still had to go through the rest of the clothing in the bedroom, but I didn't believe Isabella would have tossed the journal in with the ratty bundles piled on the huge bed. No. She'd obviously wanted to hide the book from the authorities. She'd done a great job.

I pushed my hair back from my damp brow and stared at the ceiling. Did I need Anton's help? Anxious, I got up and paced the living room.

Should I trust Anton with Isabella's first journal? I chewed on my fingernail and watched the boats chug down the Seine with their barges of coal.

No, not yet. Although I suspected Anton's motives were honorable, I still didn't want to divulge Isabella's secrets. Even this many decades after the war, I couldn't foresee all the consequences.

The next morning, I trawled through the apartment looking for places I'd yet to inspect. I dug under the day bed in Isabella's tiny bedroom and found a few old pictures stacked on the floor. A suspicious itch skittered up my spine, and I smiled. Then I sneezed.

Most of the frames were empty, a few held old prints of little value, but in the corner—hah—a small oil painting. I blew off the thick layer of dust and stared at a portrait of a woman with dark hair.

When I picked it up, it seemed too heavy, so I ripped off the old paper covering on the back and there was the journal. With a quick shout, I grabbed the leather-bound book and flipped open the pages. The same neat cursive writing.

Bingo. My pulse raced, and I did a little happy dance.

Journal clasped to my chest, I leaned the picture against the headboard and studied it.

Sophie. It had to be her—the beautiful face, the dark hair done in the wavy, close-to-the-head style of the thirties. Sitting by an open window, she wore an elegant blue silk dress and a wistful smile. I carried the picture into the living room and placed it by my favorite window. Yes. That was the same too.

I couldn't find a signature, but on the back of the canvas the painting was dated 1933. Sophie couldn't have been more than eighteen.

I fixed a cup of tea and a plate of biscuits. With Sophie by my side, I turned to the first page.

****

June 12, 1940

Sophie doesn't know I've started another journal. She would be furious. Or frightened. I will write in it late in the evening, or after she leaves on one of her nighttime forays.

I won't be able to take the books with me when I leave for home. I could be searched at any time by the Germans. I will have to hide them both and hope they survive the war.

I haven't heard from Rainier in more than two weeks. I miss him. I'm worried about him. Is he safe? Does he truly love me? Will he come to say good-bye before I must leave for home?

Sophie said I should pack and take the train south to the harbor now. She has offered me her best steamer trunk, but I have little I want to take home.

I know I should leave Paris. I'm frightened to stay and filled with despair. I have been a fool, but I will wait a few more days.

****

June 14, 1940

The Germans have arrived. They paraded down the street in their horrible uniforms, marching their horrible goose step into the square in front of L'Hôtel de Ville. I watched from the window and shivered.

They are not our friends, even though they smile at us. They're evil. I will not stand in the street waving swastikas and cheering for them, even if they hand out bread to everyone who attends their parades. I would rather be hungry.

A huge German flag now hangs on L'Hôtel de Ville. It makes me sick to look at it, so I closed the draperies. My hands shook as I wiped the tears from my eyes.

I stay indoors as much as possible, only going to the garden in the early morning or late in the evening. I'm not afraid. Really. The Germans haven't shot anyone in days. The bombs have stopped falling, but I will never forget Monsieur La Bac.

Sophie still insists I burn my diary. If the SS were to find it, they'd shoot me as a traitor. I did find a good hiding place for it.

To hell with the Germans.

****

June 17, 1940 morning

For the last four days there have been no newspapers. Every morning I stand with our neighbors at the Tabac, confused. What is happening?

Then today, the new Paris begins. The front page article in *Le Matin* addresses the people of Paris. I translated the French without thinking, and my eyes burned with bitter tears.

"The German army now occupies Paris. The city is placed under military rule. The governor of the region will take the necessary measures to secure the troops and maintain order. The orders of the military authorities are to be executed without conditions..."

****

June 17, 1940 evening

Sophie packed for me—a small suitcase, something I can easily carry.

I stood in line at the Embassy for hours today in order to be processed. Because America is still neutral, I'm allowed to travel but only with the proper papers, stamped and double stamped by the German authorities.

I have my tickets in my handbag. I take them out and stare at them ever hour to see if they're still there. I'm so nervous. My stomach has a constant case of butterflies, only they feel more like dive bombers.

I want to go home, but I don't want to leave my friends. I'm worried about Sophie and François, and Rainier.

I haven't telegraphed my parents yet. I don't know why not. I pray every night they still love me enough to forgive my sins.

Late this evening, there was a knock at the door. Sophie froze, looking very worried. I peeked through the eye hole, and let out a moan when I saw the telegraph messenger.

I fumbled as I tore open the flimsy envelope. Sophie moved closer and stood silently beside me.

"Rainier. It's from Rainier. He will come soon." My breath returned.

"He'd better," Sophie said and returned to folding my few clothes. "You have to be on the train tomorrow tonight."

"What if…?"

"No, Isabella. You can't wait. You have to leave now. We don't know how long it will take you to reach Bordeaux."

"The Champlain doesn't leave for five days. It's

only a three hour train ride to the harbor."

"Three hours in peace time," Sophie pointed out.

"Maybe it won't be so hard. At least the flood of refugees heading south has slowed now that the armistice is signed."

Sophie clicked the lock shut on my suitcase. "Do you want me to go with you on the train?"

I chewed on my lip. I did. I really did want her to come with me, but I have to be brave. I squared my shoulders and shook my head. "You're needed here."

****

June 18, 1940

I rose early this morning and hurried down the steps for one last visit to the garden. The first of the zinnias were blooming, adding color to the lettuces and beans we'd planted.

I drew in a breath of fresh air. I needed a few moments alone to gather my thoughts before we left for the train station. Would Rainier arrive before I must go? I drew in another long breath and settled on the bench. Saying good-bye to him will break my heart, but not saying good-bye would be even worse.

I hate this stupid war.

I picked a sprig of mint, and the bright scent filled my senses. After almost three years in Paris, I've changed so much. I closed my eyes and let the sunshine fill my face with warmth. No matter how difficult this time has been, it has also been wonderful. I've made lasting friends and learned more about life than I could have anywhere. I wasn't sorry I'd stayed in Paris, but I was happy to leave.

I looked around the walls of the garden and smiled, then turned when I heard footsteps on the gravel path behind me. My pulse jumped. "Rainier?"

No. Sophie stood in the shade with a look on her face I couldn't even describe. Part sadness, part terror, mixed with disbelief.

I froze. "What?" I demanded. "Tell me. Is it Rainier?"

She handed me the newspaper and pointed to the small article under War News.

June 17 1940. Ile de Re.

Champlain Sinks

S.S. Champlain, berthed on the island of Ile de Re, hit a mine last evening. At 7:30 p.m., the passenger ship, S.S. Champlain, scheduled to dock in Bordeaux next Sunday for a transatlantic voyage to New York, partially sank after coming in contact with a suspected mine. After an explosion and fire, the ship now lies on its side in the small harbor. Three crewmen were injured. Passengers will be contacted by telegram.

There is no way home.

****

June 23, 1940

Hitler came to town today. I stood at the window and watched him ride through the square in his fancy car. He was led into L'Hôtel de Ville by smartly dressed French officials, among them Marshal Petain, our new Prime Minister. Hitler was much shorter than I'd imagined.

****

June 24,1940

I woke in the night. I'd left my courtyard window open to catch what cool breeze there was. Had I heard a noise? I lay in bed for a few moments and wondered if it wasn't my usual bad dream.

I tiptoed into Sophie's room. She wasn't there.

My cheeks heated with anger, and I hissed out a few choice words. She'd promised me she wouldn't go out for a few more nights until we better understood what the Germans were up to.

Everything was new now, and the rules were all different. It was as if we lived in an upside-down world—a world filled with red and black flags and Germans who smiled and bowed and clicked their heels when they passed you on the street. These new Germans were more frightening than the bombs.

I went back to my room. There. I heard the noise again.

Metal through earth.

****

The next few pages were torn from the journal. I checked the back of the book. Not there. I dug in the remains of the Chinese vase and behind the rest of the old prints. Nope. I flopped on the couch. No fair, Isabella. I want to know what happened next.

I checked the clock on the oven when I went to wash out my tea cup. It was after midnight. I didn't have the energy to search further for the missing section.

I flipped through the remaining pages in the diary. The next entries were weeks and months ahead.

Damn. Something momentous had happened. Something so awful Isabella couldn't keep it in her diary. She'd probably written the events down but then thought better of saving them. Had she burned the pages? Or were they hidden somewhere even more secretive?

I paced the floor and scrubbed my hands over my

face, too tired to continue. I would search tomorrow.

****

I hadn't heard from Anton in a day or so, so I called him after I finished my meager breakfast. I thought up a question to ask him, so I had an excuse.

"Anton?"

"*Bonjour*, Alyssa."

"What was your great-grandmother's name?"

"Angelina. Why do you ask?"

Hah! I knew it. Angelina. My heart did a leap, and I covered my mouth so he wouldn't hear my quick intake of breath. Another connection.

"Alyssa?"

"Just something I was reading," I said, trying not to sound like that was an absolute lie. It wasn't, not really.

"Aly-ssa."

He wasn't buying it. Tough. I chewed on my lower lip.

"When can I see you?" His voice sounded urgent. "We need to talk."

"How about tomorrow?"

A long hesitation. "Are you all right?"

"Hunky-dory, Anton." I clicked off before the battery of questions could continue. And I certainly didn't want to see him yet.

He still wasn't giving me the complete truth, but then lies had become the norm for us. We were at a stalemate.

I pulled Isabella's key from its hiding place and wandered into my mostly cleaned-out living room, spying a couple small wooden boxes I had yet to tinker with. I tried the key in each of them and included the cabinet in the dining room.

Too big, too small, too short, not long enough. Frustration. I felt like one of the Three Bears.

Nothing went together. With a long, annoyed sigh, I dropped into the upholstered wing chair by the window. What should I do?

Sure, I could stay in Paris and help Anton with his mystery, but maybe it would be better to book a flight home. ASAP.

I pulled on a springy curl by my ear and twisted it around my finger.

Obviously Isabella had been involved in dangerous times. Just as obvious, Anton was not a cute pastry chef who owned a little coffee shop. He had deeper motives. Mysterious motives he'd yet to confess.

Plus, he had minions.

How many? I rubbed my thumb over my lips and frowned.

I thought about that question for a long while as the sky over the Seine went from shades of orange to golden to azure.

He'd admitted the woman with the dark hair, Claire, worked for him. Since she was no sous-chef, what was her role? Errand girl or something more sinister?

And what about the undefined man, the creepy guy who'd followed me? The man Max had seen out in front of our apartment building. Did he also work for Anton?

A cold chill settled in my heart. Had Anton sent the creep who'd broken into my apartment? I gulped back the sour taste in my mouth and closed my eyes.

The really big question still swirled in my brain. How many lies had Anton told. And would he tell me even more?

****

Better to switch cafes. No matter what Anton said, I didn't want to see him. Not until I understood more of the connections.

I walked down the Rue de Rivoli in the opposite direction and stopped at another brasserie for petit dejeuner. It was a warm day, so I sat in the pleasant morning sunlight and stirred my *café au lait.*

The waiter brought me a croissant and strawberry *confiture*, but they were a huge disappointment. The *café* was even worse. I grimaced.

Frankly, nothing tasted good right now. I pinched off the corner of the pastry and chewed distractedly. After swallowing only a few bites, I decided to leave the rest.

A shadow moved across my plate. Heart racing, I glanced up.

"May I speak with you?" the woman said in perfect, French-accented English.

I set down my cup. "It's Claire, isn't it?"

"*Oui.*" She pulled out the little metal chair across from me. "This is Hélène." She pronounced it the French way—*Ay-lin.*

Another woman, taller than Claire, put out her hand. "*Enchantée.*" Helene was beautiful in an unusual way, with strong features and a modern haircut—one side shorter than the other. A diamond stud sparkled over her dark eyebrow. Her smile was friendly, so I returned the greeting. They both sat.

"How did you know I was here?" I asked Claire.

"We watched you leave your apartment."

When I pursed my lips, she continued. "You keep a

regular schedule, Alyssa. May I call you that?" She used the soft, English "sh" sound in schedule instead of the American "sk" in the word.

Sipping my wretched coffee, I watched the pair. Something was different about them, about the way they moved together and leaned into one another. Hélène spoke in quick French, and Claire nodded.

I glanced at the ring on Claire's finger and then noticed the matching one on Hélène's.

"Yes." Claire smiled quietly. "Do you understand?"

I did.

"Do you want some tea or perhaps a horrible coffee?" I put up my hand to signal the waiter, but Claire shook her head. "*Merci*, but we both need to go to work. I wanted you to understand. The Captain…Anton spoke the truth."

I swallowed another sip and nodded. "I see."

"He could use your help," she said softly.

I dropped my gaze to my hands.

As the women rose, Claire left a business card on the table. Then they were gone, walking off together, hand in hand.

Captain Anton De Ville
Récupération d'Objets d'Art
Police Nationale
Ile de Cite, Paris

Hum. That explained a lot. A cop, not bad guy. I shoved my mediocre croissant aside and headed to the police station.

The unremarkable man met me at the entrance of the Prefecture and handed me a visitor's badge, already filled out. I suspected he knew a lot more about me than my name and address.

He led me up the marble steps and down a long hallway. He opened and ushered me through a massive, carved door that had to be fifteen feet tall. I glanced around the oversized office occupied by several desks and stacked with electronic equipment. He motioned me to continue through another large door into the next room.

He gave a quick nod, and I was left standing in an impressive office. High ceilings. Tall windows. Lots of carved bits stuck to the walls. An oil painting of a handsome older man dominated the fireplace. He looked familiar.

Pretty grand digs for a policeman, even a Captain, but what did I know about the French police? Anton stood with his back to me, and looked mildly surprised when he turned around. Obviously, he hadn't sent for me.

"Uh, hi. I mean, *bonjour*." My cheeks heated.

"*Bonjour*, Alyssa." He waited for me to continue, crossing his arms and standing back on his heels. Instead of his usual black apron, he wore a well-tailored dark suit, shirt and tie. He was clean shaven. And gorgeous. Damn. Could this conversation get any more difficult?

My cheeks grew warmer and warmer. I locked my hands behind my back to give them something to do. "I spoke with Claire."

His mouth frowned, and the worry lines on his brow furrowed. "I did not send her."

"Judging from your reaction, I kinda figured that. Your team might be working behind your back."

He grunted and rubbed his thumb and first finger

along the sides of his mouth, as if to consider whom he would guillotine first.

"Look." I took a step forward. "Why don't we begin again?"

He tipped his head to the side, and a look of relief flashed across his face. "I would be willing."

"So…how?"

Anton took a step toward me and smiled—this time, a big, toothy, I'm-getting-happier-by-the-minute smile. "Let's begin at the beginning."

****

Anton's office was too formal and my place too dangerous for this important conversation, so we voted to walk along the river and watch the tour boats motor by. We found an empty patch of grass under a flowering tree and sat side by side. Still staring out at the river, Anton shook his head.

He showed me a picture of his great-great-grandmother. "You asked about Angelina. She died suddenly of a heart attack in 1943. The family found the key and the picture in her belongings." Sadness crept across his face.

"I'm sorry."

He gave a brief shrug. "I am sorry I never met her. She was a determined woman." He narrowed his eyes at me and then smiled. "Maybe a bit like you."

"Uh, thanks, I think."

"When the family left Paris before the war, she hid the necklace. The only thing my grandfather remembered was a friendly, dark-haired woman who gave him a piece of cake."

A dark-haired woman? I gulped. Sophie?

"He only remembered her because he had not

tasted cake in more than a year. In my youth, it was a family story, told again and again, as was the description of the necklace. Rubies and diamonds. Set in the finest gold filigree. Fit for a czar." Anton repeated the words as if from memory.

"Like flowers."

"*Comment?*"

"Never mind." But I smiled at him. For the first time since this whole mess had fallen apart, I began to trust him. Maybe even understand him.

"My father spent much of his life searching for the necklace."

"The guy on the wall in your office?"

"*Oui.* He located and returned many treasures to other people or their descendants but never his own." Anton turned the key over and over in his hand, staring at it with intensity.

"So you suspect these keys are a clue somehow?" I played with the small white, daisy-like flowers that grew interspersed with the grass. I picked a few and twirled them in my fingers. I couldn't look at him right now. He would know I was keeping a secret—a very big secret.

"Yes. We suspected your aunt hid treasures for many families. We believe she protected these possessions during and after the war."

"Why? I mean, why did you suspect her?"

"Nazi records for one thing. Their strength of organization was also their downfall after the war. Over the years, we have interviewed many refugees, mostly children who managed to survive. Some remembered a young woman with dark hair. Several mentioned or had a key. No one would or could give the name. Either they didn't remember or were protecting her. I believe the key was the signal—the proof to the keeper, Sophie—that this was the rightful owner of a treasure."

I leaned back in the cool grass and covered my eyes from the bright noon sun. "Clever, really."

"My father didn't know who or where this woman was, or if she was still alive. I only tracked her down a few years ago."

"Why didn't you just ask her? She hadn't done anything wrong. Why wouldn't she tell you and let you help her?"

He smiled an understanding but frustrated smile. "We tried, believe me. We approached Sophie Delacroix several times over the last few years. Wily old girl. She wouldn't say a thing. Denied her involvement and locked her doors."

"M-m-m. And she has just a few locks."

He chuckled. "I don't think she trusted us any more than she'd trusted the damn Nazis."

"So you waited."

"What else could we do?"

Anton's shrug was so totally French, shoulders up, hands up, I had to turn my face away to hide my smile. Poor guy. He looked more than frustrated. He looked almost defeated.

He glanced out over the river. "There wasn't enough evidence for a search warrant. As you said, she had done nothing illegal. She certainly wasn't going to let us through her front door."

I licked my lips and put up my palms. "I haven't found any treasures, Anton. Other than a few rabbits."

He studied me for a long moment and then nodded. "I believe you."

"Well, that's good anyway."

I picked a few more daisies and tugged on their petals. Should I tell him about the journal? Confirm his suspicions about the keys. I hesitated and chewed on my fingernail, staring at this new man.

He was different somehow, more intense. Not the happy, carefree baker flirting with a tourist but a driven police officer on a mission. Which was the real Anton?

Chapter Twenty-Three

Anton and I are friends again, I guess, although at this point I'm still holding back on what I know. I suspect he is too. Until I have a more complete picture of everyone playing in this little treasure hunt, I'm keeping mum.

I hurried up the stairs, not even waiting for the itty-bitty elevator. I opened my door, locked it—four should do it—and hurried to the kitchen. Hot tea and a journal were the order of the day. I would finish the next part and continue searching for the missing pages.

****

April 30, 1941

I don't know where François found the rooster, but he came home one day with the huge bird, looking very proud of himself. François—not the rooster.

The poor creature was scrawny and had only one good eye. His tail feathers were skimpy and drooped in odd directions.

"Looks like he's been in a fight," I said.

"Cock fighting. A friend of mine gave him to me."

"Did he win or lose?"

François snorted. "He's alive."

I grimaced.

"You can put him with your hens and have chicks."

"Oh, François," I said excitedly. "Thank you. We can expand the pen, and I can have the children search for food for the new chicks. Everyone in the building will have more to eat." I gave him a kiss on the cheek.

We went down the stairs, and he released the big red rooster into my chicken coop. The rooster gave an echoing crow.

"What will you name him?" François asked.

I smiled. "De Gaulle."

****

May 19, 1941

Rumor has it the Germans are recording the names of every male citizen over the age of sixteen. They knock on doors and accost workmen in the street, checking the long, precise lists they carry.

No one ever knew what the Nazis were up to, but no one with any sense trusted them. Fear simmered under the surface of the city.

Although the soldiers had yet to track François down, it was only a matter of when and where they would corner him and discover who he was. Although he still walked with a limp, he refused to stay indoors, no matter how I pleaded. He would disappear for days only to return filthy and exhausted. I didn't ask where he'd been. He would never tell me.

"You must leave Paris," I said one evening.

François stared out the window, ignoring my words. The night was very dark. No moon. There were few street lights in this part of town. Rain glistened on the barren square.

"It's time, François." I closed the blackout curtains.

The look on his face cracked open my already aching heart.

He let out a long sigh and turned to me. He'd grown so tall these last months now that he was nearly twenty. I had to tip back my head to look into his lovely brown eyes. He was strong again. We both knew he could no longer hide, no longer ignore the war raging through the world.

He rested his hands on my shoulders, and then pulled me closer. I didn't resist and found comfort in his embrace. There was so little comfort these days. So little warmth.

"I don't want to leave you." He said the words in English.

"What if the Nazis come for you? What would I do then?" I asked in a hushed whisper.

He drew a hand over my darkened hair and loosened the tight bun at my nape. "I would always protect you, Isabella."

"No." I put my finger to his lips. "Don't call me that. Ever. I'm Sophia Delacroix. Our friend Isabella is gone. She went home to America—to Minnesota. We don't know where she is."

****

What? Now I was totally confused. Dammit, Isabella. What had happened to Sophie? And why had François been hurt? Those damned missing entries were driving me crazy. With a frustrated growl, I turned to the next page.

****

François nodded. "She went back to America."

"*Oui*. She left on the train. Many months have passed since we've heard from her."

"But I miss her, Sophie. I loved her." He kissed my cheek softly.

"I know." I kissed him back. "She loved you too."

He picked me up and carried me into the bedroom.

239

May 20, 1941

Morning came too early, and François stirred beside me. He rose but came back to bed a few minutes later. He'd turned on the radio. For once, quiet music crackled through the speaker instead of news.

I hadn't listened to the radio lately. Couldn't. The world was in flames. Europe in chains. London burning.

"So beautiful," I said, curling next to him. He was warm and smelled of sex. "So peaceful."

"Vivaldi." François kissed me on my head. "I will always love this music."

"Me too."

"I love you, ma bella."

"I love you, François. I'm sorry I didn't see that before."

"We are together now. That is all that matters."

Before François left that night, I attached one of Sophie's keys to his watch.

"To remember me," I said, unable to look into his face.

"Always." His heart thudded heavily in my ear as he held me one more time.

He will head north to join the French patriots in Belgium. From my window, I watched him limp across the bridge and disappear down the narrow alleys of la Cité.

My heart followed him.

****

I sniffed sadly and closed the journal. I mourned with Isabella. So many years wasted.

What had happened to François? Was he killed in the war? Did the two lovers ever meet again?

****

Anton phoned the next morning and suggested a visit from the antique appraiser as a kind of truce offering. Or did he want to look around my apartment again?

I would take the chance and trust him. A little.

The two men arrived late that afternoon. With the days longer now, the sun was still high in the sky.

The appraiser, a Monsieur Royer, was an older man. Mostly balding, very short. He spoke only a few words of English, but I could tell he was very excited by the number of '*Oh, mon Dieus*' he exclaimed when I led him into the office to see Isabella's *lapin* collection. Even after my intruder's best efforts, I still had hundreds.

He walked the tables once, then twice, hands behind his back and then went straight for the bronze sculptures. He spoke directly to Anton in a clipped, French accent I couldn't decipher. Anton translated as Monsieur rearranged my rabbits.

"Chinese," Anton interpreted. "He's not sure how old until he checks with a friend of his: Could be very early. Perhaps B.C."

"Wow." I'd suspected as much after seeing what the Museum of Decorative Arts had in the Oriental collection. The rabbit was covered with gorgeous enameling.

"Those others are later copies, done by the French in the same style."

"Valuable?"

Monsieur shrugged his shoulders, picked up his leather bound notebook, and scribbled notes with a stub of a pencil.

Next he examined each of the wood carvings gathered together farther down the table and began chattering away.

Anton continued his translation. "Most of these are from the Middle East, but none are more than a hundred years old. They're hand carved from olive wood for the tourist trade of the late nineteenth century."

The appraiser babbled in a higher pitched voice and pointed to a rough little sculpture of three small bunnies.

"Except that one. Very old."

They continued in staccato French. Anton raised an eyebrow and then whistled under his breath. "He says these little guys could be early medieval, nine or tenth century."

I picked up the smooth, blackened carving, no larger than my palm, and felt the years of loving wear rubbed into it.

"It could be a very early child's toy."

I placed it on the window ledge along with my precious Lalique buddy and smiled to myself. Aunt Isabella had an eye for a bargain. The price sticker, still attached to the bottom of Mr. Medieval said ten francs.

"It's worth thousands, maybe tens of thousands," Anton added. "The Cluny needs to take a look."

I had to sit down. "The Cluny?"

Anton gave a slight chin nod and turned to listen to Monsieur Royer.

Over the next hour, the appraiser picked up and examined every surviving ceramic bunny on my table. The Delft, Lladro and Doulton ones he set to the side.

"A hundred or two hundred euros at the most," Anton said.

"All together?"

"Each."

My turn to raise a brow. Had to be fifty little bunnies in the warren. I rubbed my hands together. Jojo would be able to choose any university he wanted. Maybe even attend a private high school.

My heart rushed along at a happy pace. Whatever remained of my cool had evaporated. I was bouncing on my toes by this point.

Monsieur stopped and said quite clearly, "*Oh, mon Dieu.*" He was staring at a small glass vase, roughly made but with the obligatory rabbits beautifully etched into the side. He continued his explanation to Anton, waving his arms around.

I shook Anton's hand. "What?"

Monsieur took a magnifier from his pocket, squinted one eye, and examined the glass. "*Oui.*"

Anton turned to me with a grin. "Roman, very early."

They conversed again.

"He says it should only be sold to a museum."

I was feeling hot again and went to open the window in the office.

"Okay?" Anton asked, looking worried.

I swallowed, but my face still burned, and my heart was jumping like…well like a bunch of terrified bunnies. "I'm a little overwhelmed."

Anton led me to the chair in the corner and brought me a glass of water. He knelt next to me and held my hand.

Monsieur started babbling. He'd worked his way down to the little drawings, etchings and paintings at the far end of the table. Through the babble, I clearly heard the name Rembrandt.

Even the wallpaper scraps were samples of designs from famous European palaces.

The preliminary total was astounding. The majolica alone was worth a fortune. The bunny tea pot—a thousand euros. The early hand-painted ceramics would fetch even more. Each.

The tapestries weren't repros but early examples from Brussels. "More Cluny," Anton translated.

"Like the *Lady and the Unicorn*?"

When Anton asked my question, Monsieur responded with barely controlled excitement, his hands gesturing wildly.

"What?"

"He says it's earlier than the Lady. Could be the same master."

Although light-headed again, I managed to walk out of the room. Monsieur continued to sort the etching and drawings, exclaiming as he went through the pile.

I drew in cool, fresh air from the window in the living room.

Anton soon followed me. "You don't want to hear about the rest?"

"I will but not now."

"A little surprising?"

I agreed and turned back to stare out the window. I watched a family push a stroller across the square, hurrying to make the bus. Suddenly, I missed my sister, Sam.

I went to the kitchen to make tea. The kettle whistled, and I added loose tea from the tin. I'd always loved Earl Grey—or *Thé de Bergamot*. The aroma filled the room, soothing my racing heart. Adding milk and stirring with my tiny spoon brought back calm and normality. My shoulders relaxed, and I drew a long, clean breath.

I glanced out the window, registering twilight. We'd spent a good part of the afternoon examining bunnies. Anton accepted a cup and added a bit of sugar.

I drank mine straight, although I wondered how bourbon would go with Earl Grey. I'd kept the bottle I'd found in Sophie's top cupboard. Booze didn't go bad, did it?

Monsieur entered the small kitchen and held out a wooden box of brooches on the flat of his palm. I'd set the beat up jewelry box to the side, thinking I'd donate the junk to the church down the street. I'd assumed the stones were paste, but when Monsieur opened the lid, I clearly heard him groan.

Suddenly, I could hardly breathe and grabbed a magazine to fan myself. "What?"

Anton listened to the little man's exclamations.

"Is it old?" I asked, trying to take a sip of my tea with shaky hands.

"No," Anton replied. "But two of the pieces are Cartier."

Monsieur had his eye piece out again and continued to mutter under his breath.

"One is Fabergé, and this little guy is a very early Van Clef and Arpel."

I smiled. "I guess my mom is getting a nice birthday present."

Monsieur spent the rest of the evening in the office, writing down everything in his funny old notebook.

Anton and I returned to the living room. I opened a bottle of burgundy. For a while, we sat drinking wine as the light on the Seine changed from twilight to moonlit.

He rose, and I watched him fidget, pacing between the windows.

"What?" I finally asked.

He glanced at me, eyebrows up, but then his gaze shifted down and left. "Nothing."

What a terrible liar. I crossed my arms and continued to stare. "You want to tell me something, but you're worried how I will receive the idea."

Anton smiled. "You're a fast read, Alyssa. I could use you in my department."

"So tell me."

"You need to have better security. The value—" he pointed to the next room with a thumb.

"No one knows about the rabbits but you and me and your buddy in there."

Anton rubbed his hand over his face.

He always did that when he was frustrated. I smiled to myself. Good to know.

He approached me, knelt, and took my hand. "And whoever broke into the apartment last month."

I pressed my lips together and blew out a long breath through my nose. He was probably right.

"They belong in a bank vault."

"They're good company."

Anton tipped his head to the side. "Keep a few of the less expensive ones."

I let out a long sigh. "Bank vault it is."

Tired but overwrought, I couldn't sleep after Anton left with the appraiser. I flipped every lock on my door, then dug Isabella's journal out from the hiding place under my mattress and continued to read.

February 4, 1942

I know I should burn these journals. If the Nazis come to interrogate me, their insidious searchers will find them, no matter where I conceal the damn things. But I need to remember these days, and so I will take the risk. The old Chinese vase works well as a hiding place for now.

February 12, 1942

I received a letter addressed to Sophie last week. I let it lie on the entry hall table for several days, unwilling to acknowledge the bad news it held inside. No one sent letters with good news anymore.

I'd recognized the return address as her father's, but the handwriting was different from that on the letters I'd seen before. Finally, on the third day, I opened it, feeling I'd once again intruded on my friend. I sat in the chair by the window and read the few words.

Dear Sophie.

Your father, Monsieur Armand Delacroix, died January 13, 1942 outside the village of St. Lô. He had been injured in the bombing of his home and had begun to recover, but he could not survive this difficult winter. I had taken care of him since his injuries.

He worried about you, Sophie. Please let your family know if you are all right.

Cousin Miriam.

I folded the thin sheet of paper and listened to the bells of Notre Dame. As the second winter of the German occupation dragged forward, many more French civilians had died. Bullets and bombs weren't needed anymore. Starvation and exposure worked just as effectively and didn't cost as much.

I'd never met her father, but I would mourn him as Sophie would. She'd always spoken of him with softened eyes and a quiet smile on her face.

The next morning, I dressed in black, walked across the bridge and through the quiet streets to Notre Dame. It was still cold outside, even though most of the snow had melted. My coat still kept me warm enough, but my shoe had another hole in it, and the cardboard soaked up the icy slush. I jumped the puddles as best I could.

Red and black swastikas hung from the police station across the street. The Nazis didn't interfere with somber worship yet, although several of the more outspoken priests who dared to criticize the Reich had disappeared. If we kept our heads down and our mouths shut, we were allowed to pray in desperate but quiet pain.

Ignoring the armed guards standing at attention outside the cathedral, I opened the tall door. I entered the cold, gothic space, sparsely lit and somber, arriving in time for Matins. The bright smell of incense calmed my nerves, and I released a battered breath.

The hymns sung in Latin sounded familiar to my ears. I prayed for Sophie in French and then under my breath in English. I prayed for her father as she would have done. I prayed for François's safety, and a tear trickled down my cheek.

After mass, I rose from the creaky wooden pews and glanced around the dark cathedral. I wandered to the front of the church and studied the wooden carvings that illustrated bible stories for the fourteenth century illiterate.

The scene of Mary hurrying to St. Anne to exclaim the existence of the Lord always drew me. I studied the joy carved into her face and searched my heart for joy. I found none.

The young priest, Father Horatio, blessed me as I left. He's so kind, so young. I should pray for him too.

Feb 26, 1942

I've torn apart the whole apartment looking for Sophie's keys. Finally, I found the ring in the bathroom. She'd buried it in an old box of dusting powder. I choked on the foul smell of stale lavender.

The keys hung on a large ring, each pair systematically wired together. On the tag, the name Delacroix *Gymnas et Boîte Débarras, St. Lô, France,* had been written in faded ink.

As I rose from the floor, more than one hundred little sets of keys jangled in my hands. I ran them through my fingers. They couldn't have been from her father's Gymnasium. He'd worked most of his life for the Government here in Paris. Maybe they'd belonged to her grandfather?

I put on a sweater and walked the mile to the library. Digging in the dusty shelves, I found a history book of the First World War. I smiled bitterly at the title. *The Great War.* Little did they know.

Much of St. Lô had been destroyed in the terrible fighting. Early twentieth century photos illustrated a picturesque town with a small market and gothic church. The after photos showed nothing but rubble and broken walls.

Despite the destruction, I smiled to myself and closed the volume. So clever of you, my friend. The old locker keys were the perfect signal to use for both the keeper and the owners of the treasures. No two keys were the same, yet no one, not even a rapacious Nazi would bother with such an insignificant item.

I hurried home and climbed the stairs. With electricity so unreliable these days, it was safer to use the steps than to be trapped inside the tiny elevator.

I walked by the mirror hung in the hallway and glanced at my reflection. I still startled whenever I saw myself. With my darkened hair, I did look a bit like my friend although my face was thinner than hers had been. I'd practiced the way Sophie walked and spoke but kept away from her old friends as well as the Nazis.

Now that François had left, I have no friends except those in my books. And *mes petits lapins,* of course. They keep my secrets.

****

The rest of the journal was blank. I forced myself to take a break. I was hungry and had nothing left to eat in the apartment.

I munched an apple on my way home from grocery shopping at the little market in the Marais. I hurried along the street near the Tour Saint Jacques and noticed an old man in a black beret sitting on a bench in the garden.

"Max?" I called over the iron fence.

He waved and folded his newspaper.

I came around the corner, entered the small city refuge through the swing gate, and followed the gravel path toward his place in the morning sunshine.

"How are you?" I sat beside him on the bench. The irises bloomed in the flower beds around us, and a hundred shades of purple dazzled my vision. The Tower St. Jacques rose hundreds of feet above us—a haunting remnant of a medieval church that had once stood on this spot.

Max grinned as I set down my shopping bags.

"You found the little market, I see."

"Yes. I love the *fromage* there. So fresh. And the vegetables are gorgeous. See? I found these baby asparagus to cook for dinner. They look like they popped out of the ground this morning." I returned his smile. "I thought California had fresh vegetables, but the Paris markets are amazing."

He nodded, dug in his coat pocket, and opened his little round tin of candy drops to offer me one. "How is the apart-a-ment coming along?"

I popped a lemon drop in my mouth and sighed. "Slowly. Very slowly. Max, may I ask you a question?"

His eyes sparked with curiosity as he nodded.

"Isabella had quite a few, uh, valuable objects in her apartment. How, I mean, she didn't seem to have a job, how did she—?"

"How could she afford to live in a beautiful apartment, in a wonderful location with no source of income?" Max understood.

"Yes. Even if she didn't have a mortgage, there would have been taxes and utilities to pay. Food. Necessities. Not to mention her serious rabbit habit."

He scratched the side of his nose. "I only knew her a short time, but I do know she was my landlady."

"What?"

Max nodded. "I guess that makes you my landlady." He chuckled in a wet, throaty way and leaned back on the bench.

"I didn't know she owned more than the one apartment."

"Not many people did."

"Her lawyer never said anything."

"They have not been forthcoming?"

I brushed a stray curl off my face. "Obviously not." Then again, neither had she. "But Max, how?"

His shrug, so totally French caused me to smile. "Of course she'd lived there a very long time—knew everyone in the building. When someone moved on, she'd purchase this apartment or that over the years. Remember, the Marais was not the pricey side of town in years past."

"How many?"

"Oh, she owns the whole building. I pay my rent to a management company who, I imagine, does all the real work."

I sucked in a breath so quickly, I choked on my lemon drop.

Max slapped me on the back a few times until I could breathe. "Explains a few things."

I sat forward and only then noticed a small brass plaque attached to the back of the bench. There are plaques all over Paris, commemorating everything that has happened in the last five hundred years. I'm always curious about them, so I looked more closely. "What does it say?"

Max translated for me.

"Henri La Bac
Born1898
Killed in the first
bombing attack of Paris,
June 3, 1940"

I rubbed my finger over the letters as chills climbed my forearms. "So sad." I recalled the story in Isabella's journal, but didn't mention this to Max.

Max glanced at the name and said quietly, "Yes, he was a nice man."

I cued in on the statement and stared at him.

He immediately looked flustered and struggled to rise from the bench.

"You knew him?"

"What? Oh, well, maybe. It was a long time ago. I forget…"

"No, you don't. Your memory is perfect."

The blush on his cheeks continued to darken.

"Why are you embarrassed about this?"

He sat down with a thump and rubbed his face with his hands. "I…"

I stared at him for a long moment until more of the puzzle pieces slipped into place.

Injured right leg, in his nineties, knew Isabella, sweet tooth.

I held out my hand. "Let me see your watch again."

Max stared across the street as if he hadn't heard me.

"Max."

Muttering, he dug in his pocket and pulled out the old timepiece but refused to meet my gaze. I traced the F on the front of the watch, almost worn off but still visible in the bright light.

"François," I said under my breath, like it was a deep, dark secret.

His eyes widened. He looked like he would panic and run—that is if someone almost a hundred years old could run.

"It is you. You're François." I was so excited, my voice rose and several people in the garden turned to stare.

Max looked pained. No. Frightened. He dropped his head on his chest and let out a long sigh. "You must have found her journals."

"Well, yes. At least two with green bindings."

"I begged her to burn them, but she was so stubborn. She would never tell me where she'd hidden them."

"Them? Are there more?"

He gave his French shrug.

I eyed him up close. "How long have you really been in Paris?"

He glanced furtively at the people enjoying the park. "Can we speak somewhere more private?"

Even more curious because of his obvious discomfort, I took his arm and helped him rise. We walked across the street to an almost empty bistro and sat outside in the sunshine. I ordered two coffees. Max added three packets of sugar to his. See? Sweet tooth.

He tapped his spoon on the edge of his cup. "After I left Paris in 1941, I fought with the Resistance for more than a year in Belgium. I was captured by the Germans late in the war and held in a work camp for the last few months of the war. When the Russians claimed that part of East Germany in '45, I had no way home until the wall came down. More than forty years."

I sipped my coffee but didn't avert my gaze.

"I worked in a factory for many years. After I was too old to work, I was granted a visa. I crossed into West Germany and made my way to France. I waited and watched. I didn't want to frighten Isabella, you see. She was elderly by then, already fragile and suspicious of strangers."

"But she would have known you," I argued.

He chuckled to himself. "I look very different."

"Why didn't you just tell her who you were?"

"I tried, but by the time I'd gathered my courage, her mind had slipped from view."

I touched his wizened hand. "Alzheimer's?"

He sighed so painfully, my throat closed around the lump. I swallowed and waited for him to continue. "I need to know, Max. I need to understand."

He put up his palm and shook his head. "It's a long story, and certain people would not be happy if they knew I was here. Or if I divulged these secrets."

"Who?"

He thinned his lips, refusing to answer.

I watched him for a moment. "The people who were following me? The people who broke into my apartment?"

His frown deepened until it took over his face. "You must be very careful, Alyssa. The war is not over for everyone. There are still many secrets."

"Please, Max. Tell me."

He stood and rapped his paper on his good leg. "No. I promised Isabella. Only she can divulge these secrets."

Chapter Twenty-Four

After leaving Max at his door, I triple-locked mine. I paced the living room as the late afternoon sunshine flowed into the windows. It warmed the apartment, so I opened all of them and enjoyed the breeze coming off the river.

Should I tell Anton who Max really was? It hardly seemed fair to involve the old man at this point. Would Anton interrogate him? Pressure him? No. I couldn't stand by and let that happen.

I knew Max, I mean François, from Isabella's journals. She'd loved him and trusted him. He'd protected her when no one else had.

I wouldn't rat him out. He deserved my protection in return.

Anton called that evening from his mother's house. "I needed to check on the place," he explained. "My mother took my sister and her family on a short trip to Arles. Would you like to come out here for the weekend? It's not far by train."

Sounded like a pretty flimsy excuse to me, but I'd never been outside Paris. I hesitated, but then decided to follow my lust instead of my good sense.

I needed to know where this relationship was headed. Maybe getting away from Paris, maybe being Anton the baker and Alyssa the tourist again, would help us find some common ground. If there was any.

I took down his instructions and promised to be on the eleven o'clock train the next morning.

That would give me time to finish boxing up the last of the most valuable *lapins* and take the final stash to the nearby bank for safe keeping.

****

I was coming out the front door of my building the next morning when I noticed Philippe and Dominique having coffee outside the little bistro on the corner.

Were they watching for me? Paranoia is a scary thing. It could be the couple wanted to meet me again 'by accident' to further their chances of marketing the apartment, but after my conversation with Max aka François, I was more suspicious than ever of everyone's motives.

Since I couldn't hide the two boxes of bunnies I had tucked in my carry bags, I decided to bluster my way through the encounter.

"Good morning," I said cheerfully as I passed their outdoor table under the striped awning.

"Ah, Alyssa," Dominique said. "We're so happy to see you. You have not answered my calls, so Philippe and I decided to have our coffee here this morning in hopes of seeing you."

That was pretty honest. "Yes, well, um, I haven't made much progress on the apartment. I didn't want anyone to see it yet, you understand."

"Would you like to join us?" Dominique held out her hand. Philippe jumped up to find me a chair.

"No, no. Thanks, anyway. I have a long list of errands today," I lied. I had a train to catch, but I wasn't letting anyone know I wouldn't be in Paris this weekend.

Philippe hadn't taken his gaze off my bags during the whole conversation. "Do you need help with those?" he asked in his overly helpful way. My hackles rose.

I glanced at my treasures. "Oh no, just some junk I'm going to donate at the church."

"We could drop it off for you. St. Paul's is on our way back to our office." Philippe held out a hand.

"That's okay." I pulled the bags back.

Dominique arched her finely drawn eyebrows with surprise. Damn. Was I too adamant with my refusal?

"Gotta go," I called cheerfully and started down the block toward Rue Victoria.

When I turned the corner, I checked over my shoulder before I entered the bank. The couple had finished their coffees and crossed the street in front of L'Hôtel de Ville.

Only after they rounded the corner, did I hurry inside the bank, knowing they wouldn't see me.

****

Lapins protected in the bank's three largest personal safe deposit boxes, I relaxed during the train ride to Port Villez. I'd sent Sam a short text, telling her where I would be, just in case, but I hadn't picked up the three times she'd called afterwards. I didn't want to worry. I didn't want to think too much. I wanted to feel.

Hopefully, Anton and I would know each other better after this weekend in different surroundings. If he didn't need to be the detective, and I didn't need to be a suspect in this twisted treasure hunt, maybe we could be Anton and Alyssa.

Could I leave Sophie and Isabella and François behind in their century and try to discover who I was in mine?

When I arrived at the tiny station, Anton waved to me from the platform. The sky was a miraculous shade of blue with only a few puffy clouds.

Dummy. Why was I thinking about clouds with Anton walking toward me? Dressed in jeans, a button down shirt and light weight tan jacket, he looked positively scrumptious. The plaid scarf draped around his neck shouted Frenchman. Only they could pull off the look. Unassuming. Adorable.

He kissed me on both cheeks and took my small weekend bag before leading me toward the village. We walked hand in hand through the tiny, cobblestone square, passed an old church built before America, and made our way along a quiet lane banked with tall hedgerows. The air was crystalline, and the birds were chirping their heads off as if they'd been hired for the job.

Anton unlocked a neatly painted gate and pushed through toward a rustic, thatched cottage.

"Oh, this is just too cute," I exclaimed as I studied the small windows and white-washed, flower-covered entry.

"I know." Anton opened the creaky front door for me. "My mother fell in love with the place years ago. After my father died, she spent most of her time and money caring for it."

"How old is it?"

We'd entered a low-ceilinged gathering room with terra-cotta floors and blackened beams partially buried in the plaster walls.

"This room was built before Napoleon." He closed the thick wooden door. "It was in ruins when my mother found it. Of course, she added onto the back of the house."

I cooed at the steep, winding staircase to the second floor and then followed Anton through an archway into a sunlit kitchen. Although blackened beams crisscrossed the ceiling and a rustic fireplace commanded one whole wall, the space had obviously been remodeled with care and attention.

I smoothed my hand across the old farm house sink—had to be original—and admired the deeply worn butcher-block island in the middle of the room. Sunlight poured in through three wide open multi-paned windows. As a breeze flowed over my face, I closed my eyes to enjoy the warmth and the smell of fresh bread.

Anton stood near the pantry, arms crossed, with a satisfied look on his face. "Do you like it?"

"Oh yes. It's a fantasy kitchen. And look, a marble baking area." I traced my hand along the gray veins of fine Carrera. "Did your mother do this? Design it, I mean?"

"She helped, but I knew what I wanted."

"You built this?"

A look of pride spread across his handsome features.

I tipped my head. Ah, had the real Anton finally appeared?

"So you do like to cook?"

"It is my passion." He drew out the ss's in that lovely French way.

I glanced around the room again, taking in the huge, red six-burner stove and the rows of glass-fronted, rich cherry cabinets. Then I moved closer to

Anton, close enough to feel his heat. "Can I kiss you?"

"But of course, *ma petite.*"

I wrapped my arms around his neck and dove in for a long, intense, I've-missed-you kiss. His heart pounded next to mine, and I could feel the heat coming off both of us. We didn't need a stove to cook.

He lifted me onto the counter, and I wrapped my legs around his waist. His groan interrupted the kiss.

He nibbled my neck and across the sensitive place just under my collar bone. I arched back and let him move toward my breast.

"Please, Anton. Please." I wanted him to touch me.

His hand reached under my shirt and up to my breast. My blood heated, the fire growing more intense. I hissed in a long sigh and smiled with my eyes still closed.

He suckled my breasts until I was panting with desire. "Please," I whispered in his ear. "I need you."

Although he replied in French, the words sounded like enthusiastic agreement.

I sat forward and ran my hands through his hair. He shivered when I nibbled on his ears with my lips. His beard, a little longer now, tickled my face. Then I kissed him again. Long, and hard, and dangerous.

I didn't care. I wanted him. I wanted this.

"Alyssa," he whispered in my ear. "My room—"

"Yes. Where?"

A key turning the door latch froze both of us in place. The sound of female voices had me back on my feet and adjusting my clothing.

"Ma mère," he growled under his breath.

Although my face burned with embarrassment, I was at least presentable by the time two women, one younger, one older, walked through the door.

His mother looked surprised to see us standing there. The younger, his sister I assumed, took one look and smirked at her brother's predicament.

I knew instantly they were all related. His mother's eyes were the identical color. The same finely-shaped eyebrows rose in surprise as she took in the scene.

"Uh, *Maman*. This is Alyssa," Anton choked out. "And Gabrielle, my sister."

A long silence ensued.

"*Enchantée*, Alyssa," his sister finally said. "Are you not the American girl?"

I cleared my throat a few times before I found my voice. "Yes, I'm from California." I shot Anton my own questioning glance.

He looked the other way.

"Your aunt, she is the one Anton has wanted to speak with," his sister said. "The one who—"

"Yes," Anton interrupted. "Alyssa is helping my team with the case."

"Have you—?"

Anton shook his head.

I watched the silent repartee between sister and brother and crossed my arms. My guess? There were few family secrets here.

Finally, Anton's mother recovered from her surprise and placed her shopping bags on the counter. She moved toward us, put out her hand to welcome me, speaking clear English in a clipped accent.

"I am sorry, Alyssa. Anton is not always forthcoming with his plans. We would have been here to greet you, if only we had known you were coming." She shot Anton a fierce look of disapproval, but then she turned to me and gave me a glorious smile, her face as expressive as her son's.

"Please. Come sit in the lounge. We will have tea and get to know one another. Anton?"

He looked about ten years old when he answered. *"Oui."*

"You will make tea."

"Of course."

"And maybe some scones?"

He rubbed his chin a moment and then smiled at me. "Blueberry?"

"Wonderful." His mother answered before I had a chance. "Alyssa and I will need some time."

I brushed a wayward curl from my face. Oh, boy.

****

"Idiot. What were you thinking, Anton?" Gabby asked in a hushed tone after Mother led Alyssa from the kitchen.

I glanced over my shoulder. "Wasn't."

She let out an older-sister snort.

"I-we…we got carried away." I never blush, but right now my ears were burning. "I thought you two were gone for the weekend."

"We changed our plans at the last moment." Gabby nibbled on the blueberries I'd pulled from the fridge. "It's supposed to rain Monday morning, and Mama didn't want to drive home in the storm."

I grunted.

Leaning against the counter, she idly watched me fill the copper kettle and place it on the stove.

"She's pretty," Gabby said nonchalantly.

"Oui."

"You like her?"

I shot her a don't-push-your-luck stare but then shrugged one shoulder and nodded. I rubbed the back of my neck. Maybe more than like?

She hummed to herself for a moment as I measured out the ingredients and prepared the scones for baking. I did the work automatically, and found my annoyance dissipating as I worked the dough with my fingers. As I shaped and cut the triangles, the tightness in my shoulders relaxed. My heart beat in a gentle rhythm. It had always been this way.

Gabby strolled over to the cupboard and pulled out four oversized tea cups from the shelf. She measured a few spoons of *Thé de Bergamot* from the tin into my mother's favorite teapot, and waited for the now bubbling kettle to hiss.

I watched my competent sister and grimaced. Four years older than me, Gabriella had always acted superior. In my mother's eyes, she'd always been an angel, married now and with a baby my mother adored beyond reason.

Although I had taken up my father's position after his sudden death, I'd never felt content with the role. Never felt the satisfaction he'd always had from the job.

Even when my team was successful in locating treasures from someone's past, I found myself wishing I could do something else. Like bake macarons. I pursed my lips. Pitiful.

"When you solve this case, Anton, you should promote Bruno and open that little pâtisserie you've always dreamed about."

I glanced at her in surprise.

"*Quoi?*" she asked with her palms up. "You think we don't know this is what you love? Mother would say the same if you asked her."

I set the timer on the oven. "I need to finish my job."

"I know. It's a matter of family honor for you—to finish what father started. One of these days, you should go and search out your own treasure."

****

After twenty minutes of polite but thorough interrogation by Madame de Ville, I pretended I needed to visit the toilette. I excused myself, but when I heard voices, I tip-toed closer toward the kitchen door and stopped to listen. I caught most of the last few words of Anton's conversation with his sister. Face it, I'm a snoop. My heart tugged at Anton's dilemma, and I leaned against the wall for a moment.

I slipped into the guest bath, smiling at my reflection in the mirror, and made the decision I'd been wrestling with for days.

Perhaps I *could* trust Anton. I'd help him solve the mystery of Sophie's treasure and after that, well, after that we'd see where things stood. I would tell him what I knew. When we returned to Paris, I would show him Isabella's journals.

Perhaps he could help me find the missing journals Max had hinted about, and the lost pages from the first green book. Better yet, the treasure itself. With the necklace returned to his family, Anton would be freed of his father's obligation.

Relief lightened my footsteps back to the parlor. The smell of scones and Thé de Bergamot sweetened the air. Anton looked up and smiled at me. My heart warmed with happiness, and I returned his smile.

****

Dinner would be unbelievable. I all but drooled as I helped Anton prepare it. Duck à l'orange and fresh, out-of-the-ground finger potatoes baked with cream and cheese until crisp and fragrant. Roasted spring vegetables, harvested from the garden outside and sizzling with fresh olive oil and garlic. Heaven.

While dinner was cooking, Anton insisted I help him make macarons. We whipped up pistachio cream to fill the crisp cookies.

"Where are those trays to bake the cookies on?" I asked, as he finished adding the sweet mixture of almond flour, chocolate and sugar to the whipped egg whites.

"*Comment?*"

"You know, the silicon trays to make the perfect round cookies? Like the kit I bought at the BHV."

There. I'd finally seen it—a Frenchman with his nose in the air. The rumors were true.

"A pâtisserie does not use such a device." He twisted the pastry bag he'd filled with dough and precisely lined the cookies along the cooking tray, each exactly the same diameter and thickness.

I leaned my elbows on the counter, watching with fascination. "And you told me you weren't precise."

He chuckled. "Do you want to try?"

I put out my palms, ready to decline, but Anton handed me the bag and held it over the pan with me. "It is in the rhythm, *ma petite*," he said quietly in my ear.

"M-m-m, I see."

Most of my efforts turned out a bit lumpy, but by the end of the second tray I was getting the hang of it.

"*Bon.*" Anton popped the batch in the oven.

I licked the spoon and sighed at the rich flavor. The

kitchen filled with the magical smell of baking chocolate.

Anton reached over and kissed me gently on the lips, drawing his hand through my thatch of curls. He studied my face for a moment. "Tonight?"

I glanced into the living room, and he understood my concern.

"I have my own cottage."

My heart leapt into my throat. I had to swallow hard, but I nodded. "Tonight."

****

Gabby left after dinner, with a knowing smirk on her face. A few minutes later, Anton's mother, whom I must now call Veronica, excused herself, saying she was tired and would retire early.

I helped Anton finish loading the dishwasher, and we cleaned up the kitchen.

"Would you like to take a walk in the orchard?" he suggested.

I pulled my sweater from my bag and followed him through the back door. The soft golden twilight held for a long time this late in spring. Budding fruit trees cast long purple shadows across the lush grass. We walked hand in hand.

"I want to make a confession," I finally said.

"I am not a priest, Alyssa."

I chuckled. "I certainly hope not."

His smile flashed in the evening light, and he swung his arm over my shoulder in a quiet, familiar way. "What is worrying you?"

"Well…" I choked, but then let the story flow. It took a while to explain Isabella's history.

Anton listened without comment.

"So I need your advice, Anton. First, I need to find the other journal, or journals. Second, I need to protect Max...I mean François. And third—"

"You need to know who watches you—who wants the treasure."

"Yes, if there is a treasure, and if I—we—can find it."

We stopped in a quiet glen at the rear of the garden. An iron bench stood under a gnarled apple tree. We sat together, still holding hands in the sweet night air.

"I think we should move you from the apartment," Anton suggested. "Then I will have my team—"

"No, Anton." I turned toward him and put my palm to his chest. "Isabella wanted me to figure this out. I'm sorry, but she didn't trust the police. Besides, now that I know Bruno was the one watching me and the one who came into the apartment, there's no real danger. François—"

He grimaced and took hold of my wrist. "Bruno was not the one who destroyed your efforts, Alyssa. Remember? Someone else, someone with a great deal of anger, knows of Sophie's secrets and probably the treasure."

"François is next door."

"That old man? He cannot protect you."

I squeezed his hand. "Give me a few days. Please. I owe Isabella at least that much. She was so..."

"Stubborn?"

"Brave." I smiled up into his eyes and kissed him gently. He pulled me closer and soothed his strong hands over my arms. Goosebumps followed his clever fingers. We touched tongues, exploring, heating.

"Do you suppose—" I whispered in his ear. "—your mother has gone to sleep?"

Without another word, Anton led me to the cottage up the hill. The passion consumed us so rapidly, we barely made it through his front door.

I pulled the jacket off his shoulders and tossed it on the floor at the same time as I shed my shoes and then my sweater.

He had my blouse unbuttoned before we reached his bedroom.

I couldn't help giggling when he picked me up and carried me to the bed. The duvet was soft, the pillows luxurious.

He kicked off his shoes and lay next to me. "Alyssa," he sighed in my ear, "I have been patient."

"Very patient," I agreed as I wrapped my arms around his strong body.

He'd found my breast and suckled gently—at first.

I moaned, reacting to the sweet tightness his touch incited.

He caressed me with more need, and I arched my back as the joyous sensations overtook me. Heat pumped through my body but soon focused at my core.

I snuggled closer, moving my hands over his strong back and shoulders. "Now, Anton. I'm not patient."

He chuckled, driving me crazy with his talented fingers and kisses.

I undid his belt and as I drew my hands over his groin he arched into me. I smiled, knowing the satisfaction that awaited me.

Then I unzipped him, very slowly.

I helped him shed the rest of his clothes, and my mouth went dry. He was gorgeous. His hard muscles and tan skin shimmered in the soft twilight.

"Anton."

Soon I was naked, and his skin was warm and smooth against mine.

Closer. I needed to be closer.

The heat between us blistered. My breath panted out short and shallow. I knew he couldn't hold out much longer. I didn't want to either.

He grabbed my hand. "Be careful, Alyssa. I am fighting for my life here."

I bent over and touched him with my tongue, slowly caressing him in my hands. He hissed, and flipped me on my back.

"You are a very wicked American."

"I hope so," I said as we kissed and joined. I couldn't help but cry out with pleasure. When he pulled back, I held him tightly to me. "Perfect."

We remained still and stared at each other for a moment. Then he smiled.

"*Très bien*?" he asked, pushing just slightly.

Frissons of pleasure coursed through me. I closed my eyes and sighed. "Oh, yes, Anton. *Très bien*."

Chapter Twenty-Five

The smell of coffee woke me in the morning. I searched my bed for Alyssa and then heard shuffling and a quiet feminine curse in the next room.

"Sorry," she whispered, peeking her head into the doorway. "I was looking for coffee cups."

I sat up. Before I could cover myself effectively, Allyssa's eyes grew wide. She sauntered into the room. Dressed only in my unbuttoned shirt, she never took her gaze off me and mine.

"I think coffee can wait." She took off her glasses and gave me a seductive smile.

With one hand on my shoulder, she pushed me down on the bed and straddled my torso with her long legs. She stripped off the shirt and shook out her hair. Wild and curly from a night of lovemaking, it glowed in a bright halo around her beautiful face.

I drew my hands down her thighs and then reached up to fondle her breasts, their soft color warmed by the morning light. I stroked and kissed them gently. Her nipples pebbled and responded to my touch. She hummed that adorable American hum of hers and arched her back.

Slowly, she took me in. For a few moments, her strokes were slow and gentle, and we enjoyed playing with the rhythm of our pleasure. Soon her eyes lost focus, and she demanded more. Faster. Harder.

She climaxed the first time in only a few more strokes, and I relished the fierce, hot pleasure that flashed across her face. I wanted my fill but more slowly this time.

She was a treasure that needed to be discovered, more than any other I had searched for. I lay beside her, caressing her as she recovered her breath, then knelt and tasted her flesh. Honey. Passion. Heat.

She arched into me, moaning softly. I kissed her gently, moving my fingers within her until she climaxed again. Harder. Higher. Only then did I take her, filling her, possessing her in deep strokes. The last rise to heaven was the longest, the slowest, the most precious.

"Look at me, Alyssa."

She opened her beautiful blue eyes and put her hands to my face. She never looked away.

We found insanity at the top and tumbled back to reality only after cresting and re-cresting.

The coffee grew cold.

****

I almost managed not to blush as I said good-bye to Anton's mother late the next morning. Unbelievably friendly, she kissed me on both cheeks and waved *au revoir* from the gate.

Anton drove me back to Paris that afternoon. What had taken more than an hour on the train took less than thirty minutes by motorway.

Avoiding the one ton rabbit sitting between us in the car, we talked about the views along the way, watching the Seine when it appeared and disappeared behind the lush green hills dotted with adorable farms and fat white cows.

The cityscape grew more dense, with apartments rising and industrial areas crowding together. This modern part of the city could have been almost anywhere, even Sereno, except for the French directional signs and the markers denoting kilometers per hour.

I rested my head against the seat back and fell into a deep sleep. It was only when Anton whispered my name that I realized we were parked near the Quai de Gevres. I stretched and smiled. "Want to come up?"

"Yes," Anton agreed, "More than anything, but I need to finish some work—a few reports." He rotated his hand and then shrugged. "Can I bring dinner later? Perhaps nine?"

"Sure." I gathered my bag and jacket from the backseat. "I need to talk to my mother on the computer and fill her in on a few things. Maybe I can finish clearing the bedroom by then?" Leaning in closer to give him a kiss, I wiggled my eyebrows suggestively.

I opened the passenger door, but Anton grabbed my hand. "Alyssa. Don't open the door to anyone."

I grimaced at his concern. "You're overreacting."

"No."

"Nothing has happened in weeks."

"Use Isabella's locks." He drew my hand to his lips. "Please?"

I let out a little sigh. "O-kay."

"Until we find the treasure."

"*If* there still is a treasure."

"Until we find it, you may be in danger."

A taxi behind us honked. I nodded, and he released my hand. With a quick salute, I hurried to the sidewalk.

****

I waved to François—I mean, Max—as I exited the elevator. My knees were still shaky from all the 'exercise' I'd indulged in this weekend. As I closed my door behind me, I stared at the orchestra of Isabella's locks and flipped more than half. There. That should satisfy my French worry-wart.

I let out a long sigh of satisfaction. No, it was more than sexual satisfaction. I closed my eyes and hummed a little tune to myself. It was happiness. Maybe joy. Maybe even…

"Don't go there, Alyssa." I cautioned my reflection. We hadn't used the L word yet. There were so many issues still to be resolved in our brand new relationship. Like Anton lived in Paris, and my life was centered in California.

One thing I was sure of. After this weekend: neither of us would be satisfied with an online, half-way-across-the-world affair.

I didn't want to think about what it would be like to lose Anton now, to walk away from him. To watch him walk away from me. I swallowed the tears in my throat and sucked in a deep breath.

"Then don't think about it," I said under my breath. "Reality will come down on us like…like World War II soon enough."

I would enjoy the moment. And the man.

I dumped my bag on the floor near the hall tree and headed for the bath, shedding my clothes while I walked through the bedroom. Hot water, bubbles, and more hot water sounded fabulous right now. I turned on the taps full force and grabbed a fresh towel as lavender scented water steamed into my tub.

****

I combed back the wet curls from my face and scrunched the bottom edges with my fingers to encourage the waves. I slipped into plaid jammy pants and a comfy T-shirt and hurried to the kitchen.

Soon the kettle sang. I longed for caffeine, and the smell of cinnamon and orange rose from my cup.

A hesitant knock at my door surprised me, but I smiled. Anton must have finished earlier than he expected.

When I peeked through the eye hole and saw Max, I didn't hesitate to open the door. "Hey, Max. What are you doing—?"

The look of fear on his face stopped me, and I gripped the doorknob nervously. Then I saw the gun. My pulse pushed higher.

"I have seen a ghost," Max whispered.

I didn't understand. Then Philippe appeared from around the corner of the stairs. With a smirk, he shoved Max toward me. I caught the old man as he stumbled into my arms.

"Philippe? I don't understand. What do you want?" I cried out as he waved his gun and marched us into the living room. He roughly pushed both Max and me down onto the couch and pointed the gun at my face. I put up my hands, and they shook with fear. Cold fear.

"He wants the treasure," Max explained. His voice shook and I noticed the bruise on the side of his head. Had Philippe hit him?

"What?"

Philippe's face, usually so composed, twisted with anger. "Don't pretend you don't know what this traitor means. The treasure—the jewels and money that old bitch hid away." His polite accent had disappeared.

"I don't—"

"Give it to me," he shouted, pointing the gun at Max. "Give it to me, or I'll kill him, just like he killed my grandfather."

"I don't have any treasure," I said as calmly as I could, but a quiver rattled my words. "Please, Philippe. You're welcome to the *lapins*, but honestly, there's nothing—"

He slapped my face, and I cried out. My cheek stung, and my eyes teared up. I gritted my teeth to control my fury.

Max cursed under his breath, and even in angry French, I caught the word Nazi in his rant.

Tall, blond...Aryan. I bit my lip. "Rainier?" I asked Max.

"His grandson."

Philippe leaned over us. "You think I don't know? You think you can keep it all to yourself? You think you can trick me, as you tricked him?"

The gun, so close to my face, was still aimed at Max. Was Philippe crazed enough to shoot my friend? I watched in horror as his finger tightened on the trigger.

"No," I shouted. I dove for Philippe's knees and toppled him to the hard floor. I heard the crack of his head against the wood. The gun fired, and ceiling plaster rained down on us, but the gun slid across the slippery wooden floor.

As I sat on the half conscious man, Max rose and picked up the weapon. He could move pretty fast in a crisis.

Max stood over us, pointing the gun at Philippe. He cocked the trigger and pointed the muzzle at the struggling man's head. "One more dead Nazi won't matter to me."

"Put down the weapon, Max," Anton ordered. He and Bruno stood in the hallway, weapons trained on us. They entered the room, and after a moment's hesitation, Max reluctantly handed the gun to Bruno. Anton helped me rise, but I didn't relax until they'd handcuffed Philippe.

"How did you know?" I asked Anton as he led me to my chair by the window.

Claire appeared from somewhere and helped Bruno lead Philippe, still stunned, out of my apartment. She gave Anton a long, silent look as they closed the door.

"Anton," I repeated. "How did you know we were in trouble?"

"They were listening," Max said from the couch.

Anton wouldn't meet my gaze.

"Listening?" The realization hit me like a marble rabbit in the face, and my stomach clenched with anger. "Bugs? You bugged me?"

"Only for your safety, *ma petite*."

I stood and moved closer to him. Nose to nose, I stared him down. "How long?"

His gaze dropped to his shoes. "Since you arrived."

He reached to take my hand, but I dodged his grasp. "*Ma petite*? You really do think I'm a little American idiot? Someone you can lie to? Someone you can use?"

"Alyssa."

"No, not again. Just get out."

****

Alyssa pointed her finger toward the door, her face a furious mask.

How could I make her listen?

I glanced at the old man sitting on the couch. Max leaned his head against the cushions. Pale, almost gray, he gasped in short breaths, and held his fist to his chest.

Before Alyssa even had a chance to look, I'd grabbed my phone and called for an ambulance.

"Max." Alyssa's voice sounded worried. "Max?" She was at his side.

The old man's head lolled sideways, unconscious.

****

Alyssa wouldn't leave the hospital. She sat outside the critical care unit and waited, hour after hour. I brought her coffee and food, a blanket and clean clothes.

She wouldn't go home, no matter what I said.

Claire sat with her at times. Even Bruno brought dinner to share one evening.

A very old man cannot survive heart surgery, the doctors said. We must wait to see if he rallied.

On the third day, when Alyssa spoke his name, Max opened his eyes for a moment. He called her Isabella but took her hand and smiled.

She kissed him on the cheek, and he fell into an easier rest.

Max woke up two days later and asked for ice cream. Alyssa brought him four flavors of Bertillon.

He smiled at her and called her by her right name. The doctors seemed surprised he had made it this far. He might have a chance yet.

While we waited those days in the hall, Alyssa shared the story of the romance between Isabella and François. To live through that much heartbreak and loneliness and still be able to smile, that took courage.

If the old man did survive, we might learn more

about the secrets he'd kept all these years. He might just make it. After all, he'd survived a world war, starvation, Nazi internment and Soviet hard labor.

Even after she relayed the stories about the couple, I suspected Alyssa was holding back some of the details she'd learned in the journals. There were secrets she had yet to share with me. I knew better than to push. She needed to trust me, and I was doing my damnedest to make that happen.

Max was discharged from the hospital a week later, still frail, still needing around-the-clock care. Alyssa hired nurses and hovered over her patient.

Philippe Simone stubbornly refused to confess or explain his motivations in the attack. I could hold him on attempted murder charges but was no closer to solving the mystery behind the threat on Alyssa's life. I still suspected Simone's wife, Dominique, of complicity but couldn't prove a thing.

Most frustrating of all? Alyssa refused to answer any of my questions.

"Wait," she insisted when I pressed her.

She wouldn't leave her apartment when I offered her protection or show me Isabella's journal, even though she spoke of it often. I could have forced the issue, procured a warrant, but where would that get me?

Arms crossed and foot tapping, she'd supervised the removal of the listening devices. She seemed most annoyed about the one in her enormous purse.

Chapter Twenty-Six

May Day. The holiday commemorates the war dead of France and the French know how to celebrate. Everyday business stops. Families get together. There are parades and ceremonies and ladies selling little white flowers on every street corner.

I slept in.

I took a late morning walk and bought a few bunches of the lilies, came home, and sat in my favorite chair by the window. Even the ripples on the Seine had taken the day off. The water looked like glass, reflecting the beautiful bridges crossing it.

Max invited me to his apartment for tea. Well, actually his nurse knocked on my door and relayed the message.

I hurried over to his apartment and found him sitting in a chair by his window. Although still pale, he looked much better than he had in weeks. The meals his nurse cooked for him, and stood over him while he ate, had filled out his face and brightened his eyes.

I took the chair positioned next to him and poured the tea his caretaker had supplied. "You look great, Max."

His eyes squinted with a smile. "Thanks to you." He tipped his head toward the day nurse now working in his tiny kitchen. "And the series of dragons you hired to order me around."

"For your own good, my friend."

Max leaned closer to my ear. "I need to speak with you, Alyssa. Alone."

His serious expression caught me by surprise. "Want me to excuse the dragon?"

"Please."

I offered the woman an extra hour for lunch, and she left without a problem. As soon as the door closed behind her, Max relaxed in his chair.

I took his hand and rubbed his paper-thin skin to warm the cold flesh. His fingernails were still slightly blue. I frowned.

"Don't fuss, Alyssa."

"I worry about you as Isabella did."

Max blinked his rheumy eyes and sucked in a long breath. "I have some information to share with you."

I waited for him to draw another breath and continue.

"Isabella did know me." He dropped his chin. "Once, anyway. She recognized me. Knew my name."

"When?" I sat forward. "You mean when you came back from East Germany?"

He nodded and brushed aside a tear. "Most days she was confused, but one day I had played a Vivaldi recording on my old stereo. My door was open to help catch the breeze, and she happened to walk by my apartment on her way out."

"Vivaldi. The music…?"

"She walked in and gave me the strangest look."

"She knew you. Knew you were François?" I squeezed his hand. "Oh, Max."

He smiled a brief smile and nodded. "She walked over to me and touched my face, then took my hand and led me back to her apartment. It was a horrible mess…"

"I know."

"But she went right to a little book on the table by her bed. An old copy of *Les Miserables.*"

My heart was beating so hard, I had to take a couple deep breaths of my own to slow my pulse.

Max stared at the ceiling for a moment as if to recreate that moment precisely, perfectly. "She said. 'It's here François. The proof. If they ever come for you, I have the proof.' "

"What did she mean?"

He looked at me and gave a long, exhausted sigh. "Go. Find that book. It's red."

"I remember it. I know which one you mean."

"Find it, and then you will know our secret. It is time." He leaned back in his chair. His shoulders sagged, and he closed his eyes.

I took his pulse, and when I was confident he was safe, I kissed him on the cheek and hurried to my apartment.

I looked around the space. Where was that book? I'd moved so many copies of *Les Miserables*, I wasn't sure where to start.

I dug through the books on the office shelf. Not there.

I searched the desk. No.

I chewed my fingernail for a moment. I hadn't taken any of the hardbacks to the church, so it must still be here.

I walked back into the living room and remembered the books on the Indian-style trunk. Under three other editions, I found one small red copy of Victor Hugo's novel. Well read, a little abused. No one would have paid a euro for it at the little green *bouquinistes.*

I opened it and noticed the back few pages were stuck together. My pulse started to kick up. With painstaking care, I pulled the glued pages apart, revealing the folded journal inside.

I sat down on the couch with a thunk. "The missing pages," I whispered to myself.

Pages in hand, I raced back to tell Max. "I found them," I called as I opened his door, but he was asleep in his chair and hardly stirred, even as I approached.

I took his pulse once more, covered him with a light throw, and then I tiptoed out. I settled on my couch and flipped through the pages of the dairy. Would I now have the answers to my questions? It began mid paragraph.

****

…I padded my way to the window and peeked out, careful not to open it farther—it would have squeaked.

Below, a small kerosene lantern glowed in the garden, and someone, a man in dark clothing, moved slowly around the courtyard.

I listened carefully and finally recognized the sound. Digging. I sat down on the cool tile floor under the window. Why was someone digging in the garden? If they wanted to steal our still-green tomatoes, they could just pick them. They didn't need to dig them up.

A man's voice grunted and cursed as if he were lifting something. "Rainier?" I whispered in the dark. Even though I recognized his voice, a cold shiver crawled down my spine.

I raced through the apartment and down the stairs. I didn't stop to dress or put on shoes. I arrived in my nightdress, breathless, and whispered his name.

He turned quickly. I knew I'd surprised him, but the look on his face frightened me. I took a step back. It had to be the upward slant of the lantern that made him look so fierce.

"Rainier, what are you doing?"

"Go back upstairs, darling. I'll join you in a few minutes." He tried to make his voice sound light and smooth, but I could hear the tension behind the words. He turned and widened his stance, as if he were hiding something.

"I've been waiting for you. Where have you—?"

"Go inside, Isabella," he hissed through clenched teeth.

The lantern light reflected off the shovel he held in his hand. For a moment I thought he might raise it. My heart pounded painfully, and suddenly there was no air in the courtyard.

Rainier stepped toward me. His coat lay on the bench. I recognized the insignia on the collar and gasped.

"Why are you wearing that uniform, Rainier?"

"Because he's a Nazi." The voice came from behind me.

François stepped out of the darkness. I stepped into the light.

I covered my mouth with my hand, but my racing heart slowed, and my breath ceased to struggle. I looked Rainier up and down, and the pieces of the puzzle formed a new and frightening picture.

Rainier sneered. "And what will you do about it, François? You and your pitiful French Army? The Third Reich has taken Paris without so much as a whimper. We will take the rest of the world—"

"Not America," I shouted, hands fisting at my sides.

"Even America, *dar-ling*. Do you think those pitiful cowards in Washington will stand long against us when they are alone in the world? We will bomb England to ruins, and then Roosevelt will buckle like every other leader now under the Third Reich's control."

I turned to François. "How long?" I pointed at Rainier.

"Years," François spat the words. "We learned a few months back that his father was very highly placed in the Nazi party. Since then Sophie and I have been watching him. Rainier isn't his real name. He's a spy."

Rainier tipped up his chin. "As are you, François."

My heart dropped to my belly. "Where's Sophie?" There was panic in my voice. I didn't care.

Rainier didn't move.

François stepped closer, and in the stronger light, I saw fear on his face. "I came to find her. She missed our rendezvous."

A click sounded, echoing through the small courtyard. We both turned. Lamplight glistened off the gun in Rainier's hand.

Although Rainier followed me with the weapon, its dark muzzle a black hole of threat, I moved slowly to the place where he'd been digging. My gaze never left his.

"Come away with me, darling," Rainier said, his voice honey smooth, like we'd just made love and were content in each other's arms. "There's no need to be afraid. I promise. I will take care of you."

I glanced down.

Sophie lay crumbled in the newly dug grave, her head positioned at a horrible angle. I cried out and covered my mouth, afraid I'd be sick. I backed away, nearly tripping over the soft mound of dirt.

Seething hatred flashed through me. "You killed her."

Rainier's smile twisted into an ugly, thin line. "Stupid bitch. She had something I needed. Wouldn't tell me, would she? I had to kill her." His eyes narrowed to glittering slits. "Perhaps you can help me, darling?"

"No."

"I know Sophie has hidden valuable jewels somewhere. We captured a Jew who lived near here as he tried to escape. After a bit of 'persuasion', the coward told us he'd left his wealth with this—this traitor." Rainier's mouth sneered in a horrible grimace.

I shivered in the warm air.

Rainier moved the gun toward François, and my skin went cold. "Tell me, darling. Where is the treasure?"

"Rainier, please." I pleaded. "We're your friends…"

François gave a short, sardonic laugh. "He's never been our friend, Isabella. He's a coward and a spy. He used us. He used you."

I shook my head, trying to clear the confusion and terror. "No. I loved him."

François stuck his chin forward in defiance. "He's married, Isabella."

"I don't believe it."

"Ask him."

I looked Rainier in the eye and knew François spoke the truth. I was a fool. There was no love there. "Why?"

Rainier shrugged. "You are beautiful, darling Isabella, but also convenient. I needed a cover to watch Sophie. She was my assignment."

I choked back my horror.

"Ironic, don't you think, my darling? You've sinned even more than you knew." He gave a bark of cruel laughter and turned a ring on his smallest finger.

Sophie's ring.

My vision went white, then red. I don't remember moving, but I grabbed Rainier by the arms and struggled with him. Cold metal pressed against my heart. Strengthened by fury, I pushed it away.

The gun went off. I heard a shout, but my anger overwhelmed my sense. I fought with him. Screamed at him. Pounded him. He was strong, but I was powered by rage.

He would have shot me, but somehow I grabbed the white-hot barrel of the gun. I cried out with pain but twisted it hard. Another deafening shot rang out.

The smell of gun powder choked me. I waited for pain. It didn't come.

Rainier's face went white, and he slipped from my arms. After he hit the ground, he drew one gasping breath. His eyes glazed over.

He was dead.

I stared at him, unable to move.

François's moan of pain freed me. I ran to him. He clutched his leg to stop the bleeding, but I could see the wound wasn't serious. I helped him tie it off.

"Is he dead?"

I gulped back a sob and nodded. I had no words. Shock washed over me, cold then hot. I had to help François, so I sucked in a few more deep breaths. My vision cleared.

"You must bury him," François said quietly.

"Can't…"

"You must. If the Nazis even suspect you killed him, they'll put you in front of a firing squad. Or worse."

I gulped again and shivered. "Here?"

François nodded. "I'll help you." He stood but leaned heavily on the bench. His face white with pain, he gritted his teeth. I helped him sit.

"Give me a minute," François grunted. Sweat dripped from his brow.

I shook my head. "I-I can do it." I pushed myself toward the body.

The hole was deep enough for two. Rainier had wanted to hide his own crime well.

I stood over the grave, crossed myself, and said a quick prayer for Sophie. "You were always so much wiser, Sophie. Now I know why you didn't like him." I picked up the shovel to move it out of the way. "I'm sorry you'll spend eternity together."

I looked at Rainier's ghastly face: his half-open eyes and dead man's slack jaw. I took his still warm hand, pulled the sapphire ring from his finger, and put it in my pocket. Tears seared my face. At least he wouldn't carry Sophie's precious ring into hell with him.

It took all my strength to roll Rainier's body into the grave. It landed with a horrible thud, and I shuddered. Bile rose in my throat. I gritted my teeth and fought down the revulsion.

I had work to do. Although my hand burned with pain, I shoveled the loose soil over the bodies.

"Hand me the gun," François ordered, his voice rough.

I complied, but reached for it when he started to clean it off.

"Isabella, let me do this." He clamped his fingers tightly to the handgrip and then returned it wrapped in his shirt. He relaxed and laid his head back on the bench. "This way no one will ever blame you."

I stepped toward the grave to hide my actions from François's view. I wiped off the gun with the shirt and tossed them both in the grave. Now there would be no fingerprints. No proof. No one to blame.

My throat seared with pain. I expected tears, but none came. I shoveled the rest of the dense, wet soil into the grave. In order to enlarge the space, Rainier had dug up the paving stones around the back edge of the garden. I stamped the soil with my bare feet and replaced them the best I could.

Perhaps I would plant an even larger garden. Something Sophie would be proud of. I brushed off my filthy hands and slipped the sapphire ring onto my finger.

Sophie had died protecting the people she loved. Now I must protect them. It was the least I could do for my best friend.

Filthy, exhausted, and drained, I helped François up the stairs and back into the apartment. I tended his wound. The bullet had exited his thigh. He hadn't lost much blood. I washed his leg carefully and then bandaged it. It would take time, but he would heal.

When I'd finished the job, I suddenly went cold and shivered. "Do you think anyone heard the gunshots?" I asked as I helped François to bed.

He shook his head. "Haven't most of your neighbors left the city?"

I nodded.

He grunted as he lay down in Sophie's big bed. "I didn't see any lights come on above us, or heads pop out of a window."

I sagged onto the chair beside the bed. "Oh, François. What have I done?" My hand throbbed.

He closed his eyes. "You have joined the war, Isabella."

****

Murder. I swallowed the last of my cold tea.

No wonder Isabella was so frightened. Resting my head on the couch cushions, I stared at the ceiling. I took a few long breaths. This event had warped the rest of Isabella's life, and frozen her with gut-wrenching fear. I turned back to the last few entries.

****

June 30, 1940

I insisted François stay in bed for a week. While he slept, I paced the floor, wondering how to extricate myself from this horrible mess.

Fortunately, no one had pounded on the door, asking for Rainier. Yet.

"Why would they?" François said as I fed him soup. "I'm sure he didn't broadcast his affair."

I groaned at the thought. I had loved a man, slept with him, and all that time, he had a wife. I felt sick and swallowed hard.

"I feel sorry for his wife," François pointed out.

I nodded but couldn't say more.

Later that afternoon, I wandered into the sickroom where my patient rested.

"What else do you know about Rainier?"

His face cringed with pain, but I don't think it was his leg that was hurting. "You don't want to know."

I thought about it for a moment and then knelt next to the chaise where he was stretched out. "Yes, I do. Please. Everything."

He turned toward the wall for a moment, perhaps debating with himself, but he finally faced me and began the story. "Sophie and I didn't know in the beginning, *ma bella*, who Rainier was, what he was. We would have warned you. You must believe me."

"I do."

"You weren't the only one Rainier fooled. Neither Sophie nor I would have ever put you in danger."

With a brief smile, I patted his arm.

His shoulders relaxed. "Last summer I began to suspect Rainier was more than he said." He fiddled with his bandage for a moment. "I was jealous."

I dropped my gaze. "I know." I folded my hand into his.

"I followed him—" he continued "—at first, just around Paris when he was in town. Often he would disappear for days."

"He had business."

"No, darling. He had a wife in Alsace. Her name was Simone."

I licked my lips and swallowed. "Alsace," I repeated. "I met Rainier at the train station one time when he returned from a trip. He told me he traveled there to visit his parents."

"He probably did. His father's the local leader of the Nazi party."

"Children?"

"Yes, a son."

I drew little patterns on the floor, trying to picture Rainier with a son. Would the child look like him? Blond, blue eyed.

Aryan? Another chill washed over me.

I closed my eyes and pinched my lips. Why hadn't I seen this before? I'd let my love, my lust for Rainier blind me to his real purpose. His evil.

"Sophie and I informed the underground about him. We eventually learned he was gathering information for the Nazis."

"The clothing business?"

"A well fleshed-out cover. He was charged with the collection of information on valuable objects, paintings, gold—"

"Jewels?"

François's face looked grim. "Hitler wants it all."

****

July 8, 1940

For days François and I waited for *that* knock on the door, but still no one came looking for Rainier. Since Sophie was often absent, none of the returning neighbors suspected anything had happened to her.

François slowly healed. Eventually I could look at myself in the mirror again. One morning as I brushed my hair, a thought struck me.

Before that horrible night in the garden, I'd broken nine out of ten commandments—some unknowingly. Counting my latest sin—killing Rainier, I'd completed the number.

I pinched my lips together. Even if the Germans didn't know what happened to him, sooner or later someone would ask about Sophie. I twisted my hair between my fingers and stared at its pale length.

Then I knew how to fight my war.

Chapter Twenty-Seven

Alyssa invited me to dinner at Le Bouquet. She said she would meet me there. I ducked through the narrow corridor into the main room precisely at eight. She smiled at me. She'd already ordered wine.

I sat across from her. This was her gig, as the Americans say. I waited for her to begin.

She took a sip of her wine. "I know where the real Sophie is. And Philippe's grandfather too."

I frowned. "Did they run off to Argentina together?"

"No, silly." She opened her menu. "Shall we have frogs' legs again?"

I dropped my head into my hands. "You're not going to tell me, are you?"

"Not yet." A wicked smile crossed her face.

"But you will?"

"Yes."

"Okay. Frogs' legs it is."

After dinner and a couple bottles of excellent red wine, we strolled across the bridge and stopped mid-stream to view the almost-full moon shining over the city. Its reflection sparkled in the Seine. The night smelled sweet with summer flowers.

Alyssa sighed, "So beautiful."

Finally, she allowed me to enter her apartment, the first time since the crime scene tape had been taken down. I sat on the couch. She offered me wine.

Her cup of tea in hand, she sat next to me, and curled her feet under her, and began. "According to her diary, Isabella met Sophie Delacroix, and they became friends in 1938."

"So there were two different women."

"Oh, yes. As the war heated up, Sophie began her work with the Résistance. I think she may have been a leader, but that's only a guess. Sophie's friend, François—"

"Max?"

Alyssa nodded. "Max was part of the Résistance too. Isabella only learned that later, after the war started. They kept their involvement a secret from her in order to protect her.

"Isabella also met Rainier in '38, and they began an affair. She fell in love with him." Alyssa pinched her lips into a firm line. "She didn't know he was married."

I rubbed my chin. This had been a hot spot for Alyssa. From the forbidding expression on her face, it obviously still was.

I toyed with my wine glass. "Philippe is the grandson of this Rainier. After he attacked you, Claire and Bruno delved into Philippe's family history. Rainier had one child, a boy named Adolf."

"Yikes."

"He changed his name after the war but remained loyal to his father's twisted ideals. Philippe was raised by this man."

"And his mind was probably poisoned by him."

"Did Dominique—was she in on the plot?" Alyssa asked.

"She denies it, and we can't prove complicity. She

was out of town the night Philippe attacked you."

"I think he used her, just like Rainier used Isabella."

"Could be. You said you knew where Sophie and Rainier were."

"Yes."

"Are you going to tell me?"

"Eventually." She stood, stepped back into a provocative pose and began to unbutton her blouse. I hardened instantly.

"Later?" She tugged my hand, and I stood to kiss her. "That okay with you?"

"Fine."

She led me into the bedroom. I'd never seen the room as anything but a hoarder's haven. Now, lamplight glowed over a huge antique wooden bed I recognized from somewhere. Gorgeous wood and sensual curved lines filled the center of the room. The thing was probably worth more euros than I earned in a year.

Alyssa had been shopping again. The bed was made up with a silk comforter and a stack of inviting pillows.

A large rabbit—the one from the garden—sat in the corner. I tossed my jacket over him. Sorry, Monsieur. We needed privacy.

Alyssa pulled back the comforter and set her glasses on the night table.

I stepped up behind her and nibbled on the lobe of her ear. "Leave them on."

She hummed softly and leaned into me. I smoothed my hands over her silky arms and took hold of her waist. Turning in my arms, she combed her fingers through my hair. I kissed her, long and hard, and then tossed her on the bed. "I have been patient, Alyssa."

She laughed, raising her arms to greet me.

****

The perfect man in the perfect bed. I was in heaven. I moaned happily as he kissed my breasts.

"Anton, please." I wrapped my legs around his waist. "I've missed you."

"*Très bien*," he replied. He entered me, and I sighed with pleasure.

He *had* missed me. Our first time together after two weeks apart soon became a fiery race, each of us touching, kissing, climbing and reaching toward a ferocious climax. We shouted with pleasure and collapsed in the wreck of covers and discarded clothes, barely able to breathe.

Still joined, Anton rolled me to the top and stroked his hands over my back and through my hair. We caressed each other and cooled with long, languid kisses, then climbed again to another climax, higher, more exquisite than the last.

Finally, we slept. I woke in the middle of the night, opened my eyes and smiled into Anton's face. I turned on my side. "How long have you been awake?"

He stretched his long body. "A while, but I like watching you sleep."

"Curiosity driving you crazy?"

He held up a thumb and a finger, barely a centimeter apart. "*Un peu.*"

I pushed the pillows into a pile, sat up and folded the covers over me.

"So…?"

"Rainier and Sophie are in the garden."

Anton frowned. "You mean the little courtyard? Where you found that stupid rabbit?"

I nodded.

He pushed back his messy hair. "What are you talking about?"

"Well, I guess you might say they're *under* the garden."

His eyes went wide. "*Merde*."

****

I jumped out of bed and searched the floor. "Where's my phone?"

Alyssa chuckled but remained in bed.

I raced to the bedroom door and then looked down. "Where are my pants?"

"Here." She tossed me the inside-out trousers I'd shed in haste a few hours earlier. "There's no rush. They've been there seven decades." She followed me, stopped in the hall, and waited while I dressed.

I turned to stare at her and combed my fingers through my hair. "The treasure?"

She shrugged. "Still don't know."

In the moonlight, her skin shone like silver, and the curls in her hair reflected the bright moonlight. She stood, so relaxed in her beautiful skin that I instantly forgot about the bodies buried in the garden. Well, almost.

She was right. They could wait until morning.

When I picked her up, she laughed. I carried her back to her beautiful old bed. I still couldn't remember where I'd seen it before.

We sank into the soft sheets, and she reached her arms up for me, her face haloed in bright curls.

I kissed her. "This could take all night."

"Hope so."

****

Anton whispered in my ear, and his fingers held magic when he touched me. I swirled in a heaven of heat and desire. Wanting him. Having him. He rose over me, and I drew my hands down his strong chest.

I waited impatiently for him to enter me and sighed with pleasure as he filled me. We could be patient now. Testing our need. He moved slowly, taking time to bring on the heat, the power of our lovemaking.

I wrapped my legs around his waist to draw him closer, and our rhythm increased. I could hardly breathe, hardly see as I climaxed once and then again. Anton roared over the edge along with me.

Then my damn bed broke.

Chapter Twenty-Eight

We landed with a loud crash and a thump on the old wooden floors. Fortunately the headboard leaned against the back wall, but then the footboard tipped and fell with us.

I started laughing and couldn't stop. My sides ached, and I must have sounded slightly hysterical—but really? A broken bed?

Monsieur Gallé, you have done me wrong.

After a moment, Anton joined in with my laughter as we rolled naked onto the floor. Still chuckling, I turned on the light, and we quickly dressed.

Anton put his hands on his hips and inspected the destruction. "Doesn't look too bad. The footboard is fine." He propped it against the settee and examined the huge headboard. "I think the slats broke. There may be a few missing."

I was relieved. "Do you think we can put it back together?"

He shrugged. "Help me with the mattress."

I pulled off the sheets and comforter and piled them on the settee. It took two of us to hoist the floppy mattress. After a bit of grunting, we moved it to the doorway and left it standing upright in the narrow hall.

"Here's the culprit." I held up the splintered board that had once spanned the two rails.

"That's firewood. It can be replaced, but there's

only one other slat."

"We didn't have a chance." I started laughing again.

After I calmed myself, we re-attached the rails to the headboard and foot board and stared at the naked bed.

"There's always my single bed in the study. We can snuggle. Or put the big mattress on the floor in the living room."

Anton continued to stare at the bed. I waited for his response and then looked at him more closely. He was staring at the floor *under* the bed.

I joined him, and my heart took an enormous leap. "A rabbit." I cried out.

"*Oui.*"

I climbed over the rail and knelt to examine the floor more closely. The old wood floor boards were horribly dusty. After I brushed aside fifty years of dust bunnies—hah, I could clearly see the outline of a rabbit etched into the floor. "Holy…"

Anton climbed into the space beside me, used the light on his phone and felt the boards around the etching. He traced the larger rectangle shape with his finger. "There's a tiny key hole in the rabbit's mouth."

There went my heart again. I grabbed his arm to steady myself. "It's the treasure," I whispered.

"*Oui.*"

I leaped up and ran toward the next room. The treasure. It had to be. Just had to be.

I dug my tiny key from where I'd hidden it in the herb pot on my kitchen counter and rushed back to the bedroom.

My hands shook as I struggled to fit the key in the

lock.

Anton finally took it from me. He had better luck. The lock clicked, and we lifted the trap door.

It wasn't a huge space, only a few square feet, but it was filled to the very top with all sorts of small boxes.

"Anton," I breathed.

"I see it."

I pointed to the round-topped tea caddy. "It's your family's treasure."

He grinned. "*Oui.*"

****

The news media circled my apartment like vultures. They'd set up little tents in the square across the street and watched the place night and day.

"Still out there?" Anton asked on the third day after the treasure had been announced to the public.

I nodded toward the street. "Max is doing another interview."

Dressed in his best suit, jaunty beret, and silver topped cane, the old guy was swarmed by young newsgirls.

I leaned against the window sill. "He's enjoying all the attention."

Anton chuckled, blew and sipped his coffee. "Bruno thinks we will be done today."

I sighed. "Good. Did they find anything else under the floor boards?"

He shook his head. "I think we have it all. The cupboard behind the bed was emptied yesterday. Just over three hundred treasures in all."

I shook my head in disbelief. "Will your team be able to find the owners?"

He rubbed his chin with his thumb. He'd let his beard grow the last few days into a shadowy scruff. I kinda liked the look.

"With the media coverage on this story," he said, "we have an excellent chance. The calls have been pouring in. The unclaimed pieces will be donated to a survivors' fund."

"And Max will receive the reward?"

"Are you sure that's what you want?"

"I have enough. I'm sure Isabella would approve. This way Max can live out his life with the care he needs."

Anton hugged my shoulder and softly kissed my temple. "There were a couple items that didn't need to go into police custody." He handed me a small box containing a few dusty letters.

I glanced at the address in Minnesota and the post mark. "Oh, Anton. She wrote to her parents." I blinked back tears.

"They had already moved to California by then. She missed them by a few months."

"So sad." I undid the envelope marked Return to Sender and glanced at the letter. "She wanted to come home." I checked the postmark again—October, 1945.

"The war was over."

"Two more letters, one each year." I checked the dates. "Mailed on the same day."

"Her mother's birthday. We checked."

My heart grew heavy. "Poor Isabella. She never knew we missed her. Never knew we looked for her."

"She looked for your family too. Does that help?"

I nodded. "It will."

One tiny box remained. An old jewelry clip box. I

opened it, and my breath caught. "The sapphire." I held it up for Anton to see. "Sophie's sapphire."

He slipped the ring on my finger. "You solved Isabella's mystery. She would want you to have it."

I turned and circled my arms around Anton's neck. Reaching up, I kissed him. He tasted of coffee. "I need to go home soon."

His hands squeezed my waist and his expression grew serious. "I know."

He dug in his pocket and pulled out a small gift box, wrapped with pretty blue paper and a bow.

"What's this?"

"A little something." Anton shrugged. "Claire insisted I wrap it."

I watched the blush creep over his ears. Curiosity blazing, I pulled off the paper and peeked inside.

A lock.

"Oh, Anton."

"I thought we might take a walk to the bridge tonight."

Epilogue

I hurried through customs at SFO and out the wide glass doors to the greeting area, filled with California sunshine. Searching the crowd, I waited. Sam had promised she'd pick me up. I couldn't wait to see the new baby and get my hands on Jojo, now a big brother.

"'Llysa," a small voice called.

"There you are." I swung the little guy up into my arms. "How ya been, buddy?"

He hugged me tightly around the neck. Warm and sticky, he smelled of peanut butter. "You come home." His happy words steamed my glasses. I didn't care.

"Yes, buddy. I'm home."

Sam appeared with Jojo's new sister strapped to her chest in a carrier. My heart melted. I couldn't wait to hold her.

"That's my sista," Jojo chimed in, pointing to the wrinkle-faced little bundle with a thatch of red hair. "Mommy and Daddy and me, we named her Isabella."

"I know. She's beautiful."

Sam gave me a tearful hug. "How was the flight?"

"Long."

She looked over my shoulder and smiled. "So this must be the policeman."

Anton put an arm around my waist and grinned. "No. I'm the baker."

A word about the author...

Along with teaching, Joy began her writing career by publishing children's historical fiction. She later found writing romantic suspense fulfilled her need for travel and romance.

She lives with her husband and two dogs near Silicon Valley and the mythical town of Sereno.

http://www.ejbrighton.com

CPSIA information can be obtained
at www.ICGtesting.com
Printed in the USA
LVHW051646120421
684241LV00012B/1027